BILLIONA...

*Hot, jet-set docs at the top of their game
professionally...and personally!*

Enjoy our new 2-in-1 editions
for double the romance!

HOT-SHOT SURGEON, CINDERELLA BRIDE
by Alison Roberts

THE PLAYBOY DOCTOR CLAIMS HIS BRIDE
by Janice Lynn

Look out for our next **Billionaire Doctor** in
SECRET SHEIKH, SECRET BABY
by Carol Marinelli, coming next month
from Mills & Boon® Medical™ Romance

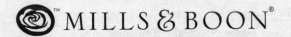

MILLS & BOON®

Dear Reader

Welcome to the new look Medical Romances!

Now we're offering you two great value editions with two stories in each, double the medical drama...and twice as many happy endings. All of your favourite authors and all the best stories will still be available—and with **two double** volumes and **two** single story books each month, you'll be spoiled for choice!

Look for these great new titles—out now!

HOT-SHOT SURGEON, CINDERELLA BRIDE
by Alison Roberts
&
THE PLAYBOY CLAIMS HIS BRIDE
by Janice Lynn

* * *

A SPECIAL KIND OF FAMILY
by Marion Lennox

* * *

EMERGENCY: WIFE LOST AND FOUND
by Carol Marinelli

* * *

A SUMMER WEDDING AT WILLOWMERE
by Abigail Gordon
&
MIRACLE: TWIN BABIES
by Fiona Lowe

To find out more, visit
www.millsandboon.co.uk/makeover.

Best wishes

Sheila Hodgson

Senior Editor, Medical™ Romance

HOT-SHOT SURGEON, CINDERELLA BRIDE

BY
ALISON ROBERTS

MILLS & BOON

First published in Great Britain 2009
Harlequin Mills & Boon Limited,
Eton House, 18-24 Paradise Road, Richmond, Surrey TW9 1SR

© Alison Roberts 2009

ISBN: 978 0 263 86859 3

Set in Times Roman 10½ on 13 pt
03-0809-41176

Harlequin Mills & Boon policy is to use papers that are natural, renewable and recyclable products and made from wood grown in sustainable forests. The logging and manufacturing process conform to the legal environmental regulations of the country of origin.

Printed and bound in Spain
by Litografia Rosés, S.A., Barcelona

Alison Roberts lives in Christchurch, New Zealand. She began her working career as a primary school teacher, but now juggles available working hours between writing and active duty as an ambulance officer. Throwing in a large dose of parenting, housework, gardening and pet-minding keeps life busy, and teenage daughter Becky is responsible for an increasing number of days spent on equestrian pursuits. Finding time for everything can be a challenge, but the rewards make the effort more than worthwhile.

Recent titles by the same author:

ONE NIGHT WITH HER BOSS
THE ITALIAN SURGEON'S CHRISTMAS MIRACLE
MARRYING THE MILLIONAIRE DOCTOR*
HER FOUR-YEAR BABY SECRET

Crocodile Creek

CHAPTER ONE

WHO on earth was that?

The conversation he'd been engrossed in a moment ago became a meaningless blur of sound for Dr Anthony Grimshaw. For just a heartbeat he had caught a glimpse of the most stunning-looking woman he'd ever seen, standing between two pillars on the far side of the ballroom.

Much to the delight of the organising committee, St Patrick's fundraiser had become *the* function of the year, and there was a sea of people moving to the excellent music being provided by a small live orchestra. The dance floor was so well populated it was inevitable that his line of vision was obscured, but Tony still found himself trying to see those pillars again as he tuned back in to the voice beside him. A well respected voice that belonged to a senior colleague: paediatric cardiologist John Clifford.

'…and anyway, didn't I see a photo of you in some gossip rag? Out and about with Morrison's daughter? What's her name?'

'Miranda,' Tony supplied absently.

'Ah, yes! So. As I was saying. The fact that Gilbert's father is on the board should be well cancelled out by you having a prospective father-in-law with the same— if not greater—power to cast a vote in favour of *you* becoming HOD.'

'What?' Tony's attention was recaptured. 'What on earth are you talking about, John?'

'You. And Miranda.'

'There is no me and Miranda.'

'But…'

'We met at some charity do. Not unlike this one but without the fancy dress.' He smiled at the rotund figure of his companion. With his genial expression and fluffy mane of white hair it was no wonder his small patients loved him. Dr Clifford had answered tonight's medieval theme by wearing a king's robe and a crown. 'That outfit suits you, by the way. Very regal. Yes, Miranda and I went out a couple of times, but it's not going anywhere.'

'Why ever not? The girl's beautiful. Wealthy. Probably one of the many that seem to find you irresistible. My word, if I was still your age, I'd—'

The direct look Tony gave his companion was enough to break a flow that would have been extraordinary if they hadn't known each other so well for many years. In his early sixties, John Clifford was a family friend and had been Tony's mentor since he'd joined the staff of St Patrick's as a surgical registrar some years ago now.

'Don't you think it would seem a little blatant to be

dating the daughter of the chairman of St Pat's board of trustees at exactly the same time I'm up for the coveted position of head of the cardiothoracic surgical department?'

John's sigh was resigned. 'But it's the fact that you're young and single that counts against you, Tony. The powers-that-be see you as someone who's going to be distracted by a wife and family in the next few years. Responsibilities that might compromise your ability to lead the department into becoming the cutting-edge facility they've set their hearts on having.'

'I'll be able to assure them that isn't the case,' Tony said with quiet confidence. He tempered any implied criticism with a grin. 'With any luck Miranda will have told Daddy she broke it off with me because she wasn't about to try and compete with my job. That I'm far more interested in research than romance.'

The smile was returned. 'Don't understand it myself. She looked perfect.'

Tony's grin faded to a poignant curl. 'Want to know a secret, John?'

'What is it?'

Tony leaned closer. 'Perfection can be very, very boring.'

His gaze shifted as he straightened. Straight back to where he'd be able to see those pillars if the dancers would just move out of the way. His eyes narrowed as he tried to see past the colourful swirl of ornate costumes, and he only turned away briefly to acknowledge the farewell as John responded to a wave from another group.

What was it about that woman that drew his line of vision so compellingly? He was too far away to recognise her, or even see her features in the soft light from the flames of dozens of gas lamps on the walls of this vast ballroom. Maybe it was something about the way she was standing? Poised. Graceful even without any motion. With an aura that spoke of being alone but not lonely. Independent.

Yes, that was an intriguing enough impression to explain the attraction.

He felt a bit like that himself tonight. Independent.

Free.

Part of it could be explained by the costume. Not that Tony had been keen on the idea of being one of the Three Musketeers when the idea had been mooted by one of his registrars, but much to his surprise he was loving it. The soft suede boots, tailored jacket, frilly shirt, and the sword dangling by his side. Even the wig and preposterously wide hat with its ridiculous feather. Not one to do anything by halves, he'd added a mask, moustache and neat goatee beard, which had the unexpected bonus of being a very effective disguise.

The rest of it could probably be attributed to the conversation he'd just been having with John. Or perhaps more to the ending of it. Not that he ever minded talking shop, but he was more than happy to forget the background tension of the career competition he was currently engaged in. He could probably avoid it for the rest of the evening, too, in this disguise. Now that he was alone he could virtually disappear into this incredibly colourful crowd, half of whom *he* wouldn't be able to recognise.

Like that woman between the pillars.

The princess with the dark dress and jewels sparkling in her hair.

He watched the crowd of dancers, enjoying the visual feast of this enormous costume party. The timeframe had been—loosely-adhered to, and the variety was impressive. There were knights and highwaymen, kings and queens and Vikings. Milkmaids and monks and jesters. Crusaders and pirates. More than one Merlin and a good crowd of peasants.

And…*yes*—there she was again!

Dancing, now. With a Robin Hood who was possibly a little merrier than he should be. Not the best dancer, in any case. But the princess…she was on another level entirely. The grace with which she had been holding herself whilst standing still had been a faint reflection of her body in movement.

The way she turned—with that subtle bend, like a leaf in a gentle breeze.

The way her hand traced a shape only she could feel in the air. The shape of the music as it danced in his ears.

There had to be a better position from which to watch the dance floor. One without the frustration of having his view constantly interrupted in this fashion. The best available seemed to be where *she* had been standing. Between those pillars.

Having chosen his desired position, Tony moved with a determination that had the customary effect of people unconsciously moving aside to clear his path.

Who on earth was *that*?

Standing there, at the vantage point she had recently vacated herself.

No—lounging might be a better word, with the padded shoulder of an ornate red jacket shifting his weight onto that pillar. On one foot with the other crossed elegantly at ankle level and just the toe of the boot touching the floor. Kelly almost expected to see him twirl the end of that fake moustache or sweep his hat off as she noticed him watching her.

Was he watching her?

Hard to tell with that mask and the flickering shadows from the atmospheric lighting behind the pillar, but it didn't matter because it *felt* as if he was watching her— and there was something incredibly exciting about the notion. Kelly wanted to be watched. To feel…desirable.

He was tall and lean. In a costume that could only be considered ideal fodder for a romantic fantasy. And that was precisely what Kelly was in the mood for.

This whole night was a fantasy as far as she was concerned. It had been ever since she had become the envied winner of the raffle for one of the astonishingly expensive tickets to St Patrick's annual ball. Not that she'd intended to actually come. That had been Elsie's doing. Her boss. Surrogate mother, almost. It had been Elsie who'd hunted down the costume hire shops and dragged her along after work.

Even then Kelly had been ready to give her ticket away. She'd barely listened to Elsie clucking on about how much she was looking forward to babysitting Flipper. Or to the pointed reminders of how much she loved to dance.

'I dance every day,' she'd told Elsie. 'Flipper lives for her music.'

'Not the same as being in the arms of some tall, dark, handsome stranger, though, is it?'

'A man is the last thing I need in my life right now.'

She'd said it with the conviction of utmost sincerity. She'd just been jumping through hoops as she tried to find an acceptable excuse to decline. But then she'd seen the dress in the shop.

Midnight-blue velvet. High-waisted, with a laced bodice over a silver chemise. Sleeves that were shaped with a long, long back to them that would almost touch the ground. Folds of soft material that shimmered when she couldn't resist touching the garment.

It was a dress that could almost dance all by itself, and as her fingers had trailed down the skirt Kelly had known she was lost.

For just one night, she *had* to wear that dress.

And dance like there was no tomorrow.

Robin Hood was an unskilled but enthusiastic dancer.

It was easy to slip from his grasp and put some of her own style into the nondescript pattern they had been locked into. Kelly stepped back, raised her arms to cross them over her head, and, with her hands held like butterfly wings, she spun herself around fast enough to make the full folds of her dress billow. Then she caught the hand of her partner, twirled beneath it, and stepped back into his arms for some more sedate steps.

'Wow!' he said. 'Do it again.'

This time Kelly kept hold of Robin's hand and turned sideways before spinning in to lean on his shoulder. For just a split second before the spin her line of vision had those pillars directly ahead of her, and it was all too easy to imagine that *he* was watching her.

That he *wanted* her.

The orchestra was in no hurry to complete this particular medley, and suddenly neither was Kelly.

Poor Robin Hood was simply an accessory. She was dancing for *him*. The stranger in the shadows. Why him? she wondered fleetingly. There was something about the way he was standing there, she decided. The way he might be watching her, as though he found her attractive. But more, it was a vehicle for unleashing a side of herself that had been neglected for so long it was virtually forgotten.

The sensuous side.

Dancing would have been enough to satisfy her if she'd been with a partner who could have challenged her ability or let her express herself completely. This fantasy of dancing to attract a total stranger was exciting enough to fill any gap this somewhat stilted movement left. The dress had already made Kelly feel beautiful. Being watched made it real.

She could dance her way into his heart.

Seduce him without touching. Without even seeming to notice him. And then she could melt into the crowd and simply disappear, to leave him wondering who the hell she was. The smile touching Kelly's lips was unconscious. It was a fitting part of this fairytale night. A bit of magic, like a tiny crystal ball she would be able to keep and look into occasionally when she wanted to remember feeling this good.

'Wow,' Robin Hood said again as the music finally faded. 'You're something else! What's your name?'

Kelly laughed. 'Cinderella.'

He grinned. 'Fair enough. Can I get you a glass of champagne, Cinders?'

'No—thank you.'

They both turned at the sound of the decisive negative, and Kelly felt a prickle run down her spine. How had he moved so fast? He must have been waiting for precisely this opportunity.

The musketeer swept a hand up in front of his chest and then moved it sideways in a graceful arc that left his fingers enticingly close to Kelly's.

'*My* dance, I think,' he said.

'Hang on, buddy!' Robin Hood was scowling. 'I was just going to get…'

Kelly could see, no—feel the commanding stare her recent dance partner was receiving. In normal life that kind of arrogance would have put her back up instantly—but this wasn't normal life, was it? It was a fairytale, and *he* wanted to dance with her.

With a totally uncharacteristic, demure downward glance, Kelly put her hand into his.

The touch of her hand was like…like nothing Tony had ever felt before when his skin had come into contact with that of another person.

Thank goodness she took his hand when she did, because Tony had been experiencing an astonishingly strong desire to say something to Robin Hood that he might regret.

No one, *nothing*, was going to take away his chance to meet this woman. He tightened his grip around that slim hand.

What on earth was happening to him? The Grimshaws never behaved with anything less that the utmost decorum in public. He cast a suspicious glance at the cause of his unusual emotional state, but she was looking at the floor and standing very still in that poised manner she had. If Tony hadn't just spent nearly ten minutes watching her dance and finding his heart rate steadily increasing, his breathing becoming shallow and his tight breeches becoming less comfortable by the second, he might have believed her to be completely innocent.

Robin Hood muttered something unintelligible as he melted into the crowd, and it was only then that the princess raised her gaze. Tony was instantly aware of two things.

That they both knew their behaviour to her last dance partner had been unacceptably rude but also unavoidable. And that something was happening here that was simply meant to be.

Something as unreal as pretending to be part of a medieval gathering.

No. He'd better make that three things.

His awareness of this woman's beauty had been overwhelming even from the distance of the pillars. This close, Tony could believe he was looking at the nearest thing to perfection in a woman he'd ever seen.

Dark, dark blue eyes. Pale skin made all the more dramatic by the fall of that glorious wig. He'd been watching the black ripples that fell to her waist lift and swirl as she danced, and was thankful she hadn't braided it, or bundled it up to wear one of those pointy hats with veils attached at the sides that some women were wearing tonight. Dark stones like teardrops lay against her forehead, and the chain of jewels was the only restraint to her loose, flowing locks.

His hand lifted of its own accord to touch a soft curl.

'Nice,' he murmured. 'It feels almost real.'

'Does it?' A tiny smile pulled up the corners of her mouth and Tony found himself staring. Trying to extinguish what threatened to be an irresistible urge to kiss her.

Right here. Right now. In the middle of a dance floor where people around them had already started to dance to a new bracket of songs. Slightly faster music at the moment. Like his heartbeat.

'Shall we?' He gave a mock bow. Play-acting seemed to be the way forward here, because none of this felt real.

'Please.' The smile had an impish quality. 'But…'

'But?'

'I'm just wondering how safe it is to dance with you.'

Oh, not safe at all, he thought, but he pressed his lips closed on the warning and raised his eyebrows instead.

'Your sword?'

'Oh…' With a slow, deliberate, one-handed movement, Tony unbuckled the big silver clasp and pulled the belt from his waist. He looked up to inform the princess of his plan to drop the accessory out of the way—by the pillars, perhaps, along with his hat.

She looked up at the same instant, from where she had clearly been staring at his hands, and when he saw the tip of her tongue emerge to run across her bottom lip it felt as if some giant vice was squeezing every last molecule of oxygen from his chest.

Yes!

She wanted him. The way he wanted her.

Desire threatened to suffocate him. He could simply walk out of this ballroom and take her somewhere more private, couldn't he? No. It was a long time since he'd been an inexperienced teenager, for whom where lust could obliterate the ability to think clearly. This combination of confidence and anticipation might be heady stuff, but experience had taught him something else as well. It was a thrill that should be savoured for as long as possible.

Somehow he sucked in a breath as he led her to the edge of the floor to get rid of his unwanted accessories. Then he drew her into his arms.

'Did I hear correctly?' he enquired politely. 'Is your name Cindy?'

Those eyes were huge and... Dear Lord, even the way she blinked so slowly was erotic.

'Yes,' she said softly.

'Cindy who?'

'Does it matter?'

'It might.'

He could feel her responsiveness as he manoeuvred them to a clear space on the floor. She felt weightless in his arms, like an extension of his own body rather than a separate partner. God, if she felt like this on a dance floor, what would she be like in *bed?*

He saw the way the soft mounds of her breasts, pushed up by the corset top of her dress, rose even further as she took a deep breath. His mouth went dry.

'Riley,' she said at last. 'My name is Cindy Riley.'

'And you work at the hospital, Cindy Riley?'

'Yes.'

'Whereabouts? Which department?'

'All over.' She was smiling again. 'A bit of everything, really.'

Ah… She must be a pool nurse. Filling in wherever they required assistance. No wonder he hadn't seen her often enough in one place to recognise her. Tony ignored the scoffing sound in the back of his mind. The voice that said he would have only needed to see her once to recognise her again.

'Favourite places?'

'Emergency,' she said without hesitation. He could see the flicker in her eyes that spoke of a real passion for her work. 'And Theatre.'

Tony pulled her a little closer. 'My kind of girl,' he told her. 'And my favourite places as well. I'm Tony Grimshaw, by the way. I'm on the cardiothoracic surgical team.'

'Mmm.' The sound seemed oddly strangled. 'Could we stop talking, please, Tony Grimshaw? And dance?'

By way of response, Tony altered the way he was holding her. He might be rusty, but already the short time of moving with this woman felt natural. He sent Cindy Riley into a brief spin and then caught her, stepping sideways so that she could bend and dip—one arm extending gracefully. Then, the instant she was back on balance, he flipped her into a dip on his other side.

She was laughing as she came upright again, those incredible eyes letting him know that she was happy.

Impressed.

That she wanted more.

CHAPTER TWO

HE COULD *dance*!

The unexpected way her body had responded to that first touch of their hands had been disturbing all on its own.

Finding out who was beneath that disguise had been so shocking part of her brain had shut down, and her only thought had been to finish this dance and escape.

Tony Grimshaw! The son of the city's mayor, no less. The rising star of St Pat's cardiothoracic surgical team. Tipped to become the next head of that prestigious department, despite being only in his mid-thirties.

One of life's golden people. Only ever seen to be accompanied by the cream of available women. The wealthiest and most beautiful. Often celebrities, and never encumbered with small dependent children.

Criteria Kelly could never aspire to attaining. Wouldn't want to, in fact.

But he could dance. *Really* dance. And within moments a forgotten joy was reborn for Kelly.

Like flying. Taking off and swooping and knowing it

was perfectly safe because there were strong arms to catch her. A lead that not only provided an impressive variety of moves but one that encouraged independence and gave opportunities to play.

Escape was the last thing she wanted now, and the music fading at the end of the set would have been utterly disappointing except that it went virtually unnoticed. The only change was that Tony slowed down. Held her close and started a tango step. And Kelly could rest her head against his and keep her eyes closed and still think of nothing but the music and the way they moved together so beautifully.

It didn't matter now that she was dancing with the physical embodiment of everything she had run from in her previous life. Or that she had lied about her identity.

It wasn't really a lie, was it?

Cindy Riley was close enough to being Cinderella to be a joke. Part of the pretence. Part of the fairytale she was living tonight. And it was…magic.

The spell they were under did odd things to the passage of time. Kelly had no idea how long they danced, and there was no way she was going to suggest a break. That would come all too soon—when the clock struck midnight and she had to flee. The lights became dimmer and the crowd on the dance floor thinned out, but still they danced on.

As if there was no tomorrow.

And maybe the spell was going to last a little longer than midnight.

At some point, drugged by the music and the movement, and barely moving in the slow, slow tango, she heard Tony murmur in her ear.

'I want to be with you,' he said. 'Somewhere else.'

She hadn't expected this. The thought was alarming. 'T-tonight?'

'Oh, yes.' The movement of his hand on her back was subtle. Nobody else would have noticed the way his thumb moved and pressed down along the bumps of her spine. But Kelly could feel the heat spread through her entire body. Into every single cell.

His voice was such a low rumble that Kelly felt rather than heard the two words he added.

'*All* night.'

His lips were right beside her ear. She felt them move like a caress. She felt the tiny coolness of his tongue touching her skin.

Yes!

No!

It was unthinkable! To spend a night with a man she'd just met for the first time? Not even met him honestly, come to that, seeing as he had no idea who she really was.

But maybe that made it less shocking somehow— because it wasn't *her* doing something so risky. So unlike anything she'd ever contemplated doing. She wasn't herself. Wasn't expected to be until around eight tomorrow morning, when she was due to collect Flipper from Elsie's house. Just for tonight—a few more hours—she could continue being part of the fairytale and do things she might never get the chance to do again.

She could believe she was someone that a man like Tony actually wanted.

'Wh—where?' she heard herself whisper.

'The owners of this hotel are family friends. I have a suite upstairs for the night.'

His head was moving as he spoke. His lips brushing her cheek. Any moment now and he might kiss her, and—God help her—Kelly wanted him to. She wanted the touch of his lips more than she had ever wanted anything. *Ever.*

It was too easy. Kelly was being led as decisively as he had been leading her in their dancing. Doubts collided in her mind, but wouldn't slow down enough to take shape. Not when he was looking down at her like this and she could see the dark eyes behind the mask.

'Don't worry,' he said softly. 'You're safe. I'll take care of you, Cindy Riley. I promise.'

And that was her undoing.

The thought of being cared for.

Loved.

It wasn't the first time Tony Grimshaw had taken a woman he barely knew to his bed. The only difference between his testosterone-laden teen years and those of most young men had been the playground he'd had available. One where the kind of holidays, clothes, cars and freedom had been a magnet for every pretty girl he'd encountered.

So why did it feel like the first time?

Tony led Cindy through the door of the best suite the Grand Chancellor had to offer, pushed it closed with his foot and pulled her into his arms, dipping his head to claim her lips with his own as part of the same, fluid series of moves.

It was all just another kind of dance, really, wasn't it? And he'd been right. Her responsiveness was… mind-blowing. The way her mouth moved under his and her lips parted. They way her tongue touched and curled against his own. And when he moved his head to deepen the kiss she tilted her own to exactly the angle he needed to explore her delicious mouth a little more thoroughly.

It was some time before he registered what his fingers, rather than his lips and tongue, were aware of.

'Your hair,' he said in amazement. 'It's *real*.'

She laughed. 'Of course it is.'

He smiled back at her. He wanted to make her laugh again because it was such a gorgeous sound. 'Mine isn't.'

It worked. 'I should hope not.' Then her face stilled. 'Take it off,' she whispered. 'I want to feel *you*. Take off the wig. And this—' She touched the moustache that was already half detached after their kisses.

She didn't seem to mind that his own hair was flattened and damp from the wig. Or that his chin felt rough because he hadn't shaved before sticking on that silly beard. Her hands shaped his head, and the pressure brought his lips back to hers for an even more intense kiss.

Tony had to slow things down. He wanted her right now. To pull up the acres of fabric in that dress and take her here, against the wall. But he'd promised to take care of her, hadn't he? And even if he hadn't made that promise, he wouldn't want to rush this. It was too special.

He dragged his mouth from hers, but he couldn't pull right back. He kissed the corner of her mouth. Then her jaw and her neck. She tilted her head back in response to his touch, and the gasp as he trailed his kisses down to the pale flesh rounded over the top of her corset made him utter a sound that was unfamiliar to his own ears.

A primal sound of pure need.

His fingers fumbled with the string at the front of her bodice and then her hands joined his, making deft, sure movements that undid the knot and loosened the lace. And all the time her fingers worked under his, her eyes held his gaze. Tony thought he was going to drown in the deep blue depths. In the desire he could see that so clearly matched his own.

Then the laces were undone and her breasts were free and his hands could hold them and he could bend his head and touch his tongue to nipples as hard as buttons.

And he was lost.

Completely and utterly lost.

Kelly wasn't a virgin, but it had been a very long time since she'd been with a man—and she'd never been with anyone as far out of her league as Tony Grimshaw.

Maybe that was why it felt like a first time.

Or maybe it was because *this* man made her feel different. Every touch made her ache for more, but even the combination of long abstinence on her part and gentleness and strength on his part, overlying the undeniable expertise of his lovemaking, couldn't explain why this felt so different.

He seemed to know her body. Just where to touch her and *how*. With his lips, his tongue, his teeth. His hands and his fingertips. His *eyes*! The way he looked at her body as he uncovered it. The way he held her gaze as he stripped off his own clothing.

And his focus. He'd stopped talking and asking awkward questions when she had wanted to dance, and now there seemed no need for any words at all. With the costumes that represented the first chapters of this fairytale lying puddled on the floor, Tony scooped Kelly into his arms and carried her to the massive bed, softly illuminated by discreet lamps.

He laid her down, took a condom from the drawer in the bedside cabinet and then knelt over her on the bed.

There was no going back now. Even if escape had been offered, Kelly would have been totally unable to accept. She looked at the beautiful body of the man she was with. The hard lines of muscle. The faint smudges of dark hair. The *size* of him in more ways than the obvious. Because Kelly could sense his generosity of spirit. His ability to care.

That recognition took her breath away.

She was completely lost. She held up her arms to welcome him, but he didn't return her faintly tentative smile. His face was so serious, so *intent*, she experienced a moment of fear that made her heart stop and then thump painfully hard.

He caught her wrists and lowered her arms until he was holding them, crossed over her head. He transferred both wrists easily to one hand and then, as he bent his mouth to hers, his free hand slipped the curtain of her long hair from where it covered her breast. Gentle fingers traced her neck, along her collarbone, and then dipped to come up from beneath her breast and skim her nipple.

The shaft of exquisite sensation made Kelly gasp, and he raised his mouth from hers, releasing her wrists and using both hands to touch her as his lips took over from his fingers on her breast. But only for a heartbeat. His mouth kept moving, his tongue finding her belly button and then leaving a line of fire as it tracked further down.

She left her arms where they were, above her head, and lay still for as long as possible. But with the first sweep of his tongue on that tiny nub of hidden flesh she came—with a shudder and a groan of disbelief. She had to touch him then. To try and give back some of the magic that was dusting this incredible night.

She cried out again later, when he finally entered her and they began a whole new dance. And when she held him after his own shuddering climax she could feel the same kind of wonder emanating from him. And it felt as if she was touching his soul.

It was a night she never wanted to end, but of course it had to.

The magic was fading when Tony finally fell asleep, one arm flung above his head, the other holding Kelly close to his side. But the luxury of falling asleep and then waking to make love yet again was one Kelly couldn't afford. With the first fingers of light reaching into the velvety darkness in the corners of the room, she eased herself from the bed so stealthily that Tony did nothing more than take a deeper breath.

She put the dress back on, but its magic had also evaporated and Kelly could feel reality kicking in. It felt wrong to be dressed like this.

Wrong to have just spent a night having the most astonishingly wonderful sex imaginable?

No.

Kelly took one last, long look at the man sprawled on the bed, deeply asleep.

Something that had felt so right couldn't be wrong.

Softly, she kissed her fingertips and blew the kiss towards the man who still didn't know who she was.

Or anything about the life she was about to step back into.

And that was the way it had to be.

The truth would only tarnish the fairytale, and Kelly wanted to keep it exactly the way it was.

Perfect.

CHAPTER THREE

'YOU'RE in luck, Kelly, love. They're short in ED today.'

'Cool. Thanks, Elsie.' Kelly was still tucking the long coil of her braid under the elastic band of the oversized shower-cap-type hat that was part of her uniform. 'For the whole shift?'

'Yep.' Elsie was giving her a curious look. 'I thought you'd be rapt. Isn't Emergency your favourite place?'

'It is.' Kelly nodded and smiled, but her brain had gone into overdrive.

No wonder Elsie had picked up on something being different. Only last week the prospect of a day in the emergency department would have been a treat.

A poignant treat, mind you—it was like having her face pressed to a shop window that contained something ultimately desirable but equally unaffordable—but still an irresistible one.

'I'm just a bit tired,' she told Elsie, by way of excusing her lack of excitement. 'I didn't sleep very well.'

'Are you OK?'

'I'm fine.' Kelly's smile was wider this time. Physically, the only thing that had disturbed her rest was the pleasure of experiencing the delicious tingles her body could conjure up with remarkable ease as she remembered the night with her musketeer. 'Maybe I just had too much excitement the night before.'

'Hmm.' Elsie looked unconvinced. 'You haven't said much about that. You did have a good time, then?'

'Magic,' Kelly affirmed.

So fabulous she couldn't begin to try describing it. And she didn't want to, despite sensing that Elsie felt left out and maybe a little hurt.

'I only went because of you,' she added. 'Thank you so much!'

It had been a night of pure magic. One that she intended to treasure for the rest of her life. And that was where the problem now lay. The repercussions that were going to affect a very large part of her life.

Reality couldn't be allowed to intrude, because she knew without a shadow of a doubt that reality would tarnish, if not completely destroy, the joy of that magic. That was why she needed to keep it private, and not diminish its perfection by talking about it. It was also why the dreadful prospect of Tony Grimshaw recognising her at work had made sleep so elusive.

'Is Flipper all right?' Briefly mollified, Elsie was now frowning anxiously. 'I did wonder if she had a bit of a sniffle on Saturday night. I noticed she was breathless going up my stairs.'

'Was she?' Kelly caught her bottom lip between her teeth, her mind whirling in a new direction. 'I'll mention it to Dr Clifford. She's got a check-up scheduled for this week.'

'But she's not sick today?'

'No. She couldn't wait to get to crèche. As usual.'

'What day's her appointment?'

'Wednesday. Sorry, Elsie. I forgot to say I wouldn't be working.'

'Not a problem. That's why I keep you on the casual list and why you get sent all over the show. Speaking of which—' Elsie glanced at her watch '—it's seven-thirty already. They will have finished hand-over.'

'I'm gone.' Kelly stood on one foot and then the other to pull disposable shoe-covers over her old, comfortable trainers.

'Report to the nurse manager when you get there. I'm not sure if they need you out front or in the observation area.'

Kelly took the shortcut of some fire escape stairs, as familiar with the layout of this vast hospital as she was with her own home. It was a world of its own in here, and she loved it despite the fact that her dream had never had her working in quite this capacity.

'Hey, Tom!' Kelly gave a cheerful wave to an orderly pushing an empty wheelchair in the opposite direction. Then she turned abruptly and chose a different direction when she saw the group of doctors coming behind Tom. She could take another route to the emergency department. She could use the service elevator and avoid any risk of recognition.

At least her uniform should be an effective disguise. The shower cap, the shapeless pink smock and the shoe-covers. Almost the same uniform the cleaners and kitchen staff wore—because, as a nurse aide, Kelly was part of the faceless army of people whose ranks stretched from groundsmen to technicians and kept this busy city hospital functioning the way it should. Making up the dark sky that allowed stars like Tony Grimshaw to shine so brightly.

Emergency should be safe enough, Kelly reassured herself as she sped down the final corridor, past the pharmacy and gift shop. It was rare for someone other than a registrar to make an initial assessment of a need for surgery. Being around the cardiology wards or theatre suites might be another matter, however. Kelly would need to stay on guard.

Not that she was likely to forget any time soon. Not when he was still in her head to this degree. When just a flicker of memory made her want to smile. Forgetting it enough to focus on her job might prove to be a problem, but it soon became apparent that her concern—for the moment, at least—was groundless.

The department was busy enough to keep her completely focussed. Fetching and carrying supplies, taking patients to the toilet or supplying bedpans, dealing with vomit containers and spills on the floor. She'd worked here often enough to be familiar with everything she needed to know. Many of the staff recognised her. One nurse looked particularly pleased to see her when she took a fresh linen bag to hang in the main resuscitation area.

'Kelly! Just the person I need. You know where everything is around here, don't you?'

'Pretty much.'

'Help me sort out this mess?' The wave indicated a benchtop littered with supplies that hadn't been put away. 'We've got an MVA victim coming in, and if it's still looking like this when they arrive, my guts will be someone's garters.'

It was fun, working under pressure. Handling syringes and bags of saline and packages containing endotracheal tubes. Things that had once been so familiar. Part of the dream Kelly had been well on her way to attaining.

'Want any sizes smaller than a seven on the tray?' she asked the nurse. 'Do you know what's coming in?'

'Something major.'

More staff were beginning to assemble in the room.

'Where's Radiology?' someone called. 'And the surgical reg—is she on her way?'

'I'd better get out of here,' Kelly said.

'No! Look!'

Kelly looked. Cupboard doors were open below the bench, with supplies spilling into a heap on the floor. They encroached over the red line on the floor that was there to keep unnecessary personnel from the area around a patient. Right at the head of the bed, too, where the person responsible for the patient's airway would be in danger of tripping over them.

Swiftly, Kelly crouched and began to stack the awkward packages back into the cupboards, so focussed on doing it as quickly as possible she barely registered the increasing level of activity behind her.

And then suddenly the double doors were pushed open and controlled chaos ensued.

'Seventeen-year-old, pushbike versus truck,' a paramedic informed the receiving doctor. 'Handlebar of the bike penetrated the left side of his chest. Intubated on scene and decompression attempted for a tension pneumothorax. Oxygen saturation's currently—'

Kelly was rising slowly to her feet, her back to the bench, and she slid sideways to get out of the way, horrified at being somewhere she had no right to be. Her gaze was none the less fixed on the scene so close to her. The transfer of the patient from the ambulance stretcher to the bed.

'On the count of three. One…two…*three*!'

There was a reassessment of all the vital signs, like heart-rate and blood pressure and respiration rate. None of them was looking good. Monitors were being hooked up and requests being called for more equipment and extra personnel. No one had time to notice Kelly, still standing in the corner.

She knew she had to leave. There was no way a nurse's aide could be any use at all in the kind of life-and-death drama about to be played out in here.

Bags of intravenous fluids were being clipped to overhead hooks. The doctor in charge of the airway was bag-masking the teenage boy, his eyes on the monitor screen that was showing him how much oxygen they were getting into his circulation. He didn't look happy with the figures he could see.

'Saturation's dropping. We're below ninety percent. And what the hell's happened to that ECG?'

An electrode had been displaced while moving the boy from the stretcher to the bed. Nursing staff were busy cutting away clothing and hadn't noticed the lead dangling uselessly, tangled up with the curly cord of the blood pressure cuff.

Without thinking, Kelly stepped forward into a gap, untangled the lead, and clipped the end back to the sticky pad attached beneath the patient's right collarbone.

'Thanks.' The doctor hadn't taken his eyes off the monitor, and Kelly could see why. The trace now travelling across the screen was erratic, and the unusual shapes of the spiky complexes suggested that this young boy was in imminent danger of a cardiac arrest.

Another doctor had his stethoscope on the less injured side of the chest. Was it proving too hard for one lung to function well enough to sustain life? Was the heart itself badly injured? Or was this boy simply bleeding too badly from internal injuries to make saving his life an impossibility?

Kelly was back in her corner. Transfixed. She could feel the tension rising with every second that ticked relentlessly past. With every command from the emergency department specialists, who were finding it difficult to gain extra IV access and infuse the blood volume that was so desperately needed, judging by the way the blood pressure was continuing to fall.

'Didn't someone page Cardiothoracic?' a doctor snapped. 'Where the hell are they?'

'Right here,' a calm voice responded. 'What are we dealing with?'

Kelly actually gasped aloud as Tony Grimshaw stepped closer to the bed, pulling on a pair of gloves. Not that there was the slightest danger of being noticed. At the precise moment the surgeon finished speaking, an alarm sounded on a monitor. And then another.

'VF,' someone called.

'No pulse,' another added.

'Start CPR.' The order came from the head of the bed. 'And charge the defibrillator to three-sixty.'

'Wait!' Tony's hands were on the patient's chest, lifting a blood-soaked dressing to examine the wound. 'Have you got a thoracotomy trolley set up?'

'Yes, I'll get it.' An ED registrar leaned closer. 'You're thinking tamponade? What about a needle pericardiocentesis first?'

'Wasting time,' Tony decreed. 'We're either dealing with a cardiac injury or major thoracic blood loss that needs controlling. Can I have some rapid skin preparation, please? We're not going to attempt full asepsis and draping, but I want everyone in here wearing a mask.

And let's see if we can get a central line in while I'm scrubbing.'

Masks were tugged from the boxes attached to the wall as trolleys were moved and rapid preparation for the major intervention of opening the boy's chest continued. Kelly grabbed a mask for herself. A perfect disguise—just in case she got noticed when she made her move towards the exit.

Except she couldn't move. A thoracotomy for penetrating chest trauma topped the list for emergency department drama, and staff who had no more reason to be here than she were now finding excuses to slip into the back of the room to observe. House surgeons, registrars and nursing staff were squeezed into the space behind the red lines, and Kelly was trapped at the back. Able to hear everything, and even find a small window between the shoulders of the people directly in front of her, that afforded a good view of the surgeon if not the procedure.

He now had a hat and mask and gown over the Theatre scrubs he had been wearing on arrival. He seemed unconcerned by his audience. Ready to use an incredibly tense situation as a teaching tool, in fact.

'I'll use a "clam shell" approach,' he told the closest doctors. 'The one you guys would be using if I wasn't here.'

'Yeah…right,' someone near Kelly muttered. An over-awed medical student, perhaps?

She saw the flash of a scalpel being lifted from the sterile cover of the trolley.

'Bilateral incisions,' Tony said. 'About four centimetres in length, in the fifth intercostal space, mid-axillary line.'

Blood trickled down the yellow staining of hurriedly applied antiseptic on the boy's chest. Kelly was struck by how frail the young chest suddenly seemed.

'Make sure you breach the intercostal muscles and the parietal pleura. With a bit of luck we might deal with a tension pneumothorax and get some cardiac output at this point.'

They didn't.

Tony took just a moment to watch the screen, however, and his voice was soft. 'What's his name?'

'Michael.'

'And he's seventeen?'

'Yes.'

'Family here?'

'His mother's just arrived. She's in the relatives' room.'

Tony simply nodded, but Kelly was allowing herself to stare at him in the wake of his rapid-fire surprising queries. How had he done that? Made this seem so much more personal? As though he cared more about the patient than demonstrating his obviously not inconsiderable skills? Maybe he wasn't as hung up on his status as rumour had led her to believe.

She held her breath, watching the swift and decisive actions of this surgeon as he used a fine wire saw to cut though the sternum and then opened the chest with retractors.

'I'm "tenting" the pericardium,' he said moments later. 'Scissors—thanks. Make a long incision like this. If it's too short, it'll prevent access to the heart. Suction…'

What would it be like, Kelly wondered, to have this man as a mentor in a career as a cardiothoracic surgeon? Or just to work alongside him as a nurse? To know him on a personal basis?

Maybe *she* knew him better than anyone else in this room.

A ridiculous thought, given the situation. Given reality. It made her memories of her time with him more dreamlike. Precious, but harder to hang onto. Kelly tucked them protectively into a corner of her mind.

Into that empty space in her heart.

Tony had both hands inside the boy's chest now, massaging Michael's heart. 'Make sure you keep the heart horizontal during massage,' he told the observers. 'Lifting the apex can prevent venous filling. I'm aiming for a rate of eighty per minute here, and I'm looking for any obvious bleeding that we need to control.'

The people in front of Kelly were murmuring in awed tones, and they shifted enough to obscure her line of vision. She heard the request for internal defibrillation, however, and could envisage the tiny paddles that would provide a minimal jolt to the cardiac tissue but hopefully restore a more normal heartbeat.

A collective gasp of amazement rippled around the room seconds later, but she could sense no let-up in control of a difficult situation from the star at the centre of this drama.

'Theatre's on standby. Let's get Michael up there while we've got a perfusing rhythm.'

There was a new flurry of activity as the open chest wound was covered, and the bed, the monitors and numerous necessary staff members all began moving as a connected unit.

Tony stripped off his gloves, dropping them to the floor and reaching for a fresh pair. His gaze scanned the assembled staff as he took a single step to put him within reach of what he needed. Kelly felt the eye contact like something physical. Almost a blow, the way it sent shock waves through her body. Despite the contact being so brief—less than a heartbeat—the connection was so strong she was sure Tony had to feel it, too. He'd glance back—with a frown, maybe. Needing a second glance without having registered why.

But he didn't look back. He barely broke his stride as he pulled fresh gloves from the slot on the box and followed his patient towards Theatre.

Maybe he hadn't seen her. She was unimportant.

Invisible.

'Wow,' came a voice beside her. 'I saw it, but I still don't believe it.'

'I don't believe the mess they've left behind. Kelly, would you mind helping clear this up?'

'Better head back to work myself.' The first nurse sighed. 'Guess the excitement's over.'

Kelly tore her gaze away from the open door that had swallowed the figure of Tony Grimshaw.

Yes. The excitement was definitely over.

'Are you sure?'

'I've checked three times since you rang this morning, Mr Grimshaw. I'm sorry, but there's no C. Riley to be found on either the permanent or the casual nursing staff databases.'

'But…'

'Are you sure she's a nurse?' The woman from Personnel was beginning to sound impatient on the other end of the line. 'St Patrick's employs hundreds of people, you know. This Miss Riley you're trying to locate might be a physiotherapist or a dietician or a social worker—or any number of other things.'

'But she said…' Tony paused. She hadn't actually said she was a nurse, had she? She'd said she worked in a lot of different areas and that her favourite places were Emergency and Theatre. He was standing in the theatre suite right now, and there were people everywhere. Nurses, orderlies, technicians. Even a girl polishing the taps on the handbasins.

There were also two registrars waiting for him at a discreet distance from this wall phone. They were running late for a departmental meeting.

'Never mind.' He'd probably started some sort of a rumour by making these enquiries in the first place, but the staff in Personnel weren't to know *why* he was trying to locate the woman. It could be to reprimand her or something. 'Thank you for your help,' he added.

'A pleasure. If I hear anything that might be helpful I'll contact you, shall I?'

Tony could squash any embryonic rumours by saying it really didn't matter.

But it did, didn't it?

Since he'd woken up on Sunday morning to reach out and find his bed empty, he'd been unable to get rid of that sense of…loss.

It should have been easy. He'd thought he had it sorted when anger had kicked in briefly. When he'd started feeling as though he'd been used and discarded. But then the doubts had crept in. Excuses his brain was only too willing to come up with on her behalf.

Maybe she'd had a good reason to leave without saying anything. Mind you, there'd have to be a good reason to justify not wanting to repeat that experience. He knew it had been just as good for her as it had been for him. Nobody could fake that kind of responsiveness. Or sincerity. The princess had been genuine and he wanted to find her.

Maybe she was married?

If that was the case, fine. Tony wasn't about to break up anyone's marriage. It was this not knowing that was frustrating him. That and the peculiar dream-like quality the whole night had taken on.

But it had been real. Utterly different from anything he'd ever experienced before, but there was no denying it *had* happened. Or that the impression it had left made it impossible to forget. Perhaps what was really pushing his buttons was the need to *prove* it had been real. So that he would know what he needed to aim for in his personal life and never allow himself to settle for what had been on offer so far.

Mediocrity. Interest that always became infected with an urge to escape.

'Thank you,' Tony said finally, preparing to hang up the receiver. 'I'd appreciate that.'

His registrar had an armful of paperwork, and there would be a lot more by the end of the usual late Monday afternoon meeting where the cardiologists presented their cases. They would listen to histories, view footage of angiograms showing coronary arteries in various stages of blockage, grade people to score the urgency of intervention and draw up the Theatre list for bypass surgery for the next week.

There would be cases left over from last week who hadn't made it to Theatre because of emergency procedures taking precedence, and there would be debate over issues such as age and lifestyle and circumstances.

A tedious meeting in many ways. Tony was tempted to leave it to his registrar and attend to something more important. Like yet another check on this morning's trauma case. Seventeen-year-old Michael was in the intensive care unit, and he was still a sick lad but he was alive. Tony knew his save was the talk of the hospital, but what concerned him was whether the boy would make it through the next critical day or two. Whether he would recover without sequelae that could ruin his quality of life.

The two men he was leading into the meeting room now had been the other musketeers at the ball. Funny how it seemed such a long time ago already. As they sat down around the long table, Tony impulsively turned his head.

'Josh, you know a lot of the nurses around here, don't you?'

His registrar grinned. 'I'm working on it.'

'Ever come across a Cindy?'

The grin stretched. 'No. No Barbies, either.'

Tony's smile felt strained. This should feel like a joke but it didn't. He nodded at colleagues entering the room, noted that the audiovisual gear wasn't ready yet, and lowered his voice.

'Cindy Riley,' he told Josh. 'Tall. Long, black hair.'

'Not the woman you spent most of Saturday night dancing with? Blue dress with a lacey thing down the front?'

Tony gave a slow nod, hopefully not overdoing the effort to appear casual. It wasn't easy. The memory of that 'lacey thing' almost exploded in his head. The way her fingers had assisted him to undo it. The way her breasts had felt when he'd finally got to touch them…

'Won't be a moment,' one of the cardiologists called. 'We just need another extension cord.'

'She told you her name was Cindy Riley?'

'Yes.'

Josh exchanged a glance with the other registrar. 'And you're trying to find her?'

'Ah...yes.'

Josh grinned. 'Did it occur to you that she might not want to be found?' he ventured.

'What on earth makes you say that?'

Josh didn't respond immediately. Computer print-outs were being passed around, listing the cases up for discussion. Tony took his copy but ignored it. He frowned at Josh.

'It just seems a bit of a coincidence.' Josh shrugged.

'What does?'

'A Cindy Riley. At a ball.'

'Thanks for coming,' the head of the cardiology department said, then cleared his throat. 'We've got a lot to get through today, so let's get started. Case one. Sixty-eight-year-old man with angina occurring with minimal exertion. Investigations so far reveal reduced ventricular function estimated at thirty-eight percent. He has moderate mitral regurgitation. A blocked anterior descending, almost blocked posterior descending, and fifty percent occlusion on his left main.'

The screen flickered into life, and views of dye being injected into coronary arteries were shown from various angles.

Tony was having trouble concentrating. A combination of words had made a loop that went round and round in his head.

Cindy Riley. At a ball.

Again and again the name echoed and merged, and finally morphed into something else.

'Good grief!'

'Problem, Tony?'

His soft exclamation had unintentionally reached the presenting cardiologist.

'Not at all. Ah…could you just rerun that last shot of the left main?'

Josh caught his gaze for a second, the quirk of his lips revealing that he knew exactly why Tony had been surprised.

Cindy Riley.

Cinderella.

No wonder this felt so different. He'd stumbled into a fairytale!

He'd found a princess in disguise.

What would the modern-day equivalent of a dropped slipper be? A mobile phone, perhaps?

Dammit. The only clue he had to go on was that she'd been at the ball alone, and had therefore acquired a ticket by being a member of staff here at St Patrick's.

The woman from Personnel had been fazed by the sheer number of employees. She hadn't been up to the challenge.

Tony straightened in his chair, clearing his throat as he prepared to redirect his focus to where it was supposed to be right now.

For the moment he was satisfied.

He loved a challenge.

CHAPTER FOUR

'I'VE got a bone to pick with you, Kelly Adams!'

'Hey, it's my day off. I can't possibly have done anything wrong.'

'You could have told me.'

'I did tell you. It's Wednesday, remember? Flipper's appointment?'

'Not about that.' Elsie clicked her tongue, but she was peering behind Kelly. 'Where *is* Flipper?'

'Crèche. We've got a two-hour gap until the ultrasound. I asked Flipper if she wanted to come out to lunch with you and me or go and play with her friends, and the friends won, I'm afraid.'

Elsie sniffed. 'I'm far too busy to go anywhere for lunch anyway. I've got rosters to sort.'

'But I really want to take you out for lunch. A nice lunch. To say thank you for babysitting the other night.'

Elsie's sniff sounded even more offended this time. 'Yes,' she said. 'The other night…' She fished in her pocket and pulled out a folded piece of paper. Kelly watched her open it, her jaw dropping as a slightly fuzzy image appeared.

'Where did you get *that*?'

'Tom was on the hospital website. He thought I might like to see some of the pictures taken at the ball. I got him to print this one off. We both thought you looked like you were having the time of your life, but neither of us could figure out who it is in that musketeer costume.'

Kelly couldn't take her eyes off the image. She was in Tony's arms, laughing up at him. He was bent over her, about to sweep her into a dip, probably, and every line of his body suggested a total focus on the woman in he was holding. It was such a tangible reminder of that night. Kelly could feel her heart rate picking up and a delicious melting sensation deep in her belly.

'Can I…have that?'

'Not unless you tell me who he is.'

Kelly grinned. 'I'll tell you if you let me take you out to lunch. Please, Elsie? I need to stop at the gift shop on the way back, because I've promised Flipper a surprise for being such a wee champion for her blood tests this morning. You can help me choose something she'd really like.'

Elsie refolded the picture and put it back in her pocket. 'I suppose I could escape for half an hour.'

'Let's get our skates on, then. I want to take you across the road to The Waiting Room.'

'You can't afford *their* outrageous prices!'

'Yes, I can. Just for a treat. Go on… Bacon and egg sandwiches. A real cappuccino…'

Elsie might be grumbling, but she was moving pretty quickly for someone in her sixties with more than a touch of arthritis.

The two women made unlikely-looking friends as they walked briskly through the main entrance of the hospital to get to the popular café on the edge of St Patrick's grounds, but there was a close bond between them. One that had been forged by a mutual love for the baby Kelly had been forced to take with her, way back, when she'd applied for the job at St Pat's.

There was a limit to how much Kelly intended to confess to the older woman now, however, which was just as well. Elsie was shocked at simply learning the name of the musketeer.

'Dr Grimshaw? The surgeon?'

Kelly cast an anxious glance around them, but other patrons, many of them in uniform or even scrubs, fortunately seemed intent on enjoying the great food and superb coffee.

'It was just a dance, Elsie.'

'*Was* it?'

Kelly pressed her lips together firmly.

Elsie ate the last bite of her sandwich in silence. Then she looked up. 'You going to see him again?'

Kelly forgot her resolve to stay quiet. 'Of *course* not!'

'What's so "of course not" about it?'

'It's ridiculous, that's why. We come from different

planets. It would be like…oh, I don't know…a member of the royal family and a servant.'

Like…a fairytale.

'Imagine if he saw me emptying a bedpan or something?'

'Did you tell him what you do for a living?'

'Hardly. I didn't even tell him my real name. I said it was Cindy Riley.'

Elsie snorted after a moment's thought. 'Very clever.'

'Very temporary.'

'Your planets aren't really so different,' Elsie said as she pushed back her chair. 'You could very easily be standing on his one by now, you know. If it hadn't been for that dreadful accident.'

Kelly picked up her handbag. 'I can't regret any sacrifice I made,' she said quietly. 'Not when it gave me Flipper. She's my family, Elsie. She's all I have that's really mine.'

'I know, love.' Neither woman had risen to her feet yet. 'And I know that you probably don't even admit it to yourself, but there must be times when you're lonely?'

Kelly ignored the gentle query. She couldn't afford to go there. It was something else that would become far too real by talking about it. It would become real and then it would grow. She stood up.

'And that's another reason I won't be seeing him or anyone else again. I'm not going to risk letting someone into my life who might not be prepared to love Flipper the way I do.'

'You'll never know if you don't give someone a chance,' Elsie persisted as she followed Kelly. 'And who said you had to marry him, anyway? Or take him home, even?'

Kelly gasped in mock horror. 'Are you suggesting I engage in an affair that's never going to go anywhere?'

'All I'm saying is maybe you shouldn't be throwing away something that's given you a sparkle I've never seen before.'

It was time to change the subject. Kelly veered towards the gift shop in the hospital foyer and the display stand of toys outside its door.

'Look! Wouldn't she love this pink bear in the tutu? Oh…what about this?' Kelly picked up a large, fluffy green frog. She hugged it, and then laughed as it croaked with a convincing 'rivet rivet' sound.

'Definitely the frog.'

The voice wasn't Elsie's. Kelly's head turned so swiftly she almost lost her balance.

Tony Grimshaw was dressed in scrubs with an un-buttoned white coat over the top. He looked fresh from a stint in Theatre, with his hair rumpled and a pink line across his forehead that must have been left by the edge of a cap. Dark eyes she remembered so well were staring at her intently, and she couldn't miss the sudden gleam of mischief in them.

'Still looking for a prince, Cinderella?' The query was deadpan. 'Try kissing the frog.'

Kelly heard a faint, "Oh, my!" from Elsie's direction,

but she couldn't turn her head because that would mean breaking eye contact with Tony.

And she couldn't do that because she was watching the corners of his eyes crinkle, and she had to see the way the smile spread across his features. She could feel her own face changing. Mirroring his with a smile that seemed to be being pulled from a place she'd never explored. A very joyous place.

'What do you say, Cinderella? Can I buy you lunch and help you decide?'

'No.' Kelly shook her head hurriedly. 'I've had my lunch. But thank you.'

'You're not working today?' His gaze flicked over the civvies—a layered tops and the snug-fitting jeans Kelly had tucked into long boots. 'Or are you doing an afternoon shift?'

'No...I just came in to—' Kelly felt a nudge in the small of her back. Elsie might be pretending to rearrange the display stand of toys but her elbow carried a very unsubtle message. It also provided inspiration. 'To look at my roster,' she finished.

'You'll have time for a coffee, at least?'

'Oooh.' Kelly would have to tell Elsie how sharp her elbows were. 'I guess a—a coffee wouldn't hurt.'

'And your friend?'

'Sorry?' Was he offering to take *Elsie* for coffee as well?

Tony patted the fluffy frog she was still clutching.

'Rivet-rivet,' the toy said obligingly.

Kelly had to fight the wild desire to giggle like a teenager. She also had to fight the acute awareness of the way his hand had brushed her fingers. This was like a scene from a comedy.

A romantic comedy?

'Here.' Tony took the frog from her hands and turned to Elsie, clearly mistaking her for the woman who ran the gift shop. 'Could you wrap this, please, and charge it to my account? I'm—'

'I know who you are,' Elsie said calmly. 'It will be no trouble at all, sir.'

'Excellent. Cinderella will be in to collect it later.'

'Cinderella?' Elsie managed to inject an amused but questioning note into her voice.

'Private joke,' Tony explained.

The statement gave Kelly a very odd kind of tingle. As though he considered them to be friends. More than friends, even.

'That'll be Miss—?' Tony raised an eyebrow at Kelly. 'It *is* Miss, I presume?'

Oh, Lord…was he asking if she was single? Standing there, in Theatre scrubs, looking just a little rumpled. Holding a fluffy toy with a look on his face that made her think that if they weren't standing in an astonishingly busy thoroughfare of a major hospital he would be kissing her senseless.

And now, thanks to Elsie, he was going to find out who she really was.

He *wanted* to find out.

'Yes,' Kelly managed. 'Miss Adams. Kelly Adams.'

'Excellent,' Tony said again. He gave the frog to Elsie. 'I'd really appreciate it if you could gift wrap this for Miss Adams.'

He led Kelly through the foyer and out of the main door on the same route she had taken with Elsie not very long ago. 'I'm sure you've made a wise choice,' he said. 'You'll love the frog.'

That brought another smile to Kelly's face. 'It's not for me,' she said. 'I wanted to find a present for a small girl who was very brave this morning, getting some bloods taken.'

'Ah…a patient. How old is she?'

'Three. Nearly four.'

'You must be fond of her. What's her name?'

'Flipper.'

He gave her another one of those intent looks. 'Like the dolphin?'

Kelly laughed. What was it about talking to this man that had her smiling and laughing so easily? Feeling as if…as if that joyous place was just around the next corner.

'Her real name's Philippa,' she said, still smiling. 'She's always called herself Flipper, so now everyone else does.'

'You sound like you know her very well?'

'Yes.'

'One of the special ones?'

'Absolutely.'

Good grief, Tony was leading her into The Waiting

Room. A staff member working behind the counter gave Kelly a surprised glance, which made her wonder how many others would notice her being there for the second time in less than an hour.

Tony sensed her hesitation. 'The coffee's so much better in here than it is in the staff café. We could go somewhere else, if you like, but there's not many places I could get away with wearing scrubs. I reckon there's more St Pat's staff in here than members of the general public.'

Yes. A quick glance around while Tony was choosing sandwiches and some fruit confirmed that. In fact wasn't that John Clifford—Flipper's doctor—with a group of other consultants on the far side of the café? Thank goodness he wasn't looking in her direction.

'There's a free table over there,' Kelly pointed out hurriedly as Tony picked up his tray.

'Perfect.'

It was. Tucked into a corner and at least partially screened by a potted palm tree. Tony might know her real name now, but Kelly could still pull a little magic around herself by keeping the rest of reality at bay.

Except that Tony seemed to have other ideas.

'So—tell me about young Flipper,' he invited. 'What's wrong with her?'

'She has…um…congenital heart problems.'

'Oh? What sort?'

It was so tempting to tell him something about her life from the safe perspective of seeming to be discussing someone else. Just to see what his reaction might be.

'It's complicated,' Kelly said cautiously. 'Patent ductus arteriosus with a major atrioventricular septal defect. Some valve abnormalities as well.'

'Poor kid.' Tony paused before taking another large bite of his ham and salad sandwich. 'She's had surgery, I suppose?'

'As a newborn.'

'Hard on the parents.'

'Very.'

'And she's been admitted again?''

'Oh, no!' The thought was horrifying.

'Why the blood tests, then? And the frog?'

'She needs regular check-ups. For all sorts of things.' Maybe it had been a mistake allowing this conversation to continue, but she had—so why stop now? 'She has Down's Syndrome,' Kelly finished matter-of-factly.

Tony couldn't know that his reaction might be under a closer scrutiny than might be expected, but his smile was very sympathetic.

'I take my hat off to parents like that,' he said. 'It's hard enough to cope with sick kids, but the ones with special needs on top of physical problems require an astonishing devotion. From everyone. Family, doctors, nursing staff…' He was smiling at Kelly now, including her in that number. Making her feel as though he understood and approved of any extra effort involved. 'She must be special to warrant a talking frog. What's her surname? I might know her.'

The belated arrival of their coffee was well timed.

Kelly had a moment to stop kicking herself for talking about something so personal, however well disguised, and to look for an escape route before she could start clouding any dream with reality and making the mistake of believing it.

'You don't do paediatric surgery, do you?'

'It's an area of interest, but I haven't had the time or opportunity to do anything about it. I did have a seventeen-year-old patient the other day.' His smile had to be the most engaging Kelly had ever seen. 'Is that close enough?'

She dragged her gaze away from his mouth. 'How *is* Michael?'

That diverted him with startling success. 'How on earth do you know his name?'

'I was there,' Kelly confessed, delighted to have a new topic of conversation. 'I saw your thoracotomy.'

'I didn't see you.'

'I wasn't inside the lines. More like part of your audience. It was…amazing.'

'It was lucky, more like it. Good timing. A successful result is dependent on the level of cardiac activity, or on how much time between when it stops and a thoracotomy is performed. I'm not boring you here, am I?'

'Of course not.'

'There've been some big studies done, and I love to keep up with the kind of results of research that relate to what I do. Chances of survival are zero if the victim's arrested at the scene of the accident. Minimal—about four percent—if it happens en route in the ambulance.

But you can expect a survival rate of about twenty percent if the arrest happens in the emergency department. Especially if it's isolated trauma to the thoracic cavity, as it was in this case.'

'So he's going to survive?'

'He's out of Intensive Care already. I'm planning to check up on him after lunch.' Tony stilled for a moment, as though struck by a new thought. 'Tell you what,' he said with a smile, 'meet me for dinner tonight and I'll give you an update.'

Kelly shook her head. 'I can't. Sorry.'

'Oh… Not a night shift, is it?'

She pulled a wry face which might easily have suggested the necessity and lack of enjoyment involved in having to work night shift, and Tony simply nodded.

'Not the easiest life, is it?'

'No.'

'But you've had a look at your roster today, yes? I've got mine right here.' A Blackberry emerged from the pocket of his white coat. 'Let's find a night we're both free.'

Kelly said nothing, aware of alarm bells sounding loudly. It was all very well for Elsie to recommend her putting some excitement in her life—and what could be more exciting than a date with the most eligible bachelor on the staff of St Pat's? In the city, even? But Elsie wasn't sitting here, realising just how easy it would be to lose sight of reality completely and make the mistake of falling for a man like this.

As if sex with Tony Grimshaw could *ever* be meaningless.

He glanced up from the electronic device, and must have seen something of what Kelly was thinking in her face because he frowned.

'I'm sorry I didn't see you in Emergency the other day. I hope you didn't think I was being deliberately rude?'

Kelly's breath came out in an amused huff. 'Hardly. Why on earth would you have been looking?'

'Well, maybe I was a little preoccupied at that precise time, but I *have* been looking—believe me.'

'Oh?' Words deserted Kelly.

Tony leaned closer. 'Do you have any idea what sort of idiot I felt like when I realised I'd been pestering the staff in Personnel to track down a Cindy Riley that I'd happened to meet at a ball?'

Kelly bit her lip. 'I never thought...'

'That I'd want to find you? And why not?' He lowered his voice. 'Why did you just leave like that, Kelly? Without even letting me know who you really were?'

'Because...' There had been a flash of something totally unexpected in his eyes. Something like bewilderment. Hurt, even? Did someone like her really have the power to dent the confidence of someone like Tony? He didn't deserve that. 'I didn't want to spoil the magic,' she whispered. 'The whole night had been like a fairytale.'

'Hmm.' The look was assessing now. Probing. She felt as if he could see right into her soul and gauge how honest she was being. But then he smiled. 'Fairytale, huh? I can buy that.'

He reached his hand across the table so that his fingertips touched hers. The tiniest connection in physical terms, but the effect was electrifying.

'It *was* magic, wasn't it?' he said softly. 'I was starting to think I'd dreamt it. Come out with me, Kelly. I'd really like more proof that it *was* real, because…'

The way his words trailed away made Kelly even more conscious of the touch of his skin against hers. It was spreading. Up her arms and into the rest of her body. Making her breasts tingle. Giving her that mind fogging curl deep in her belly.

'Because?' Her prompt came out embarrassingly like a croak.

'It was so different,' Tony said slowly. '*You're* different. I'm not sure why, but I'm a scientist and I can't just put it down to magic.' The smile flashed again. That disarmingly boyish grin. The kind that belonged to a man confident enough not to care about standing in a busy hospital thoroughfare in his scrubs, holding a ridiculous fluffy green toy. 'I think some research is called for here.' He moved his hand to pick up his Blackberry. 'How about Friday?'

'Flipper, have you still got the keys, hon?'

A small hand jangled the set of keys importantly. Three-year-old Philippa Adams was taking her responsibility seriously. She clambered up the steps to the front door of a small terraced house, and then stared at the keys, panting from the exertion of climbing.

'It's the big silver one,' Kelly prompted.

Short fingers fumbled, trying to insert the wrong key into the lock.

'Maybe I should do it this time, sweetheart.'

'No! Flipper do it.'

'I could just help,' Kelly said casually after another attempt, hopefully without making it obvious that this skill was still well above the little girl's abilities. 'It's been a busy day, hasn't it? I think we're both tired.'

'Mummy tired?' A round face appeared as Flipper peered up at Kelly. With its small nose and wide mouth and the almond shaped eyes that disappeared into slits when she grinned, she looked like an adorable pixie. One that was frowning in concern as she considered the possibility that her mother wasn't happy.

The keys were handed over. 'You go, Mummy.'

Kelly ruffled her sparse dark hair. 'Good girl. We'll both do it. You hold the key and I'll hold your hand on top. Like this.'

A moment later they were both walking down the short, narrow hallway of the tiny house. The two front rooms were the bedrooms, and a third door led to the bathroom. At the end of the hallway a single room ran the width of the dwelling—a kitchen-living area that gave an illusion of space, accentuated by French doors that opened onto a compact bricked courtyard.

Kelly peeled the anorak from the small girl, and as

soon as she was free from her outdoor clothing Flipper made a series of kangaroo hops to reach the centre of a round rug in front of a small sofa. She held her arms wide and spun herself around in circles.

'Darn!' she called. 'Darn, Mummy!'

'I can't dance just now,' Kelly apologised. 'I need to make our dinner. Want to help?'

'No.' Flipper's bottom lip jutted.

'Hey! You dropped Frog.' Distraction was needed. 'What does Frog say?'

The smile erased the discontented frown instantly. 'Ribby-ribby!' Flipper shouted.

'And why did you get Frog?'

'I was a goo' girl.'

'You sure were.' Kelly stooped to gather Flipper for a quick hug, but Flipper wriggled free of the embrace. She swooped on the toy she had dropped in order to get her jacket taken off, and a moment later she was dancing again, with the fluffy frog clutched in her arms.

The bright green toy even had to sit on the table beside Flipper's plate when they had their dinner.

'No,' Kelly had to say firmly, more than once. 'Frog doesn't eat mashed potato. It goes in *your* mouth.'

As usual, it also went all over her face and through her hair. Flipper's bath was a necessity as well as a time they both enjoyed, but again the new family member created some friction.

'No. You can't have Frog in the bath. He'd get all wet and soggy and then he wouldn't be able to go to bed with you.' Kelly tugged on the toy that was being held with a grip of iron. 'How about we put him on the toilet seat and he can watch while I wash your hair?'

'OK.'

'And we'd better try not to splash too much tonight.'

Soaping the small body after the hair-washing was attended to, Kelly's hands traced the lumpy scar that ran down the front of Flipper's chest.

'We saw your heart today, didn't we? We saw it on the special TV, going lub-dub, lub-dub.'

'Lub-dub-*dub*!' Flipper's hands hit the water with enthusiasm, and Kelly laughed, wiping soapsuds off her own face.

'You should be called Flapper, not Flipper.'

'Dub-dub-*dub*!' And Flipper joined in the laughter with peals of the delicious gurgle that was Kelly's favourite sound in the world.

'He was a nice man who looked at your heart on the TV, wasn't he?'

Flipper reached for a plastic duck.

'I had coffee with another nice man today.' Kelly squeezed a sponge to let water rinse the suds from Flipper's back. 'He wants to go out with me.'

Flipper was pushing the duck beneath the surface of the water and then letting it go so that it bobbed up. Every time seemed to create the same level of surprise and elicited another gurgle of laughter. She didn't appear to be listening to Kelly.

'It's Aunty Elsie's fault,' Kelly murmured. 'She

thinks I should go. She reckons I could hire another dress or wear one of hers. She's got all these wonderful retro frocks from the sixties and seventies she's never thrown out, and she wants me to go and try them on and she'll make them fit.'

Flipper threw the duck over the side of the bath.

'Do *you* think I should go?'

A ridiculous question to ask an uninterested child, but Kelly was simply thinking aloud here. Exploring what was, admittedly, a very tempting notion. Elsie thought she should go. She would be only too happy to babysit Flipper again.

'He wants to take me dancing,' Kelly told Flipper.

That got her interest.

'Darn!'

'Mmm.' Kelly touched the sponge to Flipper's nose. 'With the nice man. What do you think?'

'Man?'

'Mmm. A nice man.'

'Man darn?' Flipper was staring up at Kelly now, her eyes as wide as it was possible for them to get.

'Oh, yes,' Kelly smiled. 'The man can dance, all right.'

The stare continued, and then Flipper's face creased into that wonderful smile. Not that she understood what Kelly was really talking about. She was just happy because she thought her mother was happy.

Kelly lifted her from the tub, wrapped her in a fluffy towel and kissed her. 'I love you,' she said.

'Mummy darn,' Flipper said decisively.

Did she mean with her or with the 'nice man'? Could she make her own choice? Kelly kissed her again.

'You know what?' Her smile widened. 'I think I will.'

CHAPTER FIVE

THE exclusive harbourside restaurant was an intimate and discreet haven for those lucky enough to succeed in making a reservation.

It was a favourite haunt for Tony. Usually, the fact that the owner, Pierre, knew him so well and always had 'his' table ready for him was simply taken as a matter of course—by himself and by the sophisticated women who normally accompanied him.

Tonight was different.

It had been ever since he'd pulled up near the non-descript exterior of a terraced house in one of the less desirable inner city streets. One that he'd probably driven through many times with no interest in what lay alongside the road.

The surroundings had been forgotten, however, the moment the door at the top of the steps opened. Kelly had paused for a moment, scanning the limited parking spaces available for his vehicle.

Tony had also hesitated, his hand already on the door

handle in preparation for getting out to open the passenger side of his car. It wasn't because of any reluctance on his part, more from being struck by a kind of wonder at the way this woman seemed to pull light around her. Any background would have become dull and insignificant.

She…shone.

Her hair was loose again, and desire kicked in as Tony remembered burying his fingers in those luxuriant waves to draw her close enough to kiss. His breath caught in his chest, allowing no more than a soft, strangled groan as his body decided to relive the exquisite tickle of her hair on his body when he had pulled her on top of him.

Getting out of his car and getting himself on a tight leash had been paramount. Tonight wasn't about the overwhelming lust of the night of the ball. It was about getting to know the reality behind the fantasy. Kelly Adams, not Cinderella. This was a date, and he was an expert in dates.

Except this was so different.

Kelly, with her hair long and loose, and a dress that fitted close on the top but had a billowing skirt with huge blue flowers splashed all over its white background, couldn't have presented a more dramatic contrast to his usual companions with their neat, carefully streaked blonde hairstyles and slinky cocktail dresses.

For the same reason, maybe, it was a little embarrassing to have Pierre greet him personally now, and escort them to "his" table. He didn't want Kelly to think that he came here so often. With so many other women. He wanted her to think she was special. To know that *he* thought she was special.

A trio of musicians was tucked into a corner of the restaurant beside a small dance floor, but even that made Tony vaguely uncomfortable. It was way too soon to ask Kelly if she would like to dance. As much as his body craved the touch of holding her, he couldn't do it while things felt so…different.

Awkward.

Like the way her eyes widened when Pierre brought the customary French champagne to start their evening. He filled their crystal flutes and then stood back, a square of snowy linen draped over his arm, speaking in his perfect English with an accent that made most women sigh, detailing the gastronomic delights the menu had to offer tonight.

It would be easier when they were left alone, Tony decided. They could talk about the food and break the ice.

But Kelly's eyes were shining by the time Pierre had finished speaking. She didn't even open her menu.

'Pâté,' she said decisively. 'And the chicken with truffles. I've never tasted a truffle, and it sounded divine, didn't it?'

'Mmm.' Tony closed his own menu and returned her smile. He needed to find something else to talk about.

Something. Anything that would spark a conversation and give him a reason to watch her. The way those huge eyes took in everything around her, as though it was new and fascinating. The way her face moved to reveal so much of what she was thinking. She was so *alive*.

So real. Unsophisticated, perhaps. Childlike, even. Yet she was the most attractive woman Tony had ever met. And this was…astonishing.

Even more astonishing was the fact that the ice was broken by something that had always been a taboo on any date.

Him—talking about his work.

He wasn't sure how it happened exactly. He made some polite query about her day, and a responding comment about a lengthy meeting he'd been tied up with, and suddenly he was answering questions about his current research with an enthusiasm kindled by the interest he could see in her face.

'It's a drug that can preserve cerebral cellular function in patients undergoing bypass surgery.'

'Oh…' She almost clicked her fingers as she summoned the information she wanted. 'Like—what it's called?—Neuroshield?'

The surprise was a very pleasant jolt. 'That's the parent drug. When I was a registrar I worked in Christchurch under a surgeon, David James, who's married to a cardiologist. Amazing team. They collaborated in the first trials of Neuroshield and it's been in clinical use for years, but now there's a new generation and David wants me to provide an arm of the research project.'

'And you're keen?' Her smile advertised that she knew the question was redundant.

'Research is a dimension to medicine that keeps the fascination alive. The only way to keep us moving forward and improving what we're capable of doing.'

Kelly was nodding, giving every impression of being totally absorbed by the topic. Their entrees arrived, but for once the food didn't become a new focus.

'Neuroshield works by slowing the metabolism, doesn't it? Enough to preserve cellular function when it's being challenged by something like bypass?'

Tony could only nod, his mouth full.

'How do you measure the parameters of something like that?'

It was the kind of conversation he might expect to have with a bright house surgeon or registrar. The kind of junior doctor it was a pleasure to work with. Tony swallowed.

'You need extensive baseline data. Anatomical and functional assessment with a series of neurological tests including CT scans.'

'Sounds expensive.'

'Most research is. The major cost is paying the salaries of the people qualified to do it, but do you know what the real challenge is?'

She simply raised the dark eyebrows that framed those gorgeous blue eyes and it was all the encouragement Tony needed.

'It's finding people who are genuinely interested.'

'But why? I would have thought they'd be lining up to get on board.'

'It's not the most glamorous side of medicine. Not

much kudos to be gained from the enormous amount of work it takes to run a project, collate and analyse the data, and then write it up and get the results published. Unless you make a major breakthrough, of course, and that doesn't usually happen unless you're prepared to devote years and years to it.'

'But you are?'

'I… Yes, of course.' Where had that hesitation come from? Inexplicable, but apparently significant. Enough for him to see a reflection of it in the way Kelly's eyebrows flickered into a tiny questioning frown.

'I've been heading towards this for years. Ever since David got me excited about the possibilities. It's a huge goal, but it's getting closer a lot faster than I'd anticipated. It all hinges on whether or not I get the head of department position.'

'I heard that was coming up.' Her glance was shy—as though she was so impressed she wasn't sure what to say. 'It's a big step up, isn't it?'

'Huge. And I know I'm young to be considered, but it's an opportunity I can't afford to pass up, Kelly. Imagine the influence I could have. I could make research a priority for the department. Attract funding. Employ the kind of people who will help it grow and succeed.'

She was watching him carefully, her food forgotten. 'But you'll miss being so involved in the clinical side of things? Theatre, for instance?'

Tony stared at her. He'd dismissed that as being a major issue in the interview he'd had with the board of directors earlier today. He'd believed himself. Who in their right mind would miss an overload of the pressure and tension that came with too many hours spent in an operating theatre? But could Kelly see something he might not have given enough thought to?

It was time to stop talking about this. If anyone had told him he could go on a date and have a thought-provoking conversation about his research and his career, he would have snorted incredulously. She couldn't possibly be as interested as she seemed. Or have any insight he didn't have himself. Tony pushed his plate aside.

'Enough shop talk,' he decreed. 'It's time we had a dance.'

It was still there.

The fantasy.

The feel of a man's arms holding her and his body moving in perfect unison with hers as they gave their own interpretation to a superbly played medley of slow, romantic songs.

Not just any man, though. This was Tony.

Kelly glanced up, and another sense kicked in to add to her pleasure as her eyes drank in the angular lines of his face and the shadow of his jaw that the soft lighting accentuated. She could see the enviable length of his black eyelashes and she caught a whiff of rainforest from his aftershave. His formal white shirt was crisp beneath her fingers, and she could almost taste the kisses she knew would come later tonight. Every sense was heightened by movement.

Such intense pleasure. So much more than the first time they had danced together, because there was intimacy as an undercurrent now. They were playing with the physical fire they knew could be ignited between them. That they were in public again was intoxicating. Touching within proscribed limits, but the slide of his hand on the bare skin of her shoulders and arms sparking erotic images that had the memory of reality to inflame them.

His face was so close. She only needed to raise her face a little to be close enough to touch it with her lips and feel the roughness of that shadow. Touch it with her tongue, even, and taste the musky warmth that was uniquely his.

And then Tony looked down and caught her gaze. Held it for a long, long moment as he slowed their dance and drew her closer. So close she could feel his heart beating against her own. And then he smiled, still holding her gaze, and the moment was so perfect Kelly could feel herself being sucked into the fairytale.

The wedding bells.

The happy-ever-after.

Pure fantasy, of course. But what was the harm of indulging for the limited time they would be on the dance floor? The food for their main course would arrive at their table at any moment and they would have to return. To sit still and, to outward appearances at least, be in touch with reality.

But that held a new appeal for Kelly now. A kind of fantasy all of its own. She couldn't have the career in medicine she'd always dreamed of, but talking about it—wrapping herself in the edges of someone else's passion—was curiously satisfying. Intellectually stimulating. Balm to an area of her soul that had been closed off and left to wither.

Tony's ambition was palpable, but it came with an ethos that Kelly could understand and admire. He wasn't doing this for personal kudos or wealth. She had the impression that wealth meant very little, because it had always been part of his life. The desire to excel in his career was there because he cared about what he did for a living. He wanted to do his job to the best of his ability and he cared enough to want to keep raising the bar for the standard he delivered.

It was impressive.

He wasn't the golden boy she had assumed from a distance. A rich playboy who was in this profession for the status. If he was, he certainly wouldn't be planning to dedicate his career to research. Or to take on the demanding position of HOD and all the extra hours it would entail to further his dream. He certainly wouldn't be prepared to sacrifice the amount of time doing something he really loved—the hands-on battle to improve or save a life.

His research was fascinating.

He was fascinating.

Disappointingly, Tony was clearly determined not to

talk shop any more this evening, having led Kelly back to their table. Wines were chosen and plates of gorgeously arranged and delicious food arrived. Kelly sipped her wine and then tasted her truffle-infused chicken, and she had to close her eyes for a moment to savour this new sensation.

She opened her eyes to find Tony watching her. Smiling.

'Nice?'

'Heaven.'

His nod was an agreement. 'I don't think I've ever had a bad meal here. You?'

'I've never been here before.'

'Really? But Pierre's has been an institution for decades now. Are you not a local girl?'

'Yes, but this isn't the kind of place my family could ever afford to go.' It was another facet of the fantasy. The snowy linen and sparkling silverware. Champagne and music and food to die for. 'And I...don't eat out much.'

His glance was curious, but they ate in silence for a minute. Then Tony reached for his wine glass.

'So where did you go to celebrate special occasions when you were growing up?'

'We had our celebrations at home. You couldn't beat Mum's roast lamb and her melt-in-your-mouth pavlova.'

'Mmm. Lucky you. I don't think I've ever seen my mother cook.'

Kelly blinked. 'Not even toast?'

'We had a housekeeper. Betty. She was a kind of second mother to us.'

'Us? You have siblings?' It was intriguing to imagine Tony as a little boy. But a wistful desire to see photographs seemed an odd thing to experience on a first date.

And it was a first date, wasn't it? Even though Tony knew things about her that no man had ever learned before. You couldn't count the night of the ball as a first date. Fate had thrown them together, and for Kelly, at least, it hadn't felt as though she was accepting an invitation to spend time with Tony. More as if she was being carried away on a current she had no chance of successfully resisting.

And coffee? Again, that meeting had been at the hands of fate. This time, though, Tony had asked her to be with him, and she had accepted—so, yes, this had to be seen as their first date.

'I'm the baby,' Tony was telling her with a smile, as her thoughts wandered. 'I've got an older brother and a sister. You?'

'One sister,' Kelly said, hesitating only for a heartbeat. 'Four years older.'

'Your family still lives in town?'

'N-no.'

He got it, even before she'd finished uttering the single word. His fork paused in mid-air and he stilled. Waiting. There was a softening of his features that felt like a safety net. He was a step ahead of Kelly, but how on earth could he possibly know?

Could being honest destroy this fantasy? Make the romantic setting and the wonderful food and the prospect of dancing again insignificant? The reality was harsh, but how could Kelly be less than honest when he was looking at her like this? A look that felt like a touch of sympathy.

'There was an accident. Nearly four years ago.' She tried to sound matter-of-fact. 'A terrible car crash. My parents, my sister and her husband were all in the car.' A tiny quiver crept into her voice. 'There were no survivors.'

'Oh, my God,' Tony breathed. 'You lost your whole family?'

Kelly had to look away from the gentleness in his face. To press her lips together as she nodded. She felt her fingers grasped from across the table.

'Kelly, I'm *so* sorry.'

He was. The words rocked her with their sincerity. It was a gift of caring that she suddenly felt afraid to accept. She managed a nod, but then drew in a determined breath as she pulled her hand free and reached for her glass of iced water.

'Tell me about *your* family,' she said, changing the subject. 'I know who your father is, of course, but what about your brother? And sister?'

'My brother has a gift for languages. He's fluent in at least six, and did a PhD that explored similarities between some languages. Did you know that Japanese and Maori have some astonishing similarities? The same words for some things, even.'

'No.' Kelly was more than happy to be diverted. 'It sounds fascinating. What does he do now?'

'He started his career as an interpreter, and he's now living in Geneva and has an important position with the United Nations.'

'Wow. And your sister?'

'Meg did a PhD in physics. Of the nuclear variety. She lives in the States and works for NASA.'

Kelly's jaw dropped. 'Your sister's a rocket scientist?'

'Yeah. Pretty impressive, isn't it?'

'No more than what you and your brother do. Heavens, what a high-achieving family. You're all doctors! Your parents must be very proud of you all.'

'Satisfied might be a better word.'

'Oh?' Something in his tone made Kelly want to touch *his* hand. To offer sympathy.

'Failure was never an option in my family.' Tony was smiling, but there was a hint of something far less flippant in his eyes. 'My mother's a very successful lawyer with her own firm. Dad made millions with his construction company and then got bored. Local politics gave him a challenge, but I suspect he's looking for something new again now. His philosophy is that if you get a prize you don't stop. You just look around until you can spot a bigger prize.' Tony was turning his attention back to his cooling dinner. 'He's got a mayoral reception happening tonight, and I think he might be planning to announce a decision not to run for a third term in office.'

'A reception? What happens at those?'

Tony swallowed his mouthful. 'A lot of overdressed people stand around, eating fancy bits of finger food and drinking a little too much wine. They seem very interested in everybody else, but what they're really doing is networking with people who might be useful in furthering their own interests. They're astonishingly boring affairs and I was delighted to have an excuse not to attend.'

Kelly's food went down her throat somewhat faster than she had intended. 'You were expected to be there?'

'My parents are quite used to the demands of my career. It's not often I *am* available to wave the family flag.'

'But...you *could* have been there tonight.'

'I chose to be with you.'

The look Tony gave her and the tone of his voice held so much promise. Too much. Any moment now and Kelly would actually start believing in this fantasy.

'I feel guilty.'

'For stealing me away from my filial civic duty?' Tony grinned. 'If it would ease your conscience, we could always skip dessert and drop in on the way home. It's not far from my apartment.'

He was planning to take her home to his apartment? A step further into his personal life?

This felt huge.

'I...um...'

'You might like to see firsthand what a mayoral reception is like. You could meet my parents.'

Kelly simply stared. Being invited to his home was

huge in itself. Being introduced to his parents was even bigger. Reality was crowding in on the fantasy. Merging. Making those dreams on the dance floor a possibility instead of just indulgence.

This was dangerous. Exciting. Way too much to get her head around when this was moving so fast. Too fast. A romantic ride in a runaway train. One that was highly likely to crash. But there was no way off at this precise moment as far as Kelly could see.

She was caught by this man. He already had a hold on her body and her mind...and her heart.

There was no question about whether or not she could fall in love with him. She was in freefall. Was there something she could catch hold of to save herself? Did she really need or want to? This sensation was so compelling that for this moment in time it seemed worth the risk of whatever might break when the crash happened.

She could handle this. As long as Flipper wasn't involved, and it was only herself in danger of being hurt, then it didn't matter. Not in the big scheme of things.

The sensible part of Kelly was reminding her that she had responsibilities. That risk-taking should not be on the agenda. Her spirit was rebelling. Nothing ventured, nothing gained, it put forward. What if she took the safe option and spent the rest of her life wondering "what if"?

What if there was some magic out there and this *did* have a chance of working?

What if she stepped into his world and found there was a place for her?

What if he was feeling the same way about her as she was about him?

What if she said no and never saw him again?

Skipping dessert wasn't an issue. Kelly's appetite had fled and her mouth was too dry to swallow anything.

Her smile felt curiously shy. 'I'd love to,' she said.

CHAPTER SIX

IT WAS a palace.

Never mind that Kelly sat in a low-slung, luxury sports car instead of a converted pumpkin coach as she rode through ornate iron gates and up a long driveway lined with majestic trees. She was definitely back in the fairytale, and arriving at the modern-day equivalent of a palace.

Framed by manicured flood-lit gardens that featured two vast ponds with fountain centrepieces and blankets of flowering water lilies, was the biggest house Kelly had ever seen. The brickwork had been softened over time by ivy that crept up to the second storey, but there wasn't enough time to count all the windows before Tony eased his car into place with all the other sleek European vehicles accommodated in and around what must have once been a stable block.

There was enough time to do some counting as they walked towards the Georgian pillars that supported a roof designed to provide shelter whilst waiting for the massive front door to open, but Kelly was too distracted to think of it.

The lower floor of the enormous house was lit up like a Christmas tree, and heavy drapes on each side of the windows had been left tied up. Huge chandeliers hung from intricately moulded ceilings, and the light made the scenes within the frame of the windows as bright as movie clips for anyone approaching in the dark.

Someone was playing a grand piano, and Kelly could hear the muted background of classical favourites. A kind of steady foundation for the rise and fall of animated conversation and the occasional tinkle of feminine laughter.

Waiters carried silver trays of champagne flutes that caught shards of light from the chandeliers.

And there were people. So many people. Men looking glamorous in evening suits—a dark foil for the glitz of the women in their beautiful dresses.

Kelly had to fight the urge to turn and run. What on earth did she think she was doing? She didn't belong here. She would be spotted as an impostor the moment she walked through the door, and Tony would realise he'd made a terrible mistake.

He must have sensed her trepidation, because he caught her hand. But he didn't use the contact to encourage her to keep going forward. Instead, he paused, pulling Kelly close and then looking down at her without saying a word.

A second ticked past and then another. Kelly waited,

holding her breath. Had he, too, realised that this wasn't a place she ought to be? Was he searching for a polite way to make an excuse and take her away?

Just the hint of a smile touched his lips, and he bent his head very slowly and deliberately to place a feather-light kiss on Kelly's lips.

'We won't stay long,' he murmured. 'I don't think I can wait much longer to take you home.'

It was the only encouragement Kelly needed. She belonged here because this was part of Tony's world and he wanted her by his side. That was enough.

Or was it?

Fifteen minutes was more than long enough for Kelly to change her mind completely. To have alarm bells ringing so loudly she was fighting embarrassment, disappointment, and something close to panic.

It started with the way people stared as she came into the first of the crowded reception rooms. Conversations trailed into silence, and Kelly could actually *feel* the touch of eyes running from her head to her feet. The men smiled at her, but the women exchanged glances and smiled at each other.

Knowing smiles that said: *Whoever the hell she is, she has no idea of fashion or style. What on earth does Tony Grimshaw think he's doing?*

Then there were the photographers. Why hadn't she expected that, when it was some kind of civil function and the local newspapers would be duty-bound to provide not only an account but plenty of fodder for the social pages? As a mystery woman accompanying the mayor's son, of course she would be the most interesting tidbit they had discovered so far. Lightbulbs flashed. Questions were asked.

'What's your name, love?'

'How long have you known Dr Grimshaw?'

'Is it serious between you two?'

Tony steered her through the reporters with the ease of someone who found being treated like a movie star commonplace.

'Take no notice,' he said to Kelly, even while flashing an easy smile in the direction of the cameras. 'And you don't have to tell them anything.'

He turned his head, must have interpreted her stunned expression correctly, squeezed her hand and grinned.

'Tell them your name's Cinderella,' he whispered.

That made her smile. It was enough to shut out the knowing looks and the flashes from the cameras. For just a moment it shut out the whole world around them. Here they were, the centre of attention because of who Tony was, and he was thinking of *her*. Making her feel as if she still belonged by his side by using a private joke.

Their joke.

The moment passed all too soon, however, and Kelly found herself being introduced to Tony's parents.

His father was wearing his mayoral robes, and had a heavy gold chain with a huge medallion around his neck. Bernard Grimshaw was as tall as his son but more solid, and had waves of iron-grey hair. The thought that

Tony would look this good when he was in his sixties gave Kelly an odd tingle. Maybe it was the knowledge that she could spend decades with him and still find him attractive? It was more than good-looks. Bernard also had a presence that was a more mature version of Tony's charisma. One that made Kelly instinctively want to trust him.

No wonder he had done so well in politics. Kelly had her hand gripped, firmly but briefly, in a welcoming version of a handshake.

'Delighted to meet you, Kelly,' he said.

The sincerity might have been enough to chase away the horrible feeling of being a fish out of water—except all Kelly could think of as he gripped her hand was the astonished stare she was receiving from the woman who stood beside Bernard.

Tony's mother had to be the most sophisticated woman Kelly had ever seen in real life instead of in the pages of a glossy magazine. Blonde hair drawn back into an elegant chignon, with not a single hair escaping to mar its perfection. A black sheath of a dress that hid nothing of a slender body as perfect as the hairstyle.

In her billowing skirt, with its big, bright flowers, Kelly felt as if she had dressed in old curtains. Her long, loose hair felt about as appropriate as showing up to work totally naked.

'So you're a nurse,' Louise Grimshaw said after the introductions. 'How nice!'

Kelly got the distinct impression that she would have

used exactly the same tone if Tony had told her that she was a cleaner. Or a fish factory worker. Or…or an employee of an escort agency.

She didn't belong here. With these people.

A waiter offered her champagne, but Kelly shook her head. The effects of any alcohol she'd had at the restaurant had worn off enough for her to realise that a clear head might be her only hope here. She needed to keep her wits about her if she was going to deflect the kind of verbal barbs Louise and her contemporaries could fire so expertly. A glass of champagne might undermine her control, and she would feel compelled to defend herself.

However sweetly she might be able to send the barbs flying back, it might embarrass Tony—and he didn't deserve that. He had brought her here in good faith. And he had promised they wouldn't stay long. Kelly could cope with whatever was coming her way. All she had to do was hang on until escape became possible.

Kelly was hating this.

Tony could sense her discomfort in the way she was holding herself. Taller. Straighter. Her smile was different because it didn't reach her eyes. Part of him was admiring the way she was dealing with something she didn't like. A bigger part was administering an inward kick for putting her in such a situation.

He should have known.

Any woman from his past would have been revelling in this experience. A chance to meet the movers and shakers in the city. A taste of being a celebrity, thanks to the attention of the press.

For some stupid reason he'd lost sight of how different Kelly was. Maybe that was because of the time they'd just spent together in the restaurant? The way it had felt to hold her in his arms again and dance with her. The spell had been reactivated. The one that made the rest of the world so distant and unreal. There had been a new dimension added, as well, finding out that Kelly had lost her whole family so tragically.

It explained so much. Like the strength he could sense in her. You had to be strong to survive something like that.

And no wonder she gave the impression of being independent. The need to stand alone had been cruelly forced upon her.

But she was an orphan and, no matter the outward appearance, she had to feel lonely. She needed comfort whether she was aware of the need or not.

Tony watched uneasily as his mother edged Kelly away from his side.

She needed protection.

His protection.

But his father had stepped between them now, and Kelly was being moved further away. Towards a group that seemed to be eagerly anticipating introductions.

'So…' Bernard eyed his son. 'Can I find you a drink?'

Tony shook his head. 'I've had my limit for tonight.'

Bernard nodded. 'Admirable restraint—but you're not on call, are you?'

'No, but I never have more than could wear off in an hour or two. You never know when there's going to be some kind of emergency.'

'Can't argue with that kind of devotion to your career, lad. Now, tell me about this Kelly...'

'Mmm?'

'Serious?'

Tony quirked an eyebrow. An effective 'neither confirm nor deny' gesture he had learned from his father.

Bernard grinned. 'Fair enough. None of my business. But—'

'But what?' Tony's words were quiet.

Both men turned by tacit agreement to look in the direction Louise had taken Kelly. She now stood on the far side of the enormous room, with a group that included a very pregnant young woman.

'She's...different,' Bernard said. His tone was a curious mix of appreciation and puzzlement. 'It's not just the dress. She's...'

'Yes,' Tony said. A corner of his mouth lifted and he was aware of something like pride warming him. 'She is.' He turned back to his father. 'So—are the rumours true? Are you planning to announce that you're not running for another term?'

Politics was a safe topic. A guaranteed distraction. Tony didn't want his father to talk about Kelly any more. To imply, however discreetly, that she didn't fit in here.

Bernard tapped the side of his nose and smiled. 'Wait and see, son. What's this I hear about *you*, more importantly? Sounds like you made a very good impression on the board of trustees this morning.'

'Who have you been talking to?'

'CEO of St Pat's. Have you forgotten that Colin Jamieson is a golf buddy of mine?'

'What did he have to say?'

'Said he thought you were a chip off the old block. That he'd never come across a young man so devoted to his career. Did you really tell them you have no intention of any family commitments distracting you from your professional goals?'

'I did.' And he'd said it sincerely. He'd believed it. So why did it strike a strangely discordant note to hear it said back to him now?

His father gave a single, satisfied nod. 'So it's not serious, then. I thought not.'

Tony opened his mouth. He was about to say something along the lines of being capable of choosing any goals he wished, and making sure he succeeded, and if that included having a family he would make it work—but he didn't get the opportunity.

A shriek came from the side of the room where Kelly was.

And then there was a contagious, horrified silence that spread rapidly outwards.

Tony turned to see Kelly standing beside the pregnant woman, her hand gripping the woman's arm. Supporting her?

Yes. The woman was leaning forward, looking on the

point of collapse. A man grabbed her other arm, an expression of deep concern on his face.

'Paige? Are you OK?'

'Good grief,' Bernard said. 'That's Nigel Finch—my deputy.'

People were stepping back. A woman lifted the hem of her long dress, gazing down in distress at an obvious stain on the cream carpet.

'Oh, my God, Paige! You're not going to have the baby *here*, are you?'

'No!' the pregnant woman wailed. 'I can't. It's not due for more than three weeks. Nigel! *Do* something!'

Tony was moving forward as others stepped back, but it was Kelly who took control.

'I can help,' she told Paige.

'Yes.' Louise was backing away quickly now. 'She's a nurse. She'll help.'

'Could you call an ambulance, please, Mrs Grimshaw? And you.' Kelly turned her attention to a couple beside her. 'Can you please get the tablecloths from over there? You could hold them up to make a screen and give Paige some privacy.' She was easing the woman to the floor. 'We need to see what's happening,' she told Paige. 'Are you OK with that?'

'Let Tony Grimshaw through,' someone called. 'He's a *doctor*.'

A cardiothoracic surgeon, Tony was tempted to remind these people. One who'd done a minimum amount of obstetric training, a very long time ago.

Screens were being held up in the form of long white linen cloths that had been ripped off tables, scattering platters of canapés. The men holding them up had turned their backs. They opened the barrier to admit Tony.

Paige was sitting on the floor, peering forward as Kelly lifted her dress.

'Oh, my God! What's *that*?'

'The umbilical cord,' Kelly said calmly.

'Good grief.' The man kneeling beside Paige was as pale as the linen tablecloths. 'That's not supposed to come first, is it?'

'No. It's not ideal.'

Tony had to admire the calm in Kelly's voice. He might belong to a completely different specialty, but he knew damned well a prolapsed umbilical cord could be a medical emergency. And he knew what it took to stay calm in the face of an emergency. Confidence. Skill. A belief in yourself.

'We have to see how close you are to delivering the baby,' Kelly was telling Paige. 'What I need you to do is turn onto your knees, put your head down on your forearms and your bottom as high in the air as you can. Nigel, is it?' She looked towards the pale man gripping his wife's hand.

'Y-yes. I'm Paige's husband. The baby's—'

Kelly was helping Paige move.

'Why do I need to do this?' Paige was sobbing now. 'It hurts. I…I feel like pushing, and I can't do that if I'm upside down.'

'This takes the weight of the baby off the cord,' Kelly told her. 'I'm going to see whether the baby is coming and how far your cervix is dilated. If it's close, then I'm going to get you to push as hard as you can. Otherwise, you'll need to stay exactly like this until we can get you to the hospital.'

'Nigel!' Paige wailed.

'I'm here, honey. You'll be fine. This lady sounds like she knows what she's doing.'

She did indeed. Tony stripped off his jacket, flicked the studs from his cuffs and rolled his sleeves up. 'Can I help?'

'Don't suppose you've got some gloves in your pocket?'

'No, sorry.'

Tony's admiration for the way Kelly was handling this went up a notch. How often had they had personal safety drummed into them in their profession? Protection at all costs from the blood and other bodily fluids of a patient. And here Kelly was, kneeling in blood-stained amniotic fluid, oblivious to her dress being ruined, and about to give this woman an intimate physical examination.

It didn't take long.

'She's fully dilated,' Kelly reported seconds later. 'And the baby's head's engaged. Want to take over?'

'No. You're doing fine.' In the distance, Tony could hear the wail of approaching sirens. 'The cavalry's on its way.'

Just as well. With the cord emerging first, and the

baby's head now engaged, its blood supply was cut off. They were only minutes away from tragedy.

'Right. We're going to lie you down again, Paige. The safest thing for the baby is for it to be born as quickly as possible. Do you think you can push as hard as you can with the next contraction?'

'Y-yes.'

'Good girl.'

'You can do it, honey,' Nigel encouraged, but Tony could see the fear in his eyes. And the way he kept his gaze glued on Kelly as he gripped his wife's hand and waited for instructions.

'Pant for now,' Kelly told her. 'As soon as the next contraction starts, take an extra deep breath, hold it, and then push for all you're worth.'

Paige's knees were bent and Kelly was between them, her hands poised to assist a delivery that had to be fast if this baby was going to survive.

The siren got louder and then stopped. Tyres crunched in the gravel of the driveway just outside the windows. A door banged.

'They're in here,' someone was yelling in the foyer. 'Hurry!'

But Paige was pushing now.

'Keep it going,' Kelly urged. 'Harder! Push *harder*, Paige. Take another breath, grab hold of your knees and push again.'

'*Push*, honey!' Nigel's voice was strained. 'You can do this.'

Kelly's hands were hidden—presumably trying to get a grip on the baby's head and help it out quickly.

Tony heard an agonised groan from Paige, saw a rush of blood and more fluid, and then there was Kelly, holding the limp form of a tiny baby.

Paramedics appeared behind him with a stretcher laden with gear.

'Whoa!' one of them said. 'Looks like we've missed the party.'

'The cord's still pulsing,' Kelly informed them. 'But he's...' She stopped, focussed on the baby who was starting to move. Screwing up a bright red face.

The mouth opened and then shut. Tiny fists moved and the mouth opened again. This time a warbling cry emerged. The shocked and silent crowd around them gave a collective gasp and then an audible sigh of relief.

Paige burst into tears. So did Nigel.

Kelly handed the baby to the paramedics. The cord was clamped and cut, the baby wrapped in a soft towel and then handed to Paige.

'Let's get you to hospital,' they said.

'Hang on,' Kelly warned. 'The placenta's coming.'

Bernard Grimshaw was now close enough to see what was happening. Louise stood beside him. She stared in horrified fascination and then went very pale.

'What's *that*?' Her appalled whisper was loud enough for Tony and probably Kelly to hear.

'The placenta,' he told his mother. 'It's perfectly normal. You delivered one yourself three times.'

'I don't want to even *think* about that,' Louise said. 'Bernie?' Her whisper became urgent. 'Can the caterers cope with cleaning this up, do you think?'

'Shh. It can wait. It's a baby, Lou. Born in our lounge. How 'bout that?'

It was a baby, all right. A healthy-looking boy, now in the arms of his mother, who was being comfortably settled on the stretcher. A proud father reached for Kelly and gripped her hands.

'Thank you' was all he could manage, before emotion removed his power of speech.

One of the paramedics dropped a blanket around Kelly's shoulders. 'You're a bit damp,' he said. 'You'll get cold any minute. Just drop it back to the emergency department at St Pat's some time.'

Nigel turned back for another attempt at expressing his appreciation as he began to follow the stretcher.

'I... You... We're...' He gave up. 'Thank you.'

The thanks were well deserved. Would Tony have remembered the position a mother needed to be in to keep her baby safe in a case of prolapsed cord? Probably. Would he have been able to assist in a delivery fraught with potential disaster in such a calm and efficient manner?

Thank goodness he hadn't had to find out.

'You're a star,' he told Kelly. 'The heroine of the hour.'

'Hardly.' But she was glowing, and her eyes sparkled with unshed tears as she watched the stretcher disappear through the doors.

'You've had obstetric training, obviously.'

'A long time ago,' Kelly answered. 'And it was fairly limited.'

'It was enough.' Tony tucked the blanket more securely around her shoulders. 'You saved that baby.'

Kelly shook her head. She looked down at the front of her ruined dress and then scanned the room around them. It was only then that she seemed to remember where she was.

If she'd been noticed on her arrival, it was nothing to the attention she was getting now. Bulbs flashed again—and where on earth had that television camera crew materialised from?

'I have to get out of here,' Kelly whispered in horror.

'No problem.' Tony put his arm around her shoulders. 'My coach is waiting, Princess.'

Somebody started clapping as Kelly fled. Others followed suit. Then a cheer began, and the wave of sound could still be heard after the front door closed behind them. Kelly pulled the blanket more securely around herself as she climbed into Tony's car and fastened her seat belt.

'I really need a shower,' she said, as Tony started the car and headed down the driveway.

She sounded apologetic, but the mental picture of Kelly in a shower was anything but unappealing for Tony.

'That can be arranged,' he assured her.

'I'm sorry.'

'What on earth for?'

'I... Well, I need to go home and...'

For a moment they drove in silence. Tony didn't understand. Changing gear made something more than mechanical slip into place, however. He'd seen how modest the exterior of Kelly's house was. She'd just been exposed to the opulence of his parents' home. She was very wrong if she thought that a contrast in their circumstances would make any difference to him, but he had no desire to make her uncomfortable.

'I have a shower,' he said. 'It's great. Hot water and everything.'

The chuckle was encouraging.

'It's big enough for two,' he added.

She ducked her head as he sent a grin in her direction, but it was too dark to tell if his impression that she was blushing was correct.

'But… I don't have any clean clothes to put on.'

Now it was a mental picture of Kelly forced to remain naked for a length of time that was threatening to distract Tony from his driving. His words were a contented rumble.

'No problem.'

CHAPTER SEVEN

TONY'S apartment wasn't far from St Patrick's hospital. It was within the same inner city circle as Kelly's rented house, but it was a world away in every respect other than location.

The eighteenth-century, slate-roofed stone buildings had once been a boys' school, but had been converted in recent years to luxury apartments. One end of the complex included a turret, and Tony's spacious living space incorporated the upper portion of this turret as the main bedroom. It was the *en-suite* bathroom attached to this round room that Kelly was led into.

'Help yourself to towels and shampoo and anything else you need,' Tony invited. 'If you give me your dress, I'll rinse it out and put it in the dryer. If it's OK to do that?'

Kelly simply nodded. She hadn't uttered a word since entering Tony's apartment.

This was all so unreal.

Stunning.

The surroundings were a statement of wealth, but

rather than being ostentatious they gave an impression that the man who lived here was dignified and intelligent.

Floor-to-ceiling bookshelves were full, but only the bottom shelves were stocked with medical tomes. Kelly could see at a glance that Tony read incredibly widely, and enjoyed novels as well as non-fiction. A beautiful antique globe caught her eye, and it took a moment to register that it was of the night sky and stars rather than the earth and its land masses. A powerful-looking telescope stood nearby, and a glance upwards revealed a purpose built skylight.

Gorgeous Persian rugs were scattered over a richly polished wooden floor dotted with leather couches. The deepset gothic arched windows looked as if they belonged in a church rather than someone's living quarters, but, while the room was quintessentially masculine and exquisitely decorated, it had the warmth of being a home and not just a living space.

A very special home.

The round, uncovered stone walls of the master bedroom were breathtaking, and the adjoining bathroom had somehow been designed to look as if it belonged, with its slipper bath and polished brass fittings.

What was even more stunning than the apartment, however, was the fact that she was here.

That Tony had brought her into his home.

Further into his life.

Still wordless, Kelly turned, holding up her hair so that Tony could unfasten the zip on the back of her dress.

'Wouldn't want you to have to go home in a bathrobe later,' Tony said as he complied with the unspoken request.

Having undone the zip, he slipped the shoestring straps from her shoulders. The dress fell away, but Tony's hands lingered.

And then Kelly felt the brush of his lips on the bare skin where the straps had rested.

'Much later,' he murmured.

With a visible effort at self-control, Tony moved to turn on the shower. He picked up the dress.

'I'll be right back,' he promised.

Kelly was standing amongst the multiple jets in a shower that was almost the size of her entire bathroom by the time Tony returned. Her heart tripped and sped up as she saw him start to unbutton his shirt. He really did intend to share this enormous shower.

Would they make love in here? It would be a new experience for Kelly if they did, and it was just a little scary. Would it work? Could it possibly be as good as the first time they had been together?

Tony stepped into the steamy space. He picked up the soap and moved to stand behind Kelly as he lathered his hands. She could feel the whole length of his body behind her. His chest on her shoulderblades. His thighs against the back of her legs. The hard length of his erection nestled against her buttocks.

Then his hands, slippery with soap, came around her shoulders and smoothed themselves over her breasts, bringing her nipples to life with sensation so sharp it was painfully delicious. His hands travelled to her belly, but didn't linger on their downward journey, and Kelly leaned back, tipping her head so the warm rain fell on her closed eyes and open lips.

No. This wasn't going to be as good as the first time.

It was going to be even better.

Wet.

Wild.

Incredibly arousing and intensely exciting.

And just when it seemed their time together couldn't get any better, Tony wrapped her in fluffy towels and scooped her up, carried her to his bed and made love to her all over again. This time so slowly and tenderly Kelly thought her heart might break as she lay in his arms, the beat of their hearts almost audible in the quiet moments that followed her final cry of ecstasy.

She must have slept then, at least for a little while, because awareness that Tony had moved and was watching her came slowly in the wake of a gentle touch that smoothed strands of tumbled hair from her forehead.

'You're amazing.' In the soft light of the moon through the arched windows it seemed that Tony's gaze was as tender as his touch had been. Then it shifted, to follow his hand as he slowly traced the outline of her body.

Down her cheek, over her jawbone and down her neck. Kelly could feel the pulse at the side of her throat meeting his fingertips. He followed her collarbone to her shoulder and then, so softly, shaped the curve of her breast. The movements paused as he reached her belly, his touch making a tiny circle around her belly button.

A flicker of new desire sprang to life and Kelly closed her eyes, waiting for his touch to go further. To where the desire would be fanned, yet again, into overwhelming heat.

But the circle was repeated. Slighter bigger this time.

'So flat,' Tony murmured. 'So perfect.'

'It just looks flat because you saw an eight months pregnant woman not very long ago.'

The pressure of his fingers changed. As if Tony was imagining what it would be like to be touching a pregnant woman this way. Kelly's breath caught in her throat. *She* could imagine it. Just the soft bulge of early pregnancy. Knowing that there was a new life growing within her belly.

A baby.

Tony's baby.

He would touch her just like this, wouldn't he? Soft, slow strokes. And when he spoke he would have that kind of wonder in his voice—the way he had just a minute ago when he'd told her she was amazing.

'What would it be like, do you think?' Tony asked quietly. 'To have a baby in there?'

He was thinking about the same thing. Did he also feel that poignant curl deep inside that could so easily become longing?

'If it was the baby of someone you loved, it would be the most magical thing ever,' Kelly responded.

Tony was silent for a moment. His hand flattened and became heavier.

'Do you want to have babies, Kelly?'

Another silence. Lulled by the feeling of safety that being in Tony's arms gave her and by the lingering intimacy of the lovemaking they had just shared, it would have been easy to ignore any alarm bells the loaded question might have set off. Caution came simply because Kelly feared she might jinx a dream by talking about it out loud.

'One day,' she said slowly, 'I would love to have my own baby. To be pregnant by someone who loves me the same way I love him. To make a family.'

Tony was silent longer this time. Long enough to make Kelly feel just a little uneasy.

But when he spoke his voice was sympathetic. Understanding. 'You miss your family—don't you, Princess?'

'Of course.'

'And you love children?'

The prickle of unease grew. 'You don't like children?'

'They're an alien species.' Tony was smiling. 'I've had as little as possible to do with them.'

'You don't have any nephews or nieces?'

'No. I don't think my brother or sister have even considered the possibility. I guess families don't really go with high-flying careers.'

Tony had a high-flying career. Was he trying to tell her he never intended having children? Or a family? In the watch of her expressing the ultimate goal for her own life? A tiny shiver came from nowhere and rippled through Kelly's body.

'You're cold.' Tony reached out to pull the duvet over them both.

'You were lucky, you know,' he said a few moments later. 'You had a loving family and a happy childhood.'

'Yours wasn't happy?' Kelly had had that impression earlier tonight, during dinner, when he'd said that his parents were satisfied with rather than proud of their children's achievements. Asking such a personal question would have been unthinkable until now, but this had been a remarkable 'first date'. She felt closer to Tony than she had ever felt to any man before.

'It was privileged,' Tony replied thoughtfully. 'We wanted for nothing.'

'Except your parents' time?'

'We competed for their attention. Maybe that's why we've all been successful in our own fields? But…yes. Looking back, I think we all felt a certain lack. Maybe that's why none of us have had families of our own. Maybe we don't want to do that to another generation.'

'No pressure for any grandchildren from your parents, then?'

'Good grief, no!' Tony chuckled. 'My mother would have to start admitting her age if she became a grandma.'

Kelly made a sound that could be interpreted as sharing his amusement, but his words were a warning she couldn't ignore.

She'd seen his mother's horror at the mess of her carpet after the delivery of Paige's baby tonight. She'd been aware of the aura of perfection that Louise Grimshaw exuded from the first moment she'd met her.

To imagine her in the same room as Flipper, never mind accepting her, was a real source of humour. Kelly could just see Flipper whirling in circles as she 'danced'. Sending some priceless ornament flying to its doom. Her daughter had a lot to learn before her eating habits became less than messy, and she would take longer than most children to accomplish that skill. And, no matter how deeply Kelly loved her little girl, there was no getting away from the fact that, in the eyes of the world, Flipper was not 'perfect'.

It was a no-brainer. Kelly and her daughter would never fit into the kind of world Tony came from. It wasn't just his background. As a famous surgeon and head of a prestigious department, he would always have that kind of social life. And he didn't want a family anyway, so the writing couldn't be clearer on that mental wall.

This relationship was going nowhere.

But did that matter when Kelly had never felt happier than she did at this moment, cradled in the arms of the most amazing man she'd ever met? It was too late not to fall in love with him. Why couldn't she just take it as it came and enjoy their time together for what it was, without ringing a death knell because it had no future?

'I'd be hopeless with a baby.' Tony's words broke into the whirl of Kelly's thoughts. 'Couldn't get away from Obstetrics fast enough, to tell you the truth. Messy business.'

'Worth it,' Kelly said softly. 'You must have felt that magic when Paige's baby started moving. Like it was coming to life in front of our eyes.'

'It *was*, thank God.' Tony's sigh was an echo of the relief they had both experienced at the time. 'I'm just glad you knew what you were doing.'

'But I didn't,' Kelly confessed. 'If anything had gone really wrong I would have been in deep trouble. I only did a short run in O&G.'

'Run?' Tony moved so that he was looking at Kelly's face. 'I'd only expect a medical student or junior doctor to use a term like that. Not a nurse.'

Kelly could see curiosity in his face. She could also see softness. And something else. An expectation that she could do more to impress him than she already had tonight?

Kelly wanted to impress him.

She also wanted to trust him. And he had just made it possible to take another step in that direction without compromising the safety of what was most important in her life.

'I *was* a med student,' she told him.

She could *feel* him absorbing what had to be startling information. Analysing the implications. Adjusting his opinion of her? He pulled her closer again, resting his chin on the top of her head.

'Somehow,' he said at last, 'that doesn't surprise me.

You acted like a doctor tonight, Kelly. Calm and capable. How far did you get with your training?'

'To the end of my fourth year.'

'So you were ready to get right into the clinical side of things?'

'Yes.'

'You were doing well?' His tone suggested he expected nothing less.

'Top of my class.' Kelly's pride was something she hadn't felt for a very long time.

She could feel his nod. 'How long ago did you leave?'

'About three and a half years.'

'Did it have something to do with the accident that took your family?'

It was Kelly's turn to nod. 'It had everything to do with the accident. I…simply couldn't afford to continue.'

They were getting onto dangerous territory here. Kelly wasn't ready to tell him about Flipper. She could feel herself shrinking away from revealing that much, but at the same time she had to resist the pull to tell him everything.

To trust him with everything.

No. That way lay the potential for hurt that might never go away. She could take it for herself, but she wasn't going to let Flipper be rejected by anyone. Not by Tony's mother or, worse, Tony himself.

With a bit of luck Tony would interpret her statement as meaning she had had financial problems. If he was as connected to her thoughts as he seemed to be he would also realise she didn't want to talk about it any more. It was a reasonable denial. Traumatic events were downbeat, and why would either of them want to spoil this time together?

If he respected her, he wouldn't push.

The silence grew.

Tony didn't want to break it. He lay there, holding Kelly in his arms. In his own bedroom but in a place he'd never been before. With this astonishing woman who made him feel…

Tony sighed, pressing his lips against her hair as he expelled the air slowly from his lungs. He didn't know *how* she made him feel.

He just knew that being with her changed things. That she was beautiful and clever. That she had a strength of character that blew him away. That she had so much to give and that right now he was lucky enough to be a recipient.

He wasn't going to embarrass her by asking questions about the financial difficulties she must have faced in the wake of losing her family that had enforced her dropping out of medical school.

Neither was he going to dwell on any aspects of their time together that undermined his intention of spending more time with this woman. In fact, when he thought about it, the way people had been cheering when they'd left his parents' house earlier could be seen as a stamp of approval. Of acceptance that pointed to the possibility of overcoming any antipathy to her being there that had come from both Kelly and the reception attendees.

So they came from very different backgrounds.

So what?

The things they had in common mattered a lot more. Like a shared passion for medicine. *That* was why he was able to talk about his work with Kelly and not feel he was breaking unspoken rules or, worse, boring her senseless. If her circumstances were different she might return to medical school, even, and join him as a colleague. An equal.

A love of dancing was something else they had in common. They were like two halves of a single unit on a dance floor. Lifted by music and so light they could fly.

And that was part of their physical connection that could be public. The private part was like nothing Tony had ever experienced before. Her response. Her generosity. Her…

What *was* the extraordinary sensation that came at the climax of making love with her? A feeling that they almost merged. That she became an extension of his own body. A part that he didn't want to live without.

A dangerous line of thought. Ridiculously fanciful. Totally unscientific and probably no more than hormones in overdrive.

Distraction was needed here.

Or possibly further research.

Tony's lips curved. He traced Kelly's face until he reached her chin, and then he lifted her face so he could kiss her lips. He wanted to touch her again. To taste her. To lose himself inside her.

With a groan of renewed desire, Tony drew back the duvet. There was no place for any kind of barrier right now. He felt Kelly's arms come around him and then the touch of the tip of her tongue invited him to deepen their kiss.

There was no hesitation in his response.

He was lost…again.

CHAPTER EIGHT

IF FLIPPER hadn't dropped her fluffy toy frog at precisely the point they had stepped through the automatic doors at a side entrance to St Pat's that led to the outpatient department, Kelly wouldn't have spotted it.

'*Ribby!*' Flipper wailed in distress. Still hanging onto Kelly's hand, she planted her feet and dropped her weight to act like an anchor. The manoeuvre was successful.

'What is it this time?' Kelly noted the downturned bottom lip with dismay. 'We're going to be late to see Dr Clifford at the rate we're going.'

'Ribby,' Flipper sniffled.

Kelly looked behind them and sighed. She let go of Flipper's hand and stepped back to swoop on the toy whose novelty had yet to wear off. The thought of getting through a doctor's appointment with the beloved object missing didn't bear thinking about.

Straightening, Kelly flicked her gaze over the big metal box that contained copies of the city's major daily newspaper, and suddenly any anxiety about the appointment or even reaching it in time faded into insignificance. Stunned, she handed the frog to Flipper and fished for the wallet in her handbag.

'Wait,' she instructed Flipper, a little more tersely than she had intended. 'I—have to buy a paper.'

It was difficult to feed coins into the slot that released a copy of the paper for purchase because her fingers were shaking.

Small bright eyes were watching. 'Flipper do it!'

'No, hon. Not this time.' But the coin slipped and rolled to the floor, and the frog was dropped again, on purpose this time, as Flipper pounced on the coin with delight. It was too hard for her to pick the coin up from the shiny linoleum, however. Kelly picked it up. She saw the hopeful look on Flipper's face and sighed again— but this time it came with a smile.

'OK—you do it.'

She stared at the visible portion of the front page of the paper as Flipper, her tongue poking out as she concentrated, did her utmost to slot the fifty cent piece into the box.

The photograph must have been taken without a flash. Otherwise she surely would have noticed a photographer getting that close. The moment captured had been just after Paige's baby had been born. Kelly was looking down, holding the baby in her hands, and it must have been just after she'd realised it was going to be fine, because even in profile her expression was clearly one of amazement. Relief. And joy.

'Yay!' Flipper had succeeded in her task and jumped up and down with pleasure as Kelly pulled the paper free.

The main picture on the front page was much larger. A smiling Nigel standing beside a hospital bed, his arm around Paige, who was resting back against the pillows, her newborn son cradled in her arms.

'Unexpected Delivery' was the banner headline.

'Baby Arrives to Reception for Mayor' read the print a size down.

Kelly took another glance at the second photograph on the front page. The one of *her*. A renewed wave of shock kept her feet rooted to the spot. The last time she had had a personal connection to a front-page story had been the dreadful photographs of the aftermath of the accident that had wiped out her whole family.

By a strange quirk of fate here she was again, but this time the article was about the joy of a new family being created instead of the tragedy of one being lost.

Kelly ignored the tug on her skirt, her eyes running swiftly over the lines of print.

Deputy Mayor Nigel Finch's firstborn son arrived during a reception held in honour of visiting dignitaries at the home of Mayor Bernard Grimshaw on Friday evening just after ten.

'Mummy?'

'In a sec, sweetie.' Kelly tried to read faster.

'It was totally unexpected,' Nigel was quoted as saying. 'And it happened so fast. No warning at all. I don't mind admitting I was alarmed, to say the least, but all's well that ends well.'

Kelly's gaze flicked back to the main photograph and its caption: 'William James Finch, weighing in at almost six pounds, safe in St Patrick's Maternity Unit after his dramatic entrance to the world.'

She tried to find the place she'd left in the article.

'I want to express my heartfelt gratitude,' Nigel said, 'to the nurse who assisted Paige. To the ambulance crew and to the staff here at St Patrick's Hospital. They are all a credit to our wonderful city.'

But she wasn't a nurse! Kelly bit her lip, taking another look at the photograph of herself. At its caption. 'Kelly Adams' it said in tiny print. 'A member of St Patrick's nursing staff'.

'Mummy!'

'Yes. Right.' Kelly folded the paper hurriedly, glancing around as if she half expected someone to point. To say she was the fraud she suddenly felt herself to be. Except she'd never *said* she was a nurse, had she? And an aide could be considered part of the nursing staff, surely? Papers were always getting things wrong.

Her picture was in profile and her head was bent, partly screened by her hair. Would anyone recognise her? Tony would know, of course, but that didn't matter because he didn't know what her actual position on the staff of St Patrick's was. It was those who did that could make this a problem. The people who could tell him before she found the right moment to correct his assumption that she was a qualified nurse.

If only she'd said something right at the start—but how could she have? And why? The reality of bedpans and mops was on another planet from the fairytale she'd stepped into at the ball. Irrelevant. And now he was so impressed that she'd been a top student at medical school. She'd been too proud to admit the spot at the lower end of the medical spectrum that she now occupied.

The sinking sensation in the pit of Kelly's stomach suggested that she knew the fall was coming. There was just a very slim hope that she could avoid the worst of it.

'Look.' She crouched beside Flipper for a moment, showing her the picture still visible on one of the folds. 'Who's that?'

Flipper looked. She beamed. 'Bubba!'

'It *is* a baby. A really tiny one. Who's holding the baby?'

Flipper squinted. 'Bubba,' she repeated, and then turned away, any interest forgotten.

Maybe it was premature, but the fact that Flipper hadn't recognised her own mother in the picture was a comfort.

St Patrick's employed hundreds and hundreds of people. Most of the staff Kelly worked alongside only knew her by her first name because that was the only name on her badge. Most would never have seen her with her hair loose. Thanks to the horrible shower cap, most would have no idea what colour her hair was, even.

Kelly Adams? She could imagine an exchange in a nurses' locker room. *You know her?*

Never heard of her. You?

No. Doesn't work on our ward.

And then it would be forgotten. By tomorrow it would be yesterday's news and nobody would care.

Kelly hurried into the outpatient department, pausing to stuff the newspaper into a rubbish bin. If she could put this aside, who else was really going to be bothered by it?

John Clifford, that was who.

'You're a bit of a star, Kelly' was the first thing he said when she took Flipper into the consulting room a few minutes later. 'Nice photo.'

'I…um…just happened to be there.'

'Oh?' The way his eyebrows rose made Kelly flush.

'I saw you last week,' John said with a smile. 'At The Waiting Room.'

With Tony. Kelly sat down a little heavily on the padded chair. 'Oh…'

The connection wouldn't have been hard to make. Why else could Kelly possibly have gained admittance to a mayoral reception? Everybody knew who Tony was. Who his father was.

Kelly was a nobody.

Was that why she could detect something like concern in Dr Clifford's expression? Disapproval, even?

That stung. John Clifford had been Flipper's doctor

for years now. Both Kelly and Flipper thought he was wonderful. A father figure, almost, for Kelly. A source of wisdom. A rock in times of need. One of the few people who had shared the joy of the milestones Flipper was reaching. Someone who cared.

But he didn't think Kelly was good enough for Tony.

He couldn't see her in the role of partner to a renowned surgeon.

Or was it that he didn't see Flipper as being part of an acceptable ready-made family?

He couldn't be thinking anything that Kelly hadn't already thought herself, but somehow, coming from him, it was…embarrassing. Humiliating.

Kelly didn't know what to say.

Flipper, bless her, saved her from having to say anything at all.

She trotted towards Dr Clifford and held up her frog. 'Ribby, ribby,' she said, and then grinned.

Kelly watched the transformation of the cardiologist's expression. He feigned astonishment, and then crouched to put himself more on the level of the tiny girl. He returned her smile.

'What have you got there, young Philippa?'

Flipper hugged the frog and made it croak again. Her grin stretched from ear, to ear and was so happy Kelly could feel a squeeze on her own heart.

John Clifford grinned back. 'Goodness me,' he chuckled. 'Whatever next?'

Flipper gurgled with laughter and squeezed the frog

again. The doctor ruffled her hair, a smile still on his face as he moved to sit at his desk. He took another glance at Flipper before reaching for the thick set of patient case notes. The warmth in that look was unmistakable. Flipper had touched his heart the way she did everybody who knew her.

It wasn't beyond the realms of possibility that Tony could be charmed in exactly the same way. If Kelly let him into her life—trusted him enough to meet Flipper— it *could* happen. Couldn't it?

Flipper came back to Kelly and stood beside the chair, leaning on her.

Dr Clifford was frowning as he flipped open the notes, as if he knew that what was in there was a matter of concern.

A trickle of apprehension ran the length of Kelly's spine.

'Why don't you show Frog to the other toys while I talk to Dr Clifford?' she suggested to Flipper, making an effort to keep her voice light. 'Remember what's in the box over there? I'll bet Barbie would like to meet Frog.'

Flipper obligingly moved to the corner of the room and upended the plastic container of toys. She sat down and pulled her frog onto her lap before reaching for a doll.

Kelly watched the doctor flip through the notes, presumably to find the results of last week's investigations. When he looked up, however, he seemed to be thinking of something else. His stare was curious and went on just a shade too long. Then he cleared his throat.

'How *are* things for you at the moment, Kelly?'

It seemed an odd question.

'Fine,' she answered. 'We're doing really well.'

Oh, help. Would he interpret that as *Kelly* doing really well by snagging the interest of someone like Tony Grimshaw?

'Flipper's happy,' she added hurriedly. 'She loves going to crèche and she fits in so well. She's starting to learn her colours and her numbers, and her vocabulary is increasing every day. I think she'll be able to attend a normal school without any problems.'

'And physically? You haven't noticed any changes since her last check-up?'

He sounded as though he expected she would have. Kelly frowned, searching for evidence of anything she might have forgotten to mention last week.

'We're very careful,' she answered. 'Our GP's wonderful. She knows to get Flipper onto antibiotics at the first hint of an infection. It's been over a year since she was admitted with that pneumonia.'

Dr Clifford nodded. 'I'm thinking more of day-to-day stuff,' he said. 'Is she active?'

Kelly smiled. 'It's hard to keep her sitting still for long.'

'She still loves her music? The dancing?'

Flipper looked up. 'Darn!' She held the Barbie doll by its head and bounced the legs on the floor. 'Dolly darn!'

Kelly's smile widened, but then faded. 'She does get

a bit out of breath when she's dancing, and I noticed she was puffing when she got to the top of our steps last week. Elsie mentioned it, too.'

'Elsie?'

'My boss. She's a good friend. She babysits occasionally when I…go out.' Kelly dropped her gaze, catching her bottom lip between her teeth.

Elsie had babysat so she could go to the ball and stay out all night. And again so she could go out and end up at the Mayor's house, delivering a baby and getting her photograph on the front page of the paper.

But Dr Clifford seemed to have forgotten the publicity.

'The tests we ran last week have shown a significant deterioration in Philippa's condition,' he said gently. 'It looks as though more surgery will be likely rather than just possible.'

Kelly's indrawn breath was a gasp. 'No,' she whispered. 'Oh, please…*no*!'

Her gaze flew to her daughter, who had given up trying to make Barbie dance and now seemed to be getting her to try and kiss the frog. Intent on her task for the moment. Happy. She didn't need more surgery, surely? With its horrible risks and the pain and…

And she really ought to be listening more carefully to what Dr Clifford was saying.

Yes, she'd always been aware of the possible need for further surgery as Flipper grew, but it had always been in the future. A cloud that had almost vanished over the horizon after so many weeks and months of doing so well.

The cardiologist was talking about test results that showed that the valves in Flipper's heart were not coping now that she was older and more active. That she was already in a degree of heart failure that was going to need management with medication, and that the possibility of complications was of grave concern.

'If she had another bout of pneumonia it could tip her over the edge,' Dr Clifford continued. 'It might put her into an episode of failure that we wouldn't be able to treat effectively.'

Was he saying that Flipper could *die*?

Oh, *God*!

'And surgery would be the answer?'

'It's the only way we can achieve anything like normal cardiac function for her. The procedure's a common one. There's every chance that the result would be what we'd hope for.'

'But she's *had* surgery.' With the degree of medical knowledge Kelly had acquired she knew it was a pathetic thing to say, but this was Kelly as a mother talking. A mother who wanted to spare her child the ordeal of open heart surgery.

'I know.' John Clifford's tone was sympathetic. 'I'm sorry, Kelly. I wish I had better news. I'm going to refer you back to the paediatric cardiac surgical team. Brian Grieves is the best in the field. I'll make sure you get an urgent consult.'

'It's *urgent*?' Kelly felt a wave of panic. She wanted to scoop Flipper into her arms and take her somewhere else. Somewhere she'd be safe. But she couldn't protect her from this, could she? She had to trust this doctor. And the surgeons.

She closed her eyes for a moment, fighting panic. This was *so* hard. But they'd been here before and they'd come though. She had to do whatever was necessary to look after Flipper.

'Kelly?'

She opened her eyes.

'Are you all right?'

She nodded. 'Is it OK for Flipper to go to crèche today? I'm supposed to be working after this appointment.'

Dr Clifford nodded. 'In the meantime there's no reason not to carry on as usual. We'll keep a closer eye on her, and I want you to bring her into hospital if you have any concerns. If she gets particularly out of breath, for instance.'

Kelly nodded again.

'I'd like to listen to her chest again now. We'll talk about the medication I want you to start after that.'

Kelly was running on autopilot as she helped undress Flipper. Smiling a lot because she didn't want to communicate any of her fear to her child. She even managed to laugh, along with Flipper, when Dr Clifford made a show of listening to Frog's chest before he put the disc of the stethoscope on Flipper's chest. She felt dangerously close to tears, seeing how large the stethoscope looked against the tiny ribs, unable to stop herself imagining them being spread apart to give a surgeon access to her heart.

There was a prescription to take as well, and an appointment card to see the surgeons. It was all overwhelming, and Kelly felt dazed. It was a huge relief to be able to leave, but John Clifford had something else he wanted to say. He walked to the door with Kelly.

'I know this is none of my business,' he said quietly, 'but I'm a family friend of the Grimshaws and I've known Tony for a very long time.'

Kelly stared at him. She couldn't think of anything other than what lay in the near future for Flipper right now. It was actually an effort to remember the beginning of this interview, when the photograph had been mentioned.

'You know he's in the running to become Head of Department for cardiothoracic surgery?'

Kelly said nothing.

'He has an astonishingly bright future ahead of him but he's very young to be considered for a position like this.'

Kelly continued to stare. What on earth could this possibly have to do with *her*?

Dr Clifford shook his head. 'Forget I said anything, Kelly. Most unprofessional of me. I…just think you have enough to cope with without…complications.'

It wasn't until Kelly had dropped Flipper at crèche, changed into her uniform and gone to find where she was being sent for the day that she understood what John Clifford hadn't put into words.

Being associated with Kelly could undermine Tony's chances of getting the position he wanted. She was unsuitable. If Tony found out about Flipper he would end their relationship and she would be hurt, and she didn't need that on top of everything else she had to deal with at the moment.

Or maybe Tony wouldn't, but what if it made a difference to his success? He was passionate about his work. His research. What if he fell in love with her and it wasn't until later that he realised the damage it had done to his career?

Kelly had always known she had no basis other than dreams to imagine a future for this relationship. And didn't the magic of a fairytale depend on someone being given something they wanted more than anything else? Taking something away or even risking it was certainly not part of any happy ending. Now was the ideal time to call a halt. When she had far more important things to think about than her love life. John Clifford had hit the nail squarely on its head. She couldn't afford complications.

Flipper's heart was in more danger than her own.

Elsie thought she should take the day off. 'You can't work when you're so worried about the little one.'

'It's the best thing I *can* do,' Kelly said. 'Put me somewhere really busy, Elsie. Like Emergency. I have to work if I'm going to pay the bills, and if I'm busy I won't be able to worry so much.'

'They do need someone in Emergency. If you're sure?'

'I'm sure.'

* * *

'What's the blood pressure?' Tony was frowning, seconds after picking up the phone on the surgical ward's office desk.

'One-oh-five on sixty. And falling.'

'Jugular venous pressure?'

'Elevated.'

Damn. 'Have you ordered an echocardiogram?'

'Tech's on her way.'

'So am I. Check out the availability of a theatre, would you, please, Josh? We may need to take him back upstairs.'

So much for catching up with long overdue discharge summaries in his already late lunchbreak. The Dictaphone and patient notes were left strewn on the desk as Tony headed for the post-surgical intensive care unit.

He took the stairs rather than waiting for an elevator, but he still arrived after the requested diagnostic equipment, which was now set up beside the unconscious man, still on a ventilator after his extensive heart surgery that morning.

He watched the young technician as she angled the transducer, searching for any evidence that might confirm Tony's suspicion that this elderly patient was bleeding post-operatively around his heart.

'There!' she said. 'Collection of fluid in the pericardial sac. I'd estimate about fifteen mils.'

'Enough to compromise cardiac function.' Easy enough to remove, but if the bleeding continued his patient was in trouble.

'We'll do a pericardiocentesis, ' he told his registrar.

'If there's any evidence of further bleeding we'll have to head back to Theatre. You want to do this, Josh?'

'I've got ED paging me. Chest trauma.'

'You go, then.' Tony nodded. 'I'll deal with this.'

It was clearly going to be one of those days. Like yesterday had been. He wouldn't miss being on call for acutes when—*if*—he became HOD. He would find out some time this week whether his bid for the position had been successful, so it wasn't surprising it was in his thoughts a lot.

He put it aside easily enough as he started the procedure to insert a needle into his patient's chest and remove the blood that was creating pressure and preventing it beating efficiently. The beeping of his pager was an irritating interruption.

'Can you answer that, for me, please?' he asked the nurse assisting him. 'Take a message.'

She returned just as he was removing the blood-filled syringe.

'That was Colin Jamieson's secretary,' the nurse informed him, a note of awe in her voice. 'He wants you to call him as soon as possible.'

Tony simply nodded, his gaze glued to the monitors which were showing an improvement in his patient's condition. Cardiac output was improving, and the blood pressure was creeping up towards normal limits.

The only reason he could think of why the CEO of St Pat's would be wanting to talk to him was about the

HOD position. Maybe there was a new contract, waiting for him to sign?

The readings on the monitors steadied, remained that way for several minutes, but then slowly, inexorably, started dropping again.

'He's still bleeding,' Tony said grimly. 'We're going to have to open him up and find where it's coming from.'

His day had now gone from busy to impossible, but Tony knew they would all simply have to cope. As they always did. He left the ICU staff to organise the transfer of his patient and walked towards Theatre, unclipping his mobile phone from his belt as he moved. Getting some good news in the few minutes he had available right now might be just the lift his day needed.

The first words from Colin Jamieson were not quite what he was expecting, however. 'Have you seen today's paper?'

'No. Haven't had a chance to see anything yet.'

'There's a picture of Nigel Finch and his new baby on the front page. The baby that was born at your father's house on Friday night.'

'It was fairly dramatic.'

'I've got the press hounding Personnel right now. Trying to find this nurse that delivered the baby. Apparently Nigel is keen to thank her, and get some more publicity at the same time.'

Colin Jamison sounded irritated.

'She deserves the thanks.' Tony kept the phone to his ear as he pushed open the fire stop doors to gain access to the stairway. 'She did a great job. But—' He went down several steps in silence, caught by an image of Kelly. The way she hadn't been able to escape fast enough after that drama. There was a modesty about her. She wouldn't like publicity. In fact, Tony was quite certain she would hate it.

The need to protect her was an irresistible urge.

'But what?' Colin Jamieson snapped.

'I doubt that she'd be keen to co-operate.'

'I spoke to your father about this. It was Bernie who told me this woman was at the house as a guest of *yours*.'

'That's correct.'

'Then perhaps you can tell me why Personnel has never heard of a Kelly Adams.'

Tony could sympathise with the CEO's obvious frustration. He knew what it was like to have Personnel unable to track someone down. But surely trying to find Kelly Adams would be a doddle compared to looking for a fantasy character by the name of Cindy Riley?

'I have no idea,' he told Colin Jamieson. 'Maybe the data base is inaccurate?'

'I intend to find that out, I can assure you. In the meantime, will you be seeing this woman again?'

Several responses sprang to the tip of Tony's tongue.

That's absolutely none of your business, wasn't quite the thing to say to Colin Jamieson.

As often as possible for as long as possible, didn't seem advisable either, given the assurance he'd made recently in front of this man that he was a single, dedicated professional who intended to stay that way, and therefore his young age was no deterrent to his taking on the demanding position of HOD.

'Not immediately,' he said cautiously. But only because he was on call today and tomorrow.

'Do you have a telephone number for her?'

'No. I don't.' His response was a little curt. Why *had* Kelly been reluctant to give him her number? He'd had to work quite hard to get her to agree to have lunch with him, and he had to wait until Wednesday for that. Was she playing hard to get? No. As confidently as he knew she would hate publicity, Tony knew that Kelly was not into game-playing.

'Ah…' There was a satisfied note in the sound. Much the same as there had been in his father's voice when he'd decided that Tony wasn't seriously interested in Kelly.

It rankled.

Tony made his own choices, dammit. If he wanted to get serious about Kelly Adams then that was exactly what he would do.

'I've got to go,' he told the CEO. 'I'm due in Theatre.'

'No problem.' The voice was happier now. In control. 'I'll deal with this. You can forget about her.'

Really?

Tony entered the locker room to find a fresh set of scrubs. Even if he never saw Kelly again, he was hardly likely to forget about her.

Not that he was intending to get serious about any

woman, but the way she'd made him feel the other night… Holding her in his arms. Feeling she was a part of him that he wouldn't want to live without.

Funny how that feeling wouldn't quite go away. It was just there, all the time. A kind of awareness that didn't interfere with anything he needed to do but was very pleasant to tap into.

Comforting?

Tony snorted, pulling a clean tunic over his head. He was a high-flyer. His career was taking off and he enjoyed the thrill of riding a wave of success.

Comfort was the last thing he needed in his life.

Bumping open the doors that led to the scrub room, he pushed the awareness aside yet again. Right now, he needed to save a life.

CHAPTER NINE

IT WAS just as well nobody's life depended on how well Kelly could do *her* job that day.

Simple tasks like changing bedlinen and helping patients undress, or moving unobtrusively through a busy department fetching supplies or removing bedpans and vomit containers were about all Kelly was capable of managing right now.

For once it was a relief to be following orders and not having to think for herself. She could do this automatically and feel as if she had a tiny bit of control in a life that had just been derailed.

Again.

She'd worked so hard, and just when she was coping so well—when there was the new excitement of a possible future to dream about—fate had blindsided her and left her feeling helpless, in the control of forces she had no way of fighting. She had to go with the flow and try to cope with one thing at a time to the best of her ability.

Just as she had when the accident had happened.

When her dreams of becoming a doctor had been torn away from her and she'd found herself a single mother instead. She had coped then—somehow. And she had ended up with something so precious in her life that she couldn't imagine being without it now. Something precious under threat. That was all Kelly could think about. She hated being apart from Flipper, but it was another of those things she had no choice about.

Or did she? There was a mother sitting in the emergency department with her child near the bed Kelly was changing. The small boy had fallen off the couch at home and he was waiting for an X-ray to confirm a broken collarbone. He sat on his mother's knee, giving the that impression that he was used to having her with him all the time. They were playing 'I Spy'. Kelly envied the way they presented a solid unit to face the world.

Part of her mind at present was dealing with the necessity of being away from Flipper *more* in the short term. Picking up some extra shifts so that she could afford the time off when her little girl had surgery and a recovery period, whenever that might be. Her budget was too tight to cope with unforeseen events, and careful planning was needed.

'The lady in cubicle four needs a pan, Kelly,' a nurse said as she dashed past. 'And could you find a disposable nappy for the baby in two?'

'Sure.' Kelly finished stuffing the pillow on the bed she was making into its clean case and headed for the sluice room.

'Starts with "C",' the mother was saying to the small boy. 'Like "cat".'

'Car?'

'No. Good try, though, darling. Have another look. Over by the doors. It's something someone needs to walk with when they have a very sore leg.'

How wonderful would it be to spend so much time with her own child? To practise letter sounds or colours or numbers through games, accelerate her learning by having fun?

Kelly ducked into the sluice room and collected a bedpan, still warm from the steriliser. She slipped a paper cover over it and tucked it under one arm while she reached for a disposable nappy with her other hand. It was an instant reminder of caring for her own baby when the memory was in no way distant.

Had she made the wrong choices back then? To go back to work when Flipper was less than twelve months old and put her baby into a crèche?

Two medical students on an intensive emergency department run had paused just outside the sluice room door, and Kelly hesitated, not wanting to push her way between them laden with toilet necessities. And, as she often did, she eavesdropped shamelessly on their professional discussion.

'He had cardiac catheterisation four years ago, which showed mild aortic regurgitation. No symptoms until about three months ago, when he noticed blood in his urine.'

'Any investigations done?'

'Yes. He underwent cystoscopy as an outpatient and the results were normal.'

'Is he on any medication?'

'No.'

'How old is he?'

'Thirty-two. He's a vet.'

'So what's brought him into the department?'

'He's feeling very unwell. Pale and clammy, and has a fever of 38.6. Pulse is one ten and regular and BP is one forty on sixty.'

'Abdo?'

'Clear.'

'Heart sounds?'

'Diastolic murmur. Lung bases have widespread crepitations. Oh, yeah—he's got splinter haemorrhages under his fingernails as well. Quite marked.'

Kelly couldn't resist any longer. She stepped through the door and smiled at the students.

'Make sure he has some blood cultures taken,' she said. 'My guess is bacterial endocarditis.'

The students stared at Kelly, their jaws dropping.

'It's a classic combination,' she added. 'Infection, underlying valvular heart disease and splinter haemorrhages.'

She walked away, leaving the students still gaping, and for the first time since she'd left Dr Clifford's office that morning Kelly was smiling.

For just a moment she'd forgotten about her personal

life and the forthcoming stress and misery. Just for a blink of time—but it had achieved even more than a lift to her spirits. It had reminded Kelly why there was no point in revisiting the latest worry her mind had chosen to gnaw at.

Kelly knew she had chosen the life that was best for both herself and Flipper when she had taken this job. Flipper was in a place where she had a peer group. Trained teachers who loved her and resources Kelly would never be able to provide if she was at home on some kind of social welfare benefit. The isolation of being a stay-at-home single mother would have been detrimental to Flipper's development and hard on Kelly as well. She knew she was a better mother through the stimulation she got from being with other adults, being at least on the periphery of the world of medicine she loved. It was a real pleasure to remember snatches of her training and to keep learning through observation.

And sometimes there were moments, like the one she'd just had with those students, where Kelly gained a deep sense of personal satisfaction from who she was and what she knew. Never mind that she had to go and deal with the more menial tasks that working with patients demanded.

Except that she couldn't get back into the department. A stretcher was blocking the doors, and a highly distressed patient was trying to climb off it, fighting with the paramedic who was trying to hold a bulky dressing onto his wrist.

'Call Security,' the paramedic called to his colleague.

'My hand!' the patient was yelling. 'Let go! You're hurting me.'

'Arterial bleed,' the paramedic warned the triage nurse who was approaching. 'Industrial accident. Partial amputation. It's been difficult to try and keep any pressure on.'

Kelly could see the evidence of that struggle. The paramedic's white shirt was heavily bloodstained. So was the sheet on the stretcher. So was—

'Look out!'

With a wild swing the patient rolled clear of his restraint moments before two burly security guards appeared. He ripped at the dressings on his arm but then stopped, staring in horror at his hand only loosely attached to his arm. The spurt of arterial blood fanned out across the floor. And then the accident victim crumpled into a heap as he fainted. The paramedics grabbed dressings and applied pressure to the wound, and the security guards hovered.

'Get him into Resus One,' the triage nurse directed. 'I'll call the trauma team.' She took a look over her shoulder at the astonishing area the blood had managed to cover. 'Kelly—clean this up, please? As fast as you can.'

This was more urgent than bedpans or nappies. Kelly raced back to the sluice room and donned a heavy plastic apron. She made sure her hair was completely tucked under her cap and donned some bright green rubber gloves as her stainless steel bucket was filling with near boiling water. She took a large bottle of the bleach-based disinfectant needed to deal with a spill of potentially infectious body fluids, and also an armful of small bright orange plastic cones which would demarcate the area and keep people clear. She'd have to come back for the "Caution Wet Floor" sign.

Armed with all her gear, Kelly set to work. She mopped, rinsed the mop, squeezed it through the roller mechanism on top of the bucket, squirted liberal doses of disinfectant around and mopped again. The urgency of the task was helpful, because it stopped her thoughts reverting to her worry about Flipper, so she concentrated hard on finding every drop of blood and eradicating its threat.

'Kelly? Kelly Adams?'

The voice was loud enough to be startling. About to insert the mop into the steaming bucket once more, Kelly froze, turned and looked up.

A flash went off.

'What the—?' Kelly stared at the photographer. 'What the hell do you think you're *doing*?'

'You *are* Kelly Adams?'

Why was this man taking her picture? Why now, when she looked…? Oh, God! Kelly was clutching a mop, wearing an oversized apron, rubber gloves and her shower cap hat.

'You're a cleaner?' the man queried.

'No, she's a nurse aide.' Another staff member was approaching. 'Who are you and what are you doing in here?'

'I'm covering a story about St Pat's ED and its staff. Didn't anyone tell you?'

'No,' the nurse said coldly. 'Where's your security clearance?'

'Damn…must have forgotten it.' The stranger didn't sound overly concerned, however. He was checking the image he had scored on his digital camera. 'Great photo. Wanna see it, Kelly?'

'No.'

'Get out,' the nurse commanded. 'If you're not out of here in thirty seconds I'm calling Security.' She looked away from the photographer's rapidly retreating figure to raise her eyebrows at Kelly. 'What was *that* about?'

Kelly tried to damp down a nameless fear. She shook her head. 'I have no idea.'

'Neither do I, but let's hope that's the end of it. Let me know if he comes back.'

The photographer didn't come back. Kelly was left alone to get through what seemed an interminable shift when all she wanted was to get home with Flipper. To spend her evening with cuddles and stories and music and dancing and forget about the day.

Oh, God! Was it still safe to let Flipper dance? How could she know how well her heart might be coping with the stress of activity like that? What would happen if it wasn't? Kelly wished she hadn't been so dazed at the end of that appointment with Dr Clifford. She had so many questions she wanted to ask now. Would Flipper simply become more breathless with any exacerbation of her heart failure? Could she faint? Have a cardiac arrest and need CPR? The fear was going to be crippling, wasn't it?

'Kelly?' The nurse who had dealt with the photographer earlier that afternoon was staring at her with such a strange expression Kelly wondered if she had been talking out loud to herself.

'Mmm?'

'I've just had the weirdest call. From Colin Jamieson's secretary.'

'Who's Colin Jamieson?'

'The CEO of St Pat's. He wants to see you. In his office.'

'What?' Kelly blinked. 'What on earth for?'

'She didn't say. She just said it was urgent.'

Kelly could feel the blood draining from her face. Something had happened to Flipper. Something terrible. If the CEO was involved it must be bad enough for it to have potential consequences for St Patrick's.

'Are you all right, Kelly?'

'Just tell me…where do I find his office?'

Tony rapped on the door.

'Enter.'

It wasn't the first time he'd gone into the luxurious top-floor office suite that belonged to St Pat's CEO, and he wasn't about to waste time enjoying the view or the décor.

'Ah…Tony. Glad you could make it.'

'It sounded urgent. I haven't got much time,

though. I'm sorry, Colin. I'm a bit tied up in ICU with a post-op case.'

'I shouldn't need to keep you long. Come in—don't stand by the door.'

Tony took a step or two into the office, feeling somewhat out of place in here wearing his scrubs. Two wing-backed leather chairs were positioned in front of the massive mahogany desk that Colin Jamieson was ensconced behind, and it wasn't until Tony had moved forward that he realised one of the chairs was occupied.

'*Kelly*! What on earth are you doing in here?'

She looked dreadful. As white as a sheet. Her hair was bundled into a theatre-style cap, but she wasn't wearing scrubs as he was. She had a smock on like the cleaners wore and... Good grief—was that a pair of rubber gloves she had clutched in one hand?

'Take a look at this,' Colin Jamieson commanded. He tapped a sheet of paper on the desk in front of him. 'The editor-in-chief of the *Chronicle* gave me the courtesy of advance warning on the article that's been written to accompany this picture.'

It was a picture of Kelly. Looking startled. Holding a mop and standing beside a bucket. Wearing the kind of gloves she now had in her hands. Looking, for all the world, like a...*hospital cleaner*?

'I don't understand,' Tony said.

'No,' Colin snapped. 'I don't suppose you would, having told me today that you had no idea why Miss

Adams' name couldn't be found on the database of nursing staff at St Patrick's.'

Tony was staring at Kelly. She met his gaze, but only for a heartbeat. She looked terrified. Of *him*?

'Miss Adams is a member of the domestic staff here,' the CEO informed him. 'She is a nurse aide. A casual staff member. It was quite a task to track her down.'

Tony was trying to catch Kelly's gaze again. What on earth was going on here? Whatever it was, she didn't have to be so frightened, surely? He didn't believe she had done anything so terribly wrong.

'Just how long have you been masquerading as a qualified nurse, Miss Adams?'

Her chin lifted. Her voice sounded a lot stronger than Tony might have expected. 'I...I haven't.'

'Dr Grimshaw believed you were a nurse.'

'I never *said* I was a nurse.'

She hadn't, had she? 'I met Kelly at the hospital ball,' Tony told Colin Jamieson. 'I knew she was on the staff. I made an assumption about her level of qualification.'

'Which wasn't corrected?'

'I...no, I suppose not. We haven't spent much time together since then.'

And the time they *had* spent together they'd had far more important things to talk about. Like his work. His research. His family. Good grief, how much did he really know about this woman?

'You've spent enough time together for you to have taken her to your father's house as your... companion.'

Tony frowned. He didn't like whatever implication the CEO was making with that tone.

'Enough time to allow her to fraudulently practise medicine in public.'

'Excuse me?' Tony looked from Kelly back to Colin. 'What on *earth* are you talking about?'

'Obstetrics,' Colin snapped. 'Delivering a baby. One presenting with complications that could have been serious, according to the specialists I've spoken with today. The specialists that some journalist from the *Chronicle* has also been having a conversation with, I might add.'

'Kelly knew what she doing. She dealt competently with a situation that occurred well away from any hospital. She was administering first aid.'

'From what I've discovered, Miss Adams does not even hold a certificate in first aid. She has no medical qualifications whatsoever!'

'She attended medical school,' Tony snapped back. The shock of seeing Kelly dressed in a uniform that marked her as being on the lower ranks of hospital employment was wearing off. He could understand why she hadn't told him because, to his own consternation, he knew it might have influenced his decision to keep seeing her. Now he knew her well enough to know it didn't matter. 'Her marks were excellent. Isn't that right, Kelly?'

She was avoiding his gaze again. 'Yes.'

'You dropped out of medical school, didn't you, Miss Adams?'

The response was quieter this time. 'Yes.'

'So as far as the general public is concerned this baby was delivered by someone who had no right to be involved. Our city's deputy mayor is horrified. So is your father, I might add, Tony. If this actually hits the papers, St Patrick's is going to have one hell of a lot of damage control to do.'

Tony eyed the picture on his desk. '*If* it hits the papers?'

'The editor-in-chief happens to owe me a favour. I've managed to put a lid on the story for the moment. If I can deal with it to the satisfaction of all the public figures involved, it's possible we can bury this whole sorry mess. And I *am* dealing with it. Miss Adams—your employment, casual or otherwise, with St Patrick's is herewith terminated. Please collect your belongings, hand in your uniform and anything else you have which is hospital property, and be off the premises within thirty minutes.'

'Hang on!' Tony was as shocked as he knew Kelly must be. 'You can't do that.'

'It's all right, Tony.' Kelly was standing up. The stained smock, the horrible hat, even those ridiculous rubber gloves seemed to fade into the background. The fierce glow of a dignity that it must have required enormous strength to summon made her physical appearance irrelevant. 'Mr Jamieson is simply doing what he has to do. I have no intention of making trouble for St Patrick's, and I apologise for the inconvenience I've already caused.'

She cast a fleeting look at Tony as she left the room.

One that conveyed a misery that gave him a stab of discomfort in his gut. It was full of apology as well. To him.

He tried to send a silent message back. One that said this would be all right. That it was *his* fault she was in trouble and that he would do something about it.

The way Kelly continued smoothly to the door and then let herself out of the office made him feel he had failed.

He got to his feet, intending to follow her, but the clipped voice of the CEO made him pause.

'I wouldn't do that if I were you, Tony,' Colin Jamieson said coolly. 'The way I see it, this sorry business has now been dealt with.'

'I'm not so sure about that.'

'Well, be sure about this.' Colin reached for the printout of the photograph and tapped it. 'If you continue your association with Miss Adams, you can kiss goodbye to any aspirations you have to head the cardiothoracic surgical department here at St Patrick's.'

CHAPTER TEN

HER life hadn't simply been derailed.

It was travelling at alarming speed into a chasm that appeared terrifyingly bottomless.

Kelly had to push the buttons for the elevator more than once because her tears were blinding her. It took an agonisingly long time for the elevator to arrive and for the doors to open, and just when those doors were closing again and she thought she was safe a hand broke the beam and made them open again.

Tony Grimshaw stepped into the small space.

'Hey!' He was peering at her with deep concern written on his features as the doors slid closed behind him. 'Are you OK?'

A strange sound halfway between a strangled sob and laughter escaped Kelly's throat.

Tony groaned. 'Stupid question! Come here.'

He pulled her into his arms. He tugged off her cap and took the gloves from her hand and threw them into the corner of the elevator. And then he wrapped her even more closely against the solid wall of his chest.

Had he pushed the button for the ground floor? Unlike her desperate wait for the elevator to arrive, it would be no time at all before it descended. Precious seconds to feel the comfort of Tony's arms holding her.

'It'll be all right,' Tony was saying, his lips against her hair. 'You'll see. I'll talk to my father. To Nigel Finch. I'll sort this out and make sure you get your job back.'

'No.' Kelly shook her head. 'You can't.'

'Of course I can. I *want* to. This is my fault, Kelly. I took you to that reception. I stood back and let you deliver that baby. This is crazy.' She could hear an edge of anger in his voice now. 'Just because you haven't got a piece of paper to say you're qualified it doesn't mean you didn't save that baby's life.'

'No.' With a huge effort Kelly pushed away from the wonderful warmth and solidity of Tony's chest. The doors of the elevator slid open and she stepped back, breaking all physical contact.

Feeling as if her heart was breaking at the same time, Kelly took a deep breath. 'You can't involve yourself with this, Tony.'

'Why the hell not?'

'Because it will cause more trouble. You...' Kelly dragged in another breath. She had to find out if there was any truth in that unspoken warning John Clifford had been trying to give her. Lord, was it only this morning? 'It would mean you didn't get the job as HOD.'

Tony's eyes narrowed. 'What did Jamieson say to you?' His huff of breath was incredulous. 'Never mind. I can guess. Don't let him intimidate you, Kelly. I'm certainly not going to. He's not the only voice on that board of trustees.'

So it *was* true. But Tony was prepared to risk a job he wanted very badly for her sake.

God, she loved this man. Heart and soul.

Too much to let him risk ruining his career for her sake. He was angry himself, now. Outraged. He needed time to think about this. To realise how much damage defending her might bring.

A chance to decide if being with her was worth the fallout.

And if he did? What would that give them? An opportunity to continue a passionate affair that was going nowhere? Tony didn't see a family in his future, and family was the driving force of Kelly's life—wasn't it?

Family.

Flipper.

Kelly had no more choice here than she'd had years ago, when she had chosen to forsake her own career. From now on she had to focus on the most important person in her life. The vulnerable one who had only her to depend on.

Her daughter.

'It's over, Tony,' she heard herself saying in a strangely tight voice that didn't sound anything like herself. 'We can't see each other again. There's no point.' She glanced over her shoulder to check that no one in the foyer was listening to this exchange. 'There never was.'

The flicker of shock in his eyes sent a shaft of pain through Kelly.

'Because of this mess? I can sort it out. I promise.'

'I don't want you to.' Kelly stood up straighter. 'I can look after myself. I…I don't need you, Tony.'

'And you don't want me, either? Is that what you're saying?' Shock had given way to disbelief.

Was he thinking of their intimate moments together and wondering how anything in their right mind could *not* want that?

Flipper.

The name echoed in Kelly's mind. This had to be about Flipper. Forget about herself. Forget about Tony. Forget any of those dreams of what might have been.

This was agony, but it had to be done.

'Yes,' Kelly said, her tone wooden. 'That's exactly what I'm saying.'

'Oh, my dear! You look terrible!'

'Gee, thanks, Elsie.' Kelly's smile was wry. If her looks reflected the state her life was in right now, she must look a fright indeed. She had a sick child, no current means of supporting herself and that child, and she had just pushed the man she would probably love more than any other in her lifetime firmly out of her life. With a sigh, Kelly pulled her front door open wider. 'Come on in, Elsie.'

'I don't want to interrupt your day, dear.'

Kelly's laugh sounded hollow. 'Are you kidding? We've almost run out of things to do and it's only lunchtime.' She found a more convincing smile for her former boss. 'Please come in. Flipper will be delighted to see your face. Would you like a cup of tea?'

'I'd love one.' Elsie followed her down the hallway.

'Don't trip on these toys,' Kelly warned. 'The place is a bit of a mess. I'm sorry.'

More toys and a big-piece jigsaw puzzle of a clown that was half finished lay on the rug in the living area. Flipper was also lying on the rug, chewing on the lower legs of the clown. Her own lower legs were in the air, waving in time to the song a group of enthusiastic young people were singing on the television.

Kelly shoved paper and crayons to one side of the table. 'Sit down,' she invited Elsie. 'I'll put the kettle on.'

Flipper spotted their visitor. She rolled over, tried to get up too fast, fell over and then tried again. This time she managed to launch herself towards their visitor.

'Hug!' she demanded.

Elsie complied willingly.

'Darn!' Flipper tugged on the older woman's hand.

'Let me catch my breath first, pumpkin,' Elsie begged. 'I had to walk very fast to get here in my lunchbreak.'

'Oh…you're not missing your lunch, are you?' Kelly opened the cupboard over one end of the kitchen bench but it was distressingly bare. A week of not working and buying nothing but the essentials Flipper needed was already making a huge impact. A scary one. 'Can I make you some toast?' she offered apologetically. 'With some baked beans?'

Elsie's face was creased with sympathy. She understood. Kelly was dismayed to find herself suddenly very close to tears. After a week of being so strong, too. Coping. Or was she?

'I brought some sandwiches from the cafeteria,' Elsie said. 'It's nothing exciting, but I couldn't land on your doorstep at lunchtime with nothing in my bag.' She reached into the supermarket carry bag she had placed beside her chair. 'I've got some cake, too. You like cake, don't you, Flipper?'

Flipper stopped turning in circles. 'Cake!' She threw the piece of clown puzzle aside and it hit the screen of the television. Reaching up with her short arms, she tugged at another chair.

'Pick up your toys first,' Kelly instructed. 'And turn off the TV so we can hear ourselves think.'

Flipper ignored her mother. With a frown of determination she tugged harder at the chair and it tipped over backwards, knocking the small girl to the floor and landing on top of her. A frightened wail ensued.

'Oh, no!' Kelly moved swiftly from the kitchen sink. 'Are you hurt?'

'She's fine,' Elsie said. 'It was just a little bump.'

Don't make too much of a fuss, her tone warned. *You'll only blow it all out of proportion and make Flipper think she's hurt herself.*

Kelly froze. She wouldn't normally be rushing to her child like this, would she? She *was* overreacting. Elsie was helping Flipper to her feet and onto her knee, but Flipper was still crying and the sound cut through Kelly like a knife. She'd be crying a whole lot more after she had her surgery, wouldn't she? This was nothing compared to—

'The kettle's overflowing,' Elsie warned.

'Oh, God!' Kelly had forgotten to turn the tap off. Water was pouring over the top of the electric jug and running over the bench to trickle down the cupboard doors and puddle on the floor.

It took a few minutes to sort the mess out. By then Flipper had completely forgotten the bump from the chair. She climbed off Elsie's lap and stood in front of the television, singing loudly and tunelessly along with the song.

Kelly put a mug of tea in front of Elsie and sat down with another sigh.

'Sorry.'

'What about, love?'

'This…' Kelly's hand made a gesture that was intended to cover the mess, the noise of the television and the small upset with Flipper, but she felt as if she was pointing to her entire life. 'I…I thought I was actually coping, you know?'

'You are, love. You have every right to feel stressed. You're worried. How *is* Flipper?'

'I'm watching her too carefully. Reading too much into small things. It's driving us both nuts, I think.'

'It would do you both good to have some time away

from each other. There must be a crèche nearby? Or a playcentre?'

'They cost. And I'm going to have to be really careful until I find a new job.'

'I've written a reference for you. It was one of the reasons I came today.' Elsie's eyes looked suspiciously bright. 'I just wish there was more I could do.'

'Thank you, Elsie. You're a good friend. But you can't fix this. Nobody can.'

'I'll bet your Dr Grimshaw could. It's because of *him* that you got into all this trouble.'

'He's not *my* Dr Grimshaw, Elsie. And he's not going to do anything to try and help.'

Elsie looked offended. 'Why not?'

'Because I told him not to. I said I didn't need him. That I didn't want anything more to do with him.'

Elsie was silent for a moment, searching Kelly's face. 'Oh, my dear! It's not true, is it?'

'Yes. No…' The tears that had been kept at bay successfully for a week now were gathering strength. A single drop escaped and trickled down the side of Kelly's nose. 'It's impossible, Elsie. It could never work.'

'Love can find a way of making all sorts of things work. Oh, love, you *are* in a misery, aren't you?' Elsie put her hand on top of Kelly's and gave it a squeeze.

There were thumping sounds behind Kelly. Flipper was whirling round and round to the music on the children's programme.

Kelly scrubbed at her face and sniffed. 'Things will get better. I'll make them better. I'll get another job and find a new crèche for Flipper. I've got all the paperwork to apply for benefit until then. I just haven't got round to filling it in. And your reference will be a help, I'm sure. I—'

Elsie wasn't listening. She had turned her head to watch Flipper.

Kelly turned as well.

Just in time to see her daughter's strangely blank expression, and the way her eyes rolled back as she crumpled and fell to the floor with a dreadful thump. She just lay there. A tiny and very still shape in the middle of the rug.

Another chair tipped over backwards as Kelly made a dive towards Flipper, but it went unnoticed. Kelly turned the little girl gently onto her back. She tilted her head to open her airway and then bent over her, her cheek beside Flipper's nose and mouth and one hand resting on her chest to feel for air movement. Her other hand was on a chubby neck, searching for a carotid pulse.

'She's not breathing,' she whispered in horror, seconds later. 'There's no pulse! Oh, my God… Elsie— call an ambulance, please. *Hurry!*'

Kelly bent her head to breathe into Flipper's mouth and nose. She put her hand in the middle of the tiny chest and began compressions.

The huge whiteboard in the main corridor of St Patrick's operating theatre suite was a series of boxes.

Theatre numbers were listed on the left hand side. The scheduled start time for surgery in that theatre came in the next column, then the names of the surgeons, the procedure being done, and the name and age of the patient. Special details like allergies or MRSA status that could affect protocols could go in the last column.

Tony rubbed at the ache in his neck as he paused to check the start time for his third case of the day. Two p.m. He looked at his watch. Was thirty-five minutes time to snatch a drink and a bite to eat? Check on the latest lab results on that woman on the ward that Josh was concerned about, and check his e-mail to see if there was any word on an announcement regarding the HOD position? Colin Jamieson had put the matter on hold until there was no further threat of any adverse publicity for St Patrick's, but it had been days now. Long, challenging days.

Being this busy was the way he wanted things, however, wasn't it? It was the best way in the world to stop him thinking about anything other than his work.

Mind you, the hurt was wearing off. Had he really been prepared to lose his chance of being HOD for the sake of a relationship? Given the way Kelly had dumped him with such apparent ease, it was just as well he hadn't travelled any further down *that* road.

Yes. There was a good smear of relief at the silver lining of that particular cloud. He was getting good at simply burying such errant thoughts, in any case. An extra glance at his watch did the trick. Sent him straight back to thinking about the afternoon workload. He probably had a little longer than the scheduled time. He would get beeped when the theatre was free of its current case and being set up for the next, and that would give him at least thirty minutes' grace to get back, change into fresh scrubs and scrub up.

The case in Theatre 3 looked complicated, so it could well run over time. The writing in the box for the procedure was tiny to fit it all in. Valve replacements and a heap of other work on a three-year-old girl. Good grief! The name leapt out at him. Philippa Adams.

Flipper?

His gaze flicked to the end column on the right. Yes. Down's Syndrome was recorded as a special detail.

Adams? The child was related to Kelly?

God! It was so easy for his mind to skip. Like a damaged disc or something. It would catch on a memory and replay it until he made the effort to jolt it forward—or, preferably, switch it off.

This time it took him straight back to the night when the things that would send their relationship pear-shaped had been put into place by fate. When the Finch baby had been born.

He remembered the conversation. He could actually *hear* Kelly's voice in his head. Soft and clear and... warm. Saying that one day she would love to have her own baby. To make a family.

And then Tony had to close his eyes for a moment, as another, far more powerful memory superimposed itself. The way he had touched her belly, marvelling at its flat perfection. He could feel her skin now. His fingers actually prickled at the memory of how electric that touch had been.

Jolting his mind forward took a huge effort this time. The glance at his watch was automatic. He was wasting time he couldn't afford to lose. Turning away from the board, Tony strode decisively away. He pushed open the fire stop door, walked a little further, and then stopped dead in his tracks. He was right beside the relatives' waiting area.

The unanswered question was not going to leave him alone, was it? If Kelly was related to that child she would be in there, wouldn't she? Two steps took him to the door of the area. And there, curled into an armchair near a window, staring out with no apparent focus, sat Kelly.

She looked so…so small, curled up like that. Frightened. And alone. Completely alone. There weren't even any other relatives waiting for their cases to finish, to share the space and tension with her. He couldn't leave her like that. She might tell him to go away. He might have to hear once more that she didn't need him or want him. But there was no way he could keep going with the image of her sitting like that on his mind.

He walked quietly into the room. Kelly was obviously waiting for news, because she sensed his approach and turned. The fear in her eyes hit Tony like a physical blow.

'Tony!' Kelly's chest heaved as she drew in a shudder-

ing breath. She licked dry-looking lips. 'I thought it was…
You haven't come to tell me about Flipper, have you?'

'No. I'm sorry, I don't know how the case is going.
Would you like me to go and find out?'

'Yes, please. No!' The catch in her voice made Tony
turn back instantly. 'I…'

'Want some company?' Tony held her gaze. He
couldn't have looked away, no matter how much he
might have wanted to. And he didn't want to. It didn't
matter what Kelly had said to him. Her need to have him
here with her right now was in her eyes. She needed
him, and that was all that mattered.

He sat down beside her. Took hold of her hand.

'What's going on?' he asked gently. 'Do you want to
talk about it?'

'How did you know I was here?'

'I saw Flipper's name on the whiteboard.'

'But…' Confusion was added to the mix of fear and
misery in her eyes.

Such a deep, dark blue at the moment. And there
were deep furrows in her brow that Tony wanted to
smooth with his thumb.

'But how did you *know*?' Kelly asked. 'About…'

Nobody could look as Kelly did at that moment unless
they cared passionately about the outcome of a life-threatening operation. He'd seen this kind of fear before. In the
eyes of parents. It wasn't much of a guess.

'About Flipper being your daughter?'

'Y-yes.'

'I didn't. Oh, Kel. Why didn't you tell me?'

'I…couldn't.'

'But why not?' Tony didn't understand. 'You told me about your family. About the accident. Was that really why you had to leave medical school? Didn't Flipper have more to do with it?'

'It was the same thing.'

Tony didn't jump in with another question. He could sense that Kelly wanted to tell him now. She needed time to collect herself.

Which she did. She took a deep breath and then let it out in a long sigh. She didn't look at Tony, but she did grip his hand tightly.

'My sister Karen was pregnant at the time of the accident. Close to full term. The reason they were all in the car together was because Mum and Dad were taking them shopping. To buy baby stuff, like a really nice pram.' Kelly swallowed audibly. 'Karen was the only one in the car who didn't die at the scene. She arrested in the emergency department, though, and…they couldn't get her back. She was just too badly injured.'

She was holding his hand so tightly Tony's fingers were going numb. He didn't move.

'They did a post-mortem Caesarean. Right there in the department. It was…just terrible.'

'My God, you were *there*?'

Kelly simply nodded. 'I'd been in a tutorial in the orthopaedic department. Just down the corridor.' Her voice wobbled precariously and she struggled for control.

'They gave me Flipper to hold as soon as they'd checked her breathing. I think they already knew there was something wrong, but I was allowed to hold her for a few minutes. While I...while I said goodbye to Karen.'

Not only to Karen. She'd had to say farewell to her entire family.

'That tiny scrap of a baby was all I had left of my family,' Kelly continued in a voice that was no more than a whisper. 'And then I found out that she had major heart problems and would need surgery when she was no more than a few days old.'

Kelly had had to organise and attend multiple funerals. She'd had to add the stress of a baby needing open heart surgery to the horrendous grief she must have been suffering.

God. No wonder he had sensed the enormous strength of this woman.

'I gave up medical school because there was no way I could do justice to raising my niece otherwise.' Kelly looked up and met Tony's gaze steadily. 'I don't regret my choice. I'd do it again in a heartbeat. She's my little girl and I love her to bits. I'd do anything for her. Even—'

Even what? Sacrifice a relationship?

Tony frowned. 'Even what?'

She looked away from him. 'Even if other people see her as being...um...less than perfect.'

'What does it matter what other people think?' His frown deepened. 'Did you think it would make a difference to me? To how I saw you? *Us?*'

'Of course.' Kelly gave her head a tiny shake, as if the question was ridiculous.

And Tony knew that he had his answer. Nothing was as important to Kelly as her child. Her next words confirmed that.

'You have no interest in children, Tony. You're the same as your brother and sister. You have a high-flying career that doesn't leave space in your life for a family. Let alone a family that includes a child with special needs.'

'And that's why you said there was no point? That there never had been?'

Something cold inside Tony was melting. She hadn't told him the truth when she'd said she didn't need him. That she didn't want him.

His career! How many of his relationships had foundered already because of his wonderful career? All of them. But he'd thought things were different with Kelly. The way he could talk to her about his work. Share his passion. And it hadn't really mattered in the past. This was different.

Kelly was different.

'It's not just your career, Tony,' Kelly said quietly, as if she could guess where his thoughts were leading. That he could change something in his life to make it possible to include a family. 'Your family only accepts success. Perfection, preferably. Can you imagine your mother's reaction if she knew you were having a relationship with a woman who had a Down's Syndrome child?'

He could. All too well. The only times Tony had ever

felt loved as a child had been when he'd been able to produce evidence of distinction. A prize or a certificate or a silver cup. Kelly was right. His mother would never accept such a child.

But why did that have to be so important? Tony was an adult. The opinions of his parents shouldn't actually matter. Or the opinion of his peers. It was the combination of his background and his career that had been too much for this unexpected diversion his life had taken. The Grimshaw world was one where Kelly and her daughter would never fit. He wouldn't want them to. Because that would make them the same as everybody he'd ever known, and what he loved most about Kelly was how different she was.

No wonder she'd hated being at that reception so much.

No wonder she hadn't told him about Flipper. Her precious daughter.

He tightened the grip on her hand. 'Are you sure you don't want me to go and find out how thing's are going?'

He could feel Kelly flinch. Could feel her gathering new strength. Then she nodded. 'Yes, please.'

'Will you be all right? On your own?'

The faint smile was all the answer he needed. She'd been on her own before, through the worst times in her life. She would be all right.

Tony pulled a mask from the box on the wall outside Theatre 3. He went inside, just far enough to see how things were going. Judging by the atmosphere in here, the lengthy and complicated surgery had gone very well.

Tony would have easily picked up the smallest signals from the body language of the paediatric surgeons, and there was no hint of tension.

Parameters being measured, like arterial blood gas and acid-base balance and urine output, were all satisfactory, but he'd arrived at the moment of truth. They were preparing to take Flipper off the bypass machine.

The surgeon was using a syringe to remove all the air that had entered the small heart.

'Clamp can come off,' he said. 'How's her temperature?'

'Coming up nicely.'

Now there was tension in the room. Everybody was waiting to see if defibrillation would be needed to coax the heart to start beating again. Whether the end of this life-threatening procedure would be smooth sailing and the result what they had all spent the last several hours working towards.

'VF', the anaesthetist said quietly, for the benefit of those not leaning over the table with the heart in direct vision. Those people would actually be able to see the uncoordinated movement of the heart. A helpless wriggling that would be fatal if it couldn't be changed.

The anaesthetist's gaze was glued to the monitor. Tony moved a little closer so he could watch the trace. A blip appeared through the squiggle. And then another.

'Here we go,' the anaesthetist said finally, satisfaction in his tone. 'She's in sinus rhythm.'

Within a few minutes Tony was able to leave the

theatre. He ripped off his mask and walked so quickly towards the exit that a nurse gave him a startled glance.

'Is something wrong, Dr Grimshaw?'

'Not at all,' he said, without breaking his stride. 'Quite the opposite.'

Kelly jumped to her feet as though she'd been shot as he entered the waiting area.

'It's almost over,' he said as he walked towards her. 'It's gone really well. She'll be on her way to Recovery very soon and then you'll be able to go and sit with her.'

Tony thought that Kelly might be about to faint. He closed the final distance between them and caught her in his arms. She clung to him, silent sobs racking her body, and all Tony could do was hold her.

And feel…responsible.

Thanks to him, she'd lost her job and her means of supporting a child she'd already sacrificed so much for.

Including him. She did need him, whether she was prepared to admit it or not. She wanted to be with him the same way he wanted to be with her.

Maybe there was no way they could be together again, but it wasn't good enough to leave things like this. Tony had come into her life and had made it harder, and Kelly *so* didn't deserve that.

Somehow he had to try and fix this.

CHAPTER ELEVEN

THE worst was over.

It had to be.

Kelly was far too exhausted to consider any of the potential complications Flipper might still be facing.

She had wrapped herself in the reassurance Tony had given her, and the words from the surgeon a little later had been a ribbon to tie up the most precious gift ever.

'It all went superbly well, Kelly,' he'd told her. 'She's a tough little thing, your daughter. I'm confident she'll bounce right back, and the future's looking very much brighter.'

The time in Recovery had morphed seamlessly into this new vigil that the paediatric intensive care unit represented. Kelly was in a glass-walled cubicle, not far from the main central desk, as much a part of the setting as the bank of monitors and the spaghetti junction of tubing and wires surrounding Flipper's bed.

A nurse brought a figure, gowned and masked, to the door of the cubicle.

'I'm only allowed to stay for a minute or two,' Elsie whispered, clearly overawed by her surroundings. 'I told them I was family.'

Kelly looked up from where she was sitting, holding Flipper's hand, and smiled. 'You *are* family, Elsie.' She kept her voice low as well. Not that it was going to disturb Flipper, but there were other parents nearby keeping watch on their critically ill children. 'I couldn't have got through the last few days without you.'

Elsie made a snuffling noise behind the mask, but she didn't step any closer. 'I've brought your clean undies. And those DVDs for Flipper. But I still can't find that frog toy.'

'Oh…' Kelly's heart sank.

It had been three days now since Elsie had come for lunch and ended up being part of that dreadful emergency with Flipper. Elsie had been back to the house several times since, to get whatever Kelly needed so that she didn't have to leave Flipper's bedside, and every time she had conducted a search for Ribby the frog. Flipper had been tearfully begging for the toy ever since that miraculous moment when she'd started breathing for herself again, and had opened her eyes and recognised her mother.

'Did you check at the bottom of her bed? Under the sheets?'

'Yes. And under the couch cushions and in the cupboards. He's vanished. I'm sorry, Kelly.'

'Don't be. You've been a rock. I'll be able to slip home myself before too long. In a day or two, I should think. Maybe a fresh pair of eyes will spot something.'

For a moment both women were silent. The sound of the monitors beeping and the rhythmic hiss of Flipper's breathing, currently controlled by a ventilator, filled the small space.

'Poor wee mite,' Elsie murmured, her voice catching.

'She's doing really well.' Kelly stroked a few strands of hair from Flipper's forehead with her free hand. Her other hand still hadn't moved from where it was curled gently over Flipper's. 'Her cardiac output's better than it's ever been and her blood pressure's normal. Kidney function is good, and her oxygen levels are perfect.'

Elsie's frown showed the medical terminology meant little. 'Has she woken up yet?'

'She's still sedated. They'll lighten it tomorrow, and if she keeps this up she'll be back on the ward in a day or two. It's amazing the way kids can get over this sort of thing.'

'That's good to hear,' Elsie nodded. 'I'd better go, love. That nurse is staring at me. Unless you'd like me to sit with Flipper for a while, so you can get some sleep?'

Kelly shook her head. 'I'm good.'

'You look done in.'

'I am, but I'm still good. There's no way I'm leaving her, Elsie. Not yet.'

When Elsie had gone, and many more quiet minutes had ticked past, Kelly stroked Flipper's forehead again. And again. A feather-light touch. A movement that spoke of exhaustion and relief. Of a mind-numbing state that didn't allow for conscious direction of thought.

Instead, Kelly found herself thinking in snatches of the rollercoaster her life had been over the last few weeks.

When had she stepped onto that wild ride?

When she'd purchased the raffle ticket for entrance to the ball?

Or had it been the ball itself? That moment when she'd seen Tony watching her from between the pillars and she'd been dancing. For *him*.

That had certainly been the start of the upward sweep.

Rediscovering the joy of dancing. Learning for the first time what it was like to really fall in love.

There had been smaller dips. Like meeting Tony's parents and knowing that she could never fit into his kind of world. That conversation about babies and realising that a family didn't fit into Tony's future. The results of Flipper's tests and the worry that had come in their wake.

Losing her job had to have been the stomach curdling moment when she'd known the downward rush was just about to begin.

Then rock bottom. When Flipper had collapsed and Kelly had thought she'd lost her.

And now?

Now it felt like an upward roll again. One that had begun when Tony had been holding her as she sobbed out the relief of hearing that Flipper's surgery had been a success.

And here she was, touching her little girl. Feeling her

warmth. Watching the rise and fall of her small chest with every breath. Hearing the reassuring soft beeps of the monitors.

It was all she could ask for right now.

All she wanted.

It was late.

The longest day in the longest week of Tony Grimshaw's life, but he couldn't go home just yet.

He went to the paediatric intensive care unit instead.

To the central desk, to find which of the dimly lit cubicles Kelly and Flipper would be in. He'd spoken to the surgeon not so long ago, so he knew how well Flipper was doing. It wasn't enough to hear that Kelly was also coping well. He needed to see for himself.

The nursing staff were quietly occupied elsewhere, but Tony didn't need to ask or even check the list he knew would be on the desk somewhere. As soon as he reached the central area he could see her, straight ahead of him.

His forward movement ceased and Tony simply stood there for a minute, his gaze riveted on the scene in that cubicle.

Kelly was sitting beside the bed but her body was tilted inwards, almost curling over the tiny girl to offer protection. He could see her brushing back Flipper's hair. Again and again.

So softly.

A gentle touch he knew so well he could feel it himself as he watched.

But what really transfixed him, brought a lump to his throat and actually threatened to bring tears to his eyes for the first time in living memory, was the expression on Kelly's face.

Fierce, pure love.

The kind that would let nothing and no one harm the beloved if it was within human power to offer protection.

The kind that Tony hadn't really believed existed outside a fairytale. Not like this. Not when someone had chosen to bestow it, despite obstacles that would have turned many people away.

It was partly the physical problems Flipper had, partly that she was a special needs child, but mostly Tony could relate to the fact that Kelly had sacrificed her career to bestow this love.

He knew so well the passion and dedication it took to become a doctor. His parents had both had careers. Would his mother have considered *him* more important as a baby than her law practice? Would his father have given up his political aspirations?

No. Tony had never been loved like this.

Flipper had to be the luckiest little girl in existence. Even with everything she had been through and was going through now, she had experienced that kind of love. The best that life could offer anyone. Celebrations in her life would be with home-cooked food prepared with love. Not in a fancy restaurant where no more effort was required than making a choice from a menu. Where someone else dealt with the mess. Tony knew what was real. He knew what he would have chosen for the child that had been himself.

And it was too late.

Or was it?

It beggared belief that Kelly could love her daughter this much and still have the same kind of love to offer someone else, but he knew she did. He could hear her voice again, softly expressing her wish for a family. To have a baby with someone who loved her as much as she loved him.

Someone who would be the luckiest man in the world. Someone who hadn't been programmed to think that what mattered in life was success. Public accolade.

It took a moment or two to recognise the ugly feeling that the thought of that person generated.

Someone other than himself being loved by Kelly.

Making love to her.

Making a baby.

Jealousy. That was what it was.

The idea was so abhorrent. It was unacceptable. It couldn't happen. Tony wasn't going to allow it to happen.

Somehow he would have to convince Kelly that they could make it work. But not right now. He couldn't disturb her. The bond with her daughter was too tight at the moment. And too important.

The rest of his life was at stake here. Being patient for a day or two was a small price to pay if it was going to improve the odds.

* * *

'You've just missed her, I'm afraid.' The nurse's badge was a bright flower, with "Jo" written in the centre.

'When will she be back?'

'Not for a little while. She's gone home to find a toy that Flipper's been begging for.'

'*Ribby!*' said the small girl in the cot.

Tony smiled. 'Ribby?'

He was rewarded with the grin of a pixie.

'Ribby's the name of the toy,' Jo explained. 'I believe it's a frog, and it's been lost for a few days.'

Tony nodded, but he was still looking at the small face. The way this little girl was standing up and hanging onto the top rail of the cot with such a determined grip. It was only three days since her surgery. 'She's doing well, isn't she?'

'She's fabulous.' Jo leaned over and ruffled Flipper's hair. 'Aren't you, tuppence?'

'Darn!' Flipper held up both arms.

Jo laughed. 'You'll be dancing again soon enough, pet.'

Tony found himself stepping closer. 'You like to dance, Flipper? Your mummy likes to dance too, doesn't she?'

Flipper was holding his eye contact. Smiling so hard her face was a mass of crinkles. She nodded, and moved along the cot like a crab, holding on with only one hand. The other hand was stretching towards Tony.

'Darn!' she commanded.

'You can't run around yet,' Jo reminded her. 'How about I put on one of your DVDs? Or read you a story?'

Flipper shook her head. Her grin was fading rapidly and her bottom lip quivered.

'Is she allowed to be picked up?'

The nurse gave him an astonished look.

'I like dancing myself,' Tony said with a grin. 'Maybe…'

Jo sucked in a breath. 'It's OK to pick her up, and if anyone knows what they're doing I'm sure you do, Dr Grimshaw. But—'

'I'll be gentle,' Tony promised. 'And quick. We don't want tears, do we?'

Without giving the nurse time to argue, Tony leaned over the cot and found two chubby arms wound trustingly around his neck. He held the child with one arm, and with the other he kept the IV pole close. He stepped back, then forward, then turned in a small circle.

'See?' He smiled at Jo. 'Dancing!'

'Faster!' Flipper said. She thumped Tony on his back.

There was a new spring in Kelly's step today.

It was only a week since Flipper's surgery, and she was doing so well they were talking about letting her come home.

And Kelly had a new job. Flipper's nurse, Jo, had thought of it. She had a friend who worked in an old people's home that happened to have a crèche right next door. It was quite a long way from where they lived, but they could catch the bus every day and it might even be fun.

Jo had been so excited when she'd arrived at the hospital this morning. She'd seen her friend the night before, and apparently they were looking for a new staff member at the home. So Kelly had dashed out this afternoon and gone for an interview and they'd loved her. She didn't have to start right away. Not until Flipper was ready to go to the crèche. It was perfect.

A short detour into a corner shop was made, so that Kelly could buy some of the jelly snakes that were Flipper's favourite treat. Having made the purchase, she found a sense of urgency in getting back to the hospital and picked up the speed of her walk. Not that Flipper would be missing her unduly. She was having a ball on the ward. Other children were drawn to her friendly grin, and the staff could never resist the freely given cuddles. Every day her condition had improved noticeably—to the point where it was getting hard to keep her anywhere near her bed. Both the surgeon and Dr Clifford had laughed about it this morning.

'Time to think about sending her home, I think,' the surgeon had said. 'Are you happy with that, Kelly?'

Happy? She couldn't get any happier.

With the little bag of jelly snakes clutched in her hand, Kelly sped through the hospital corridors towards the paediatric ward. Flipper's room was near the entrance to the ward, but she wasn't a bit surprised to find it empty. Flipper would be down in the playroom, probably, with the other children. She turned to go in that direction, down the wide corridor.

It was late in the afternoon now. Sunshine poured in through this side of the building at this time of day, so the figure down at the end of the corridor was a dark shape. An oddly lumpy shape, that was moving in a very peculiar fashion.

Stepping forwards and backwards rapidly. Spinning.

Dancing!

The peal of childish laughter was instantly recognisable. Someone was whirling around with Flipper in their arms. Spinning and—dear Lord—dipping now. Holding her precious little girl sideways, with her head almost touching the floor.

Kelly's heart missed a beat, and then kicked in at a ferocious speed. Her feet picked up the same rhythm as she hurtled down the corridor to rescue her daughter. But then the speed ebbed as fast as she'd turned it on. Her jaw dropped and she came to a complete halt.

The person dancing with Flipper was *Tony!*

And he wasn't just dancing the way you might with a small child, with token moves and a lot of laughter. He was seriously dancing with her. As though he was enjoying it. As though it *mattered*.

Kelly knew what it was like to be held like that. To have Tony so focussed on holding her. To feel the sweep of movement and the beat of his heart. Not that there was any music happening here.

So why was her heart singing?

Why did this, more than any of the joy of watching

Flipper's rapid recovery over the last week or so, make her throat close up and tears sting the back of her eyes.

'Mummy!'

Flipper had spotted her. Tony stopped the dance abruptly and bent to let the small, wriggling person escape his hold. She ran to Kelly and wrapped her arms around her mother's knees.

'Darn, Mummy!'

'You *were* dancing, darling. I saw you.'

But Kelly wasn't looking down at Flipper as she spoke. Her gaze was caught by the man in front of her. By the expression in his eyes. He looked...hopeful? Was he expecting her to be angry at the level of physical activity he had been encouraging? Or the fact that he was dancing with her daughter?

Kelly had to clear her throat. She rested her hand on the top of Flipper's head. 'It was beautiful dancing,' she said softly.

'Wasn't it just?' Jo appeared from the shadows further down the corridor. 'She's come along a treat in her dance lessons in the last few days.'

'Few days?' Kelly's eyebrows shot up. 'You've been doing this for *days*?'

'We're dance partners,' Tony admitted. There was a faint upward tilt to the corners of his mouth. 'Only because you weren't here.'

Kelly was really confused now. 'You came here to *dance* with me?'

Flipper had bent her head backwards so she could

stare up at Kelly without letting go of her legs. 'Darn, Mummy?'

'I came here to *talk* to you,' Tony said. 'But you weren't here. You'd gone home to get Ribby. He was lost, wasn't he? Where did you find him?'

This was so weird. Hearing Tony say that ridiculous name as though it was perfectly ordinary. The man who had no interest in children. In families. Talking about a fluffy toy as though it was important.

'He was in the washing machine,' Kelly said cautiously. 'I think Flipper thought Ribby needed a bath—didn't you, sweetie?'

'Ribby!' Flipper repeated happily. She let go of Kelly's legs. 'Wanna play with Ribby.'

She trotted off and disappeared into her room.

Kelly stared at Tony, a curious bubbling sensation happening deep inside. 'You wanted to talk to me?'

He nodded. 'I kept coming back. I always seemed to miss you.' His gaze held hers as it softened. 'I *do* miss you, Kelly. Too much.'

Jo's jaw dropped. 'I'd better go and see what Flipper's up to,' she said hurriedly. 'And the dinner trolley's going to be arriving any minute.'

'I miss you, too,' Kelly said softly. 'I've been hoping I'd see you.'

'You have?'

'Mmm. I wanted to thank you for being with me the day of the surgery. It was a…a very special thing to do.'

'I wanted to be there,' Tony said. 'I want to be with you, Kelly.'

'But…'

She didn't get time to articulate why it wasn't a good idea. Why they'd both end up getting hurt if they tried something that had no hope of working out. Flipper was back. Ribby the frog dangled from one hand. She stopped and looked up at Tony. Then she looked up at Kelly.

'Darn?' she asked hopefully. Her mouth widened in a confident smile that brought the prickle of tears back to Kelly's eyes. Thank God she was this happy. This healthy now.

'Sure.' Kelly reached down. 'I'll dance with you.'

'No.' Flipper pushed Kelly away. '*You* darn.'

She grinned up at Tony. When neither of the adults moved, she marched forward, took hold of Tony's thumb and dragged him towards Kelly. She dropped Ribby so she could also take hold of Kelly's hand, and then she pulled both the much larger hands together.

'Darn,' she commanded, clearly satisfied that she had sorted the matter.

'Your daughter wants us to dance,' Tony murmured. 'With each other.'

'Mmm.' Kelly's fingers were curled loosely inside Tony's palm. She could feel his fingers moving. Taking hold of hers. She could feel that grip tighten around her heart as much as her hand.

'Shall we?'

Kelly turned by way of response. So that she was

facing Tony and they were only inches apart. She lifted her free hand and put it on his shoulder. He stepped in so that their bodies were touching.

And then he started moving. Leading her in a dance. A slow kind of tango, where their heads stayed close enough for a quiet conversation to continue.

Now was the time to say something. Before she was sucked into this feeling of completeness so deeply it would be impossible to say anything to end it.

'It could never work, Tony. Everybody knows that I was a nurse aide. Pretty much the same thing as being a cleaner. You'd never live it down.'

Tony dipped her. He leaned over her with his face just above hers. 'And you think that what you do is what really matters?'

Flipper hooted with glee. 'More!' she shouted.

'It's who you are that's important to me,' Tony said as he lifted her upright again. 'The woman I love is strong and independent and loving. She's the most amazing woman I've ever met. Or ever will.'

He *loved* her?

The wave of sensation was so intense it made Kelly's head spin, so she rested it on Tony's shoulder. It didn't matter that they had no music to dance to. They could still keep a perfect rhythm.

Flipper was holding Ribby by his fluffy front legs. She was dancing beside them and singing tunelessly. Dancing with her toy in her own little happy world.

A world that couldn't be allowed to be tarnished.

'Can you imagine Flipper living in your home?' she asked Tony quietly. 'Singing and dancing like this when you've got some kind of reception you have to hold as Head of Department?'

'I'm not the head of department. I never will be. Well, maybe in twenty or thirty years, when I don't have more important things to keep me busy.'

'What?' Kelly lifted her head. 'But—'

Tony grinned, swirling her in a circle. 'I pulled out of contention,' he told her. 'I realised where I'd gone wrong. *You* made me realise.'

He gave her a series of swirls that made Flipper laugh in delight, but Kelly was feeling alarmed. He'd given up wanting to be HOD because of *her*?

'My life has been one long series of ambitions,' Tony said, pulling her close again and slowing the dance. Moving her to one side of the corridor to let the dinner trolley get past. 'One goal after another. I've chased them and I've caught them, but they've never been enough—and do you know why?'

'No,' Kelly whispered.

'They've been the wrong goals. I never knew what the most important goal of all was until I met you. Until I saw you with Flipper.'

Some more children had joined Flipper.

'What are they doing?' one of them asked.

'Darn—sing,' Flipper enunciated proudly.

'Cool.' The children lined up to watch.

'What's Flipper got to do with *us*?' Kelly asked in wonder.

'Everything.'

That was the right answer. Kelly could feel her smile starting. Growing.

'She's the luckiest little girl in the world, being loved so much.' Tony sent her out, made her spin around, then drew her back so fast she landed against his body with a soft thump. 'More particularly because she's loved by *you*.'

Kelly caught her breath. Tony could be too, if that was what he wanted.

He *looked* as though that was what he wanted.

She wanted to tell him. She wanted to stop moving just for a moment, so she could find the right words to tell him how much she loved him. But there was movement everywhere. All the children who had been watching were dancing now as well. Even a boy on crutches was hopping in small circles.

'Dinnertime!' Jo's cheerful call cut into Kelly's whirling thoughts. 'Or are you lot planning to dance all night?'

'I wish,' Tony muttered. But he let Kelly go. 'Flipper needs you.'

So do you, Kelly wanted to say. *We need each other. All of us.*

But Tony was turning to leave. Then he turned again. To wave at Flipper and smile at Kelly.

'I'll be back,' he promised. 'Later.'

* * *

How late was 'later'?

Flipper had been asleep for hours now. Ten p.m. came and went. Eleven. The minutes ticked past and Kelly tried to stop herself watching the door.

Waiting.

He'd promised he'd come back and he would. The trust was there.

The hope.

As the figures on her watch changed to show midnight, Kelly became aware of an odd sound.

A kind of swishing outside the door.

She got up and peered into the dimly lit corridor. A janitor was mopping the floor.

Disappointment coursed through her so intense she just stood there for a few seconds, watching the mop as it swept in arcs that brought it closer and closer to her door.

And then the janitor in the stained grey coat looked up, and Kelly gasped.

'Oh, my God! *Tony!*'

He grinned.

'What on earth are you doing?'

'Cleaning.'

'Why?'

Tony propped the mop back into the bucket. He stepped towards Kelly and took hold of both her hands.

'Because I love you, Kelly Adams, and I couldn't think of a better way to show you.'

'By mopping the floor? I don't understand.'

'It's about who we are, not what we do,' Tony told

her quietly. 'It's about being real. Cleaning floors seems pretty real.'

'What if someone had seen you?'

'Someone *did* see me.'

'Oh, no! Who?'

'You.'

Kelly gave a soft huff. 'But that's not embarrassing. I don't matter.'

'On the contrary.' Tony's thumbs made circles on the backs of Kelly's hands. 'You matter more than anyone else could ever hope to. Except maybe my other dance partner. The short one. Is she asleep?'

'Yes. With Ribby clutched in her arms, of course.'

'Ah. The frog prince.' Tony smiled, and suddenly Kelly understood.

'You're doing this because of the way we met?' Kelly bit her lip, not quite ready to release the bubble of joy inside her in the form of a smile. 'The Cinderella thing?'

'Yes. I know it's the wrong way round, and I'm not the one who should be doing the cleaning—but, hey, I'm no prince either. I'm nowhere near perfect enough.'

The smile began to escape. He was perfect enough for *her*.

'What I am is a bit older and wiser than I've ever been before,' Tony continued. 'And I have to thank you for teaching me something I might never have learned otherwise. For teaching me about love.'

The look on Tony's face was so tender it made Kelly want to cry. Her smile wobbled.

'I think I fell in love with you the first time I saw you,' Tony said. 'I fell in love with a princess.'

'I'm no princess.'

But Tony didn't seem to be listening. He had let go of her hands and was fishing in the pocket of the horrible grey coat he was wearing. 'I know this is all inside out and upside down, but I really wanted to do this.' He pulled something out of his pocket. 'It's the slipper,' he said sombrely. 'And I'm really hoping it fits.'

Kelly's laugh was a gurgle of pure joy.

'It's a disposable theatre bootee,' she whispered. 'It would fit anyone.'

'But it's you I want it to fit.' Tony dropped to one knee and touched her foot. 'Will you try it on?'

Kelly just smiled down at him. 'I love you, Tony Grimshaw.'

He stayed on his knee. He fished inside the bootee. 'If you won't try the shoe on,' he said, 'could you see if this fits instead?'

'Oh!'

Tony was holding a ring. A simple, solitaire diamond ring that could only mean one thing.

The intensity of what she was feeling made Kelly's knees distinctly wobbly. She sank down. And there she was, kneeling on the floor in front of Tony.

'I love you,' he said softly. 'More than I can ever say, but I'm going to keep trying. Every day for as long as I live. If you'll let me.'

'Oh…' Kelly still couldn't find any words. She held

out her hand, aware of the moisture on her cheeks as
Tony slid the ring onto her finger.

'Will you marry me?' he asked. 'And dance with me
and clean floors with me? Now and for ever?'

'Yes,' Kelly managed. 'Oh, *Tony!*'

He kissed her. A long, tender kiss that made her tears
fall even faster. Tears of joy. He kissed her again, and
then brushed her cheeks with his thumbs. 'Don't move,'
he smiled. 'I think I'd better get my mop.'

THE PLAYBOY
DOCTOR CLAIMS
HIS BRIDE

BY
JANICE LYNN

MILLS & BOON

First published in Great Britain 2009
Harlequin Mills & Boon Limited,
Eton House, 18-24 Paradise Road, Richmond, Surrey TW9 1SR

© Janice Lynn 2009

ISBN: 978 0 263 86859 3

Set in Times Roman 10½ on 13 pt
03-0809-42667

Harlequin Mills & Boon policy is to use papers that are natural, renewable and recyclable products and made from wood grown in sustainable forests. The logging and manufacturing process conform to the legal environmental regulations of the country of origin.

Printed and bound in Spain
by Litografia Rosés, S.A., Barcelona

Janice Lynn has a Masters in Nursing from Vanderbilt University, and works as a nurse practitioner in a family practice. She lives in the southern United States with her husband, their four children, their Jack Russell—appropriately named Trouble—and a lot of unnamed dust bunnies that have moved in since she started her writing career. To find out more about Janice and her writing, visit www.janicelynn.com

Recent books by the same author:

SURGEON BOSS, SURPRISE DAD
THE DOCTOR'S MEANT-TO-BE MARRIAGE
THE HEART SURGEON'S SECRET SON
THE DOCTOR'S PREGNANCY BOMBSHELL

To my grandparents, Floyd & Janie Green

CHAPTER ONE

DR. KASEY CARMICHAEL typed clinical data into the medical record on the hypertensive patient she'd just seen. When finished, she sent his prescriptions electronically to the in-house pharmacy of the Rivendell Medical Center.

Knocking on the open door, Dr. Jonathan Douglas stuck his blond head into the exam room. The pretty-boy doctor flashed baby blues and a row of pearly white teeth that had women swooning all over northern Kentucky. "You got a minute?"

Kasey shot a coolly professional smile at the physician she'd worked with for two years.

"I'll be right there." She hit "Save" and closed her patient's file. Standing, she smoothed the crisp lines of the unbuttoned white lab coat she wore over her navy slacks and linen blouse.

She loved her job in the ambulatory clinic of the large multispecialty Rivendell Medical Center. Loved that it provided the opportunity to give back to the community, to help others the way she'd once been helped.

Rivendell's sheer size gave her the opportunity to achieve the professional and personal success she craved. Success that dangled within her reach.

When Dr. Herbert stepped down from the board, Kasey was a shoo-in to replace him. Everyone said so.

Smiling, she stepped into the clinic's hallway to see what Dr. Douglas was up to this time. Although an excellent doctor, he'd never held any appeal. Probably due to his tomcat ways reminding her of the men who'd constantly come in and out of her childhood in the form of her mother's latest loser.

"What can I do for you, Dr. Doug—?" Her voice stalled, stuck in her rapidly tightening throat. Her gaze froze on the man standing with her colleague.

The room spun.

Please let her be hallucinating.

"Eric?" Her one-and-only-ever one-night stand stared at her with similar shock. Her pulse hit a rapid, brain-frying boil. "What—? How—? Why are you here?" she sputtered.

"Hello, Kasey." Quickly recovering from his surprise at seeing her, his dark eyes glistened as if he'd stumbled upon the pot of gold at the end of the rainbow. A huge smile split his handsome face.

A smile that stole Kasey's ability to breathe just as it had on the night they'd met.

She took a step back, placed her hand on the door frame to steady her wobbly, turned-to-water legs.

"What are you doing here?" she asked again, feeling hazy.

"Funny, I was just going to ask you the same thing," Eric answered in that smooth-as-silk voice that had whispered sweet praise to her two months ago. Recalling what else they'd done, Kasey struggled to remain on her feet. Her body threatened to slide to the floor in a gooey, deoxygenated pile of shocked, blue mush.

"You two know each other?" Dr. Douglas took a step back, his gaze flicking from Kasey to Eric.

"We've met." Eric's eyes narrowed as he regarded her, a mixture of suspicion and pleasure in his eyes.

"I've never heard either of you mention the other," Dr. Douglas mused. For all his playboy ways, no one could accuse him of being slow on the uptake. No doubt her colleague had already worked out just how well she and Eric had known each other.

Probably because even though her brain was in embarrassed denial of Eric being here, her libido was dancing a happy jig of remembered pleasure.

Kasey wished the tiled floor would open up and swallow her. Anything to escape Eric's predatory male look. Anything to escape Dr. Douglas's knowing curiosity.

If word got out she'd had a one-night stand, the news would hurt her chances of being asked to join the clinic's medical board. The older board members would look unfavorably on a potential member behaving in such a feckless manner. Even if her lapse of judgment had been on the night of her mother's funeral.

Hadn't she learned how quickly one could lose everything they held dear following the gigantic mistake she'd made with Randall Covington III? Oh, yeah, she'd paid dearly for that error in judgment.

Now her only one-night stand stood in her workplace.

Panic clutched at her throat, rendering her speechless.

This wasn't really happening. History would not repeat itself. Not that she'd had a one-night stand with Randall. No, she'd given the bastard an entire year of her life. A whole wasted year where she'd dreamed of them being the perfect couple, having the perfect life together. Boy, had she been wrong.

About them being a perfect couple at any rate. With or without a man in her life, she was going to have the perfect life. She'd set goals and worked long hours to make sure they came true.

"When did you meet?" Delight sparkled in Dr. Douglas's blue eyes.

"A few months ago." Eric's gaze bored into Kasey. Was he waiting for her to acknowledge the night they'd spent together? Did he really think she'd do that? Lord, she just wanted to forget that night had ever happened. Had spent two months trying to forget.

Unfortunately, forgetting the best sex she'd ever had wasn't proving an easy task.

Images of that best sex flashed into her head like candid shots portraying the man standing before her in living color.

Hot, lurid, take-her-to-another-world best sex images.

Fire engulfed her face. She lifted her hand to fan the burn, realized what she was doing, and stopped.

"You met Eric and didn't tell me?" Jonathan's dark blond brow arched.

This wasn't happening.

Kasey roped her uncooperative vocal cords into submission. "Why would I mention we'd met? He was just someone I met—" *mere hours after laying my estranged mother in the ground* "—and I didn't know the two of you knew each other." *Because he and I really didn't do a lot of in-depth talking.*

Eric's smile slipped. "Why indeed?"

She tried not to look at him, but an inner force compelled her. His chocolate eyes appeared thoughtful, as if he was trying to read her, to gauge how to take her response.

What would her sexy lover have said, done, had she still been in his bed when he'd awakened?

Hello, she'd been a one-night stand. No doubt he was grateful she hadn't made a scene, that she had slipped out in abject humiliation prior to him waking that morning.

She was humiliated. She'd been the one thing she'd always sworn never to be. Easy. Like her mother.

She'd had one night of passion.

With a stranger.

A stranger she'd met in a bar and later accompanied to his hotel. A stranger who now stood in her clinic making a sham of her memories by looking so much better than she'd recalled.

Much to her abhorrence, she recalled way too much all too often.

God, he was gorgeous.

The strong, handsome planes of his face had surely been sculpted by a goddess intent on tempting mortal women with a glimpse of heaven. The sun had kissed his dark wavy hair with gold and his skin with a bronze hue.

At six-two or -three, he towered over her five-eight. Beneath his tailored suit, his shoulders stretched broadly, tapering into a trim waist and powerful, narrow hips. As he'd been the night they met, he was so well dressed that if testosterone didn't ooze from every pore of his fine body she'd think he must be gay. But in vivid and exquisite detail, she knew testosterone oozed.

An image of his naked body over hers, melted into hers, popped into her mind, short-circuiting her nerve endings.

Kasey swallowed. Just as she'd done many times over the past two months, she forced memories of him from her mind.

Only how was she supposed to force him from her mind when he stood a few feet away, eyeing her as if he'd like to push her into the exam room she'd just stepped out of and pick up where they'd left off? Naked and tangled together with frantic desire. When her body was all too willing.

No. She didn't want him at her workplace.

Didn't want him anywhere near her.

She had a great life.

One that didn't need a complication of his magnitude. No pun intended.

"This is interesting." As the silence continued, a grin lifted the corner of Dr. Douglas's mouth. "I call out my esteemed coworker to introduce her to my old university roomie, and they've already met."

"Dr. Douglas is who you were supposed to meet that night?" Kasey asked, winced and slapped her hand over her mouth in the most giveaway oops motion a person could make.

Eric nodded, then turned to his *old university roomie.* "I met Kasey on the night you got hung up here at the clinic. We shared a few drinks, a few dances."

A zillion amazing orgasms.

Heat slammed into Kasey's body.

"Right," she agreed on a breathless note, averting her gaze to stare at a body mass index chart stuck on the wall. "A few drinks and dances. No big deal."

Eric had been a big deal.

A very big deal.

She winced. What was wrong with her? She was at work. She wasn't supposed to be having a hot flush of sexual awareness.

That wasn't who she was. She was calm, cool, collected Dr. Kasey Carmichael.

Dr. Douglas's bushy brows rose so high they brushed the stylishly tousled hair atop his head. "You were in a bar? Had drinks? As in alcohol rather than a wheat-germ shake?" A new light shone in his eyes as he looked at Kasey. Possibly for the first time ever he was seeing her as a woman rather than the uptight doctor he worked with. "And you danced? Did I miss something?" He drew his brows into a V. "Like hell freezing over?"

Squelching the urge to growl at him, Kasey took a deep, exasperated breath. She pushed her glasses up the bridge of her nose to give her hands something to do.

Otherwise she might curl her fingers into a fist and punch his straight nose. "I happen to like wheat-germ shakes and, of course, I dance."

Not well, but she could pull off the slow numbers she and Eric had swayed to without any problems. Usually too self-conscious to let herself relax, she'd moved in rhythm to Eric's lead. On the dance floor and in the bedroom. He'd been perfect. And something she'd desperately tried to stop thinking about because Kasey was not like her mother.

"In case you hadn't realized—" she kept her voice smooth, calm, professional, like she wasn't dying inside "—I am over the legal drinking age."

Dr. Douglas burst into laughter. "You've totally shattered my image of you, Kase. I didn't think you drank. Or hung out in bars. Or talked to men who weren't paying you for their fifteen-minute appointment slot of your time." He placed his hands over his heart. "Shattered, I tell you."

Her nerves grated at how he shortened her name. She glared.

Eric cleared his throat, calling their attention back to him.

Kasey turned to the man who'd held her so tenderly on the night she'd felt so alone. He looked perturbed.

Was he upset that he'd run into his weepy bedmate who'd practically ripped off his clothes? That his friend knew he'd had drinks with the office wallflower who preferred wheat-germ shakes to cosmos?

Lord, she wanted out of here.

A cool blast of realization froze the blood chugging through Kasey's veins.

Why was Dr. Douglas introducing her to his old university mate here at the medical clinic?

University mate.

"You're a doctor, aren't you?" She'd heard some benefactor's son had been visiting the clinic that morning. A doctor. She held her breath, waiting for Eric's answer.

The corner of his mouth lifted in an ironic twist. "I did mention my profession on the night we met."

Had he? She'd been so upset when she'd gone into the bar, upset and unable to face the realization that her mother, her last blood relative, had died.

Eric had been sitting on the bar stool next to the one she'd plopped down on. She hadn't noticed him or anyone except the flashing neon beer advertisement behind the bar. Apparently he'd noticed her, though. He'd been concerned and kept talking, trying to draw her into conversation. She couldn't recall much of what he'd said while they'd sat there.

All she'd been able to think about was that she'd buried Betsy Carmichael that afternoon. That the woman who'd given birth to her, made her childhood a living hell, had died. That she was alone in the world now that her only family was gone.

In reality she'd felt alone a long time before her mother had drawn her last breath.

"You're who the administrator has been with today, aren't you?" *Please say no. Please don't let him be the bigwig son of the clinic's benefactor.* "You're applying for a job here, aren't you?"

"Applying for a job?" Dr. Douglas burst out laughing. "As if. Eric can write his ticket at this place."

"That's enough," Dr. Eric Matthews interrupted his friend. He'd rather not have his family connection to Rivendell Medical Center pointed out to the woman he'd met two months ago. Had she known who he was? Used him in hopes of advancing her career at Rivendell?

He hadn't thought so but, hell, he'd been wrong about women before.

Still, he'd really believed Kasey was different. Certainly the fact that he'd awakened to an empty bed had been a new twist. Had she known why he'd returned to Kentucky? Like so many from his past, had she seen him as a ticket to easy street?

Her eyes held dark shadows. She'd been startled to see him. No more so than he'd been when he'd looked up to meet his best friend's "boring, career-driven ice queen" colleague.

Jonathan was a fool. Kasey was no ice queen. She

was hot. His psyche had the scorch marks to prove it. His entire body caught fire just at being near her again, at memories of how their bodies had meshed together.

But Kasey wasn't happy to see him.

He honestly wasn't sure how he felt about seeing her. At least not at Rivendell Medical Center. Had he run into her in a social setting he'd have been thrilled, but the last thing he needed was an involvement with someone at the clinic.

He'd come home a different man than the one who'd left four years ago. He didn't engage in one-night stands or living for the moment. He'd changed. For the better. Or so he'd thought.

His first night back in Rivendell, Kasey had reduced him to habits he'd sworn were deeply buried in the past.

He wasn't a love-'em-and-leave-'em kind of guy anymore. Hadn't been for years. He sure wasn't going to be a loved-by-'em-and-left-by-'em kind of guy. Hell, no.

Dr. Kasey Carmichael had loved him and left him.

She didn't look the same as she had the night they'd met. Her shoulder-length brunette hair was pulled harshly away from her face. She wore trendy black-rimmed glasses. Her light makeup was impeccably dusted over her high cheekbones and wide green eyes, but not in a way to draw men to her. More of a shield against letting anyone see the real her. She looked like a woman downplaying her femininity to appear all business, to appear cold and unreachable.

But Eric had seen behind the mask. If she hadn't disappeared before he'd awakened, he'd have spent more time with her, gotten to know her. Why had she snuck out before dawn? He'd never had a woman leave him with no strings attached. Even the pickups from his youth had usually hinted at wanting money or jewelry or trips to fancy restaurants.

What did Kasey want?

"Tell me," she prompted. Desperation shone in her eyes, but her voice sounded coolly professional, as if she was used to hiding her emotions. "Tell me why you're here."

"I met with Clive and several members of the board on the day after we met. That's why I was in town that night."

She winced, causing the glasses to scoot up the bridge of her pert nose. "Because?"

His fingers itched to slip the heavy frames off her face. The glass didn't appear to be corrective, just distractive.

"They offered me a position at the clinic." An over-simplification, but the truth.

Kasey closed her eyes, looking like she wanted to disappear. Was she really so horrified that they'd come face-to-face again?

She visibly shuddered, then opened pain-filled eyes. "You knew who I was, didn't you? You knew I worked here. This was all a big joke to you."

Fathoms of hurt welled in her eyes. He didn't understand the depth of pain. Why would she think he'd tricked her? She'd been the one to disappear without even a goodbye or thanks for a fun night. Besides, she was the one with everything to gain from sleeping with the son of the clinic's primary stockholder.

"Nothing between us was a joke. Not to me," he assured her, carefully choosing his words. "I didn't know you worked here, Kasey. How could I? You never told me you were a doctor."

A couple of nurses stood just out of line of sight, trying to busy themselves but allowing curiosity to get the better of them. Eric sighed. He'd come home to take on his responsibilities, to be near his mother, not to immediately immerse the clinic in gossip about his personal life.

"Is there somewhere we can talk in private?"

"No." Kasey shook her head, her eyes narrowed into accusatory slits. "I don't want to talk to you, in private or otherwise. You aren't supposed to be here." She enunciated each word with great emphasis. "I don't want you here."

Had she audibly hissed at him, he wouldn't have been surprised. What did surprise him was her reaction to seeing him. He was the one who should be feeling betrayed. She'd given him the best sex of his life, left without a trace, and then showed up as an employee at his family's medical center. Why was she so upset?

He racked his brains, trying to recall what he'd last said to her during the night. Kissing the top of her head and whispering that she was amazing didn't seem like something that would make her so prickly. Saying how beautiful she was, how special, how glad he was that she'd sat beside him at the bar, nope, that shouldn't have agitated her, either.

Yes, she'd been upset about something on the night they'd met. And, yes, had he been a true gentleman he would have driven her home and gotten her phone number, not carried her to his hotel room and made love to her over and over. But, hell, he'd wanted her with an undeniable desperation and it had been a long time since he'd been with anyone. A long time since he'd wanted to be with anyone. Kissing Kasey, touching her, had felt right.

"What happened that night?" Jonathan asked, gawking at them, his lips twitching with laughter. "Sounds like more than drinks and dancing."

Kasey shot Jonathan a lethal look. "Don't you have a patient to see or something?"

"Right. I'll go see a patient." Jonathan nodded with a gleam in his eye that said he'd grill Eric for the low-down later.

"We should talk," Eric said, still trying to figure out why she was in attack mode. Sure, she'd left his bed without waking him, but she'd enjoyed the night, had been willing, more than willing. She'd been interesting, funny, sweet and sexy when they'd talked in the bar. Besides the phenomenal sex, he'd genuinely liked her. He'd planned to see her again, had been disappointed to wake, find her gone and realize he only knew her first name.

Having a woman use him hadn't been a new experience, but he'd never been used in that particular way before.

"This isn't the time or place for this conversation."

Kasey took another step back, looked like she might take off, but didn't. Visibly, she pulled herself together, transforming before his eyes into a calm vision of cool professionalism. She stood with her shoulders high, regal. Only her expressive eyes betrayed the hint of inner turmoil.

"I have patients to see, too." Expression pinched, Kasey reached up and pulled the stethoscope off her neck, fingering the tubing. "It was unexpected to see you, Dr. Matthews."

She emphasized the word *doctor*, making it sound dirty, almost like an insult. Damn it, he had told her he was a doctor. He was more proud of his degree than anything else he'd done in his sorry life.

She turned, took a step away from him.

His breath caught. He didn't want her to walk away. "Have dinner with me."

She paused, then shook her head. "That wouldn't be a good idea."

"Why not?" He hadn't consciously made the decision to ask her to dinner, but now that he had, he wanted her to say yes. Besides, they needed to talk about what had happened two months ago.

She hesitated, momentarily looking uncertain. "You're coming to work at Rivendell, aren't you?"

Now that he knew she was here, neither hell nor high water would keep him from Rivendell. A factor that shouldn't have any influence at all, but suddenly did. "Yes."

She leveled him with the steely green gaze beneath her glasses. "That's why having dinner together isn't a good idea. Fraternizing with colleagues is not conducive to my career goals."

Battling a myriad of emotions, Eric watched her disappear into an exam room. At least this time he'd been awake when she left.

"Tell me everything." Jonathan pounced the moment the door closed behind Kasey. Where had he been hiding? Behind a plant?

"I thought you were seeing a patient," Eric pointed out, leading his friend toward Jonathan's private office. "Besides, we're in the hallway of the clinic where we work. Use some tact."

He closed Jonathan's office door. "I met Kasey two months ago, liked her and want to go out with her again."

"And?"

"There's nothing more to tell."

Not that he was willing to share. Not even with someone he'd shared secrets with for years and who knew him better than anyone. Jonathan knew his darkest moments and had seen him through them. But some things were private. His night with Kasey fell into that category.

His friend leaned against his desk, arms crossed, expression confused. "You really want to go out with the Ice Queen?"

"Don't call her that." Eric glared, feeling oddly defensive of the woman who'd elicited strong emotions from the moment she'd plopped down next to him looking as if her world had crashed. "Why wouldn't I want to go out with Kasey? She's a beautiful woman."

Jonathan looked flummoxed. "Yeah, but—"

"She's intelligent, witty, has a great sense of humor and is a lot of fun to be around," Eric interrupted before Jonathan could say anything else. What was wrong with his friend? He'd been working with Kasey for heaven only knew how long and yet he hadn't noticed what a sexy misnomer she was? That she hid her passion behind too-tight hairstyles, don't-touch-me designer clothes and I'm-smart-not-pretty glasses?

"Are we talking about the same woman?" Jonathan shook his head. "Don't get me wrong. Kasey's a great coworker—steady, dependable, thorough—but she's not your type. Too uptight and career oriented."

"Those aren't bad qualities you're describing," Eric pointed out.

"She has her sights set on the top, pal. She's made no secret that she wants a seat on the board and she's put in the long hours to make sure it happens," Jonathan warned, pretending to shiver. "Plus, she gives off those subzero vibes. Could give a man permanent frostbite."

Frostbite? Eric had come closer to suffering heatstroke in Kasey's company than frostbite. Jonathan and apparently every other man in Kasey's life were blind fools.

Just so long as she didn't plan to use him as her stepping stone to the top, Eric had no problem with a career-minded woman. Particularly when that woman attracted him the way Kasey did.

"She's all business, rarely smiles," Jonathan continued, listing all the reasons he thought Kasey was wrong for Eric.

She didn't smile? Why did that make his chest hurt? Why did it make him want to do everything in his power to make her smile, and often? Just as he'd done on the night they'd met.

"Your loss, bud, because I've seen her smile." She hadn't smiled at first. But before they'd left for his hotel she'd laughed out loud several times. "She has an amazing smile that makes a man automatically smile back."

He wanted to experience her smile again.

Jonathan's gaze narrowed, but a smile tugged at the corners of his mouth. "I think you're suffering from brain freeze. Either that or you worked in that African desert for so long you can't handle hot anymore."

Eric grinned. Oh, he could handle hot all right. And he planned to.

Just as soon as he could convince Kasey.

CHAPTER TWO

ERIC leaned back in the expensive leather chair meant to impress guests invited into Rivendell Medical Center's administrator's office. With its original wall prints, expensive furnishings and lush greenery, the office screamed success.

"I know Dr. Douglas has already shown you around the ambulatory clinic, but would you like a tour of the rest of the facility prior to officially starting?" the lanky man he'd spent the morning with offered. "I know you practically grew up at the center, but that was before we moved to the new location."

That had been three years ago while Eric had been in Africa as part of the medical mission team he'd joined straight out of medical school. A lifetime ago. Eric didn't even feel like the same person who'd once lived in Rivendell.

He wasn't the same person.

"The entire building is state-of-the-art. The in-house referral system streamlines care with great efficiency.

We have close to a hundred providers of various special-
ties on staff now." Clive gave Eric a grin. "Your grandfather would be proud. I know your mother is."

His maternal grandfather would be proud of how far
the clinic had come. The facility comprised a three-
story building with multiple specialty departments, a
fully equipped laboratory, radiology department, pharmacy and a same-day surgery wing that bore Eric's
grandfather's name.

His mother was proud of the clinic, too, but Eric
refused to let thoughts of her into his mind. He'd barely
been home a week and already she was trotting Kentucky
debutantes in front of him at every opportunity.

Eric shook his head at his mother's matchmaking
and at the administrator. "Jonathan showed me around
the center when I was here two months ago."

Just as it had then, the center felt right.

Like this was where he was meant to be despite years
of adamant and rebellious denial of his heritage. Despite
his mother thinking his move home meant he was ready
to settle down and produce heirs.

"If there's anything Rivendell can do to make your
move smoother, let me know," Clive went on, no doubt
in an effort to impress Lena Woolworth's only child.

"Actually…" Eric rocked back in the chair, eyeing
the administrator through narrowed eyes. "There is
something."

Clive's temple jumped with a nervous spasm. "Oh?"

"I'm going to work in the ambulatory clinic."

The man's unease faded into confused relief.

"The ambulatory clinic? But…" Remembering who he was talking to, the administrator nodded. "Of course. I should have realized you'd want to work directly with Dr. Douglas."

Perhaps he should feel guilty for using his influence to change where he'd be working at the last minute. Hadn't he sworn not to let moving home corrupt him? That he'd remain true to the man he'd grown into while thousands of miles away? But working in the ambulatory clinic appealed enough for him to ignore any doubts about his motives.

He had no doubts.

He wanted to be near Dr. Kasey Carmichael.

Whether or not wanting to be near her was a good thing remained to be seen.

Early that evening, Kasey finished seeing her afternoon patients and slouched into the comfy ergonomic chair at her desk.

Her office wasn't much larger than a broom closet, but she'd been allowed to decorate the room to her taste. She'd gone with crisp white walls and black furniture. A vase of colorful Shasta daisies, looking so real people often reached out to touch a petal just to see, sat on the top of her bookshelf along with a model of a human kidney and a two-foot-tall skeleton she'd nicknamed "Bones".

She kept a vanilla-scented air freshener plugged in

to drown out the antiseptic smell that permeated the rest of the clinic.

The room wasn't fancy, but at least she had a small private place to call her own.

Right now, she desperately needed privacy.

Eric was here. At the clinic.

Maybe he'd work on a different floor and she'd never see him. What kind of doctor was he anyway?

Dropping her face into her palms, she massaged her temples.

This couldn't be happening.

Just seeing Eric in the hallway had made her want to push him into a room and perform a thorough examination of all his many attributes, right down to taste-testing him from head to toe.

Which shocked her.

She'd never been adventurous sexually. She and Randall had shared a good enough sex life, but they hadn't been the stuff to burn down buildings.

One night with Eric and smoke still clouded her mind.

Intoxicating smoke that made her want to inhale deeply and give in to sweet fantasy.

Sweet? There hadn't been anything sweet about her fantasies. Hot, enthusiastic, sweaty, yes, but not sweet.

Kasey's fingers dug deeper into her scalp.

No way would she risk her career because of a man a second time. Not at Rivendell, where she'd made her fresh start and the potential to achieve her lifelong dreams dangled in front of her like the proverbial carrot.

A knock sounded at her door and she looked up. Eric watched her.

Realizing she was massaging her temples in overtime, she dropped her hands to her desk and tapped the sleek black surface. Which was no less nervous appearing than her temple massaging. Taking a deep breath, she flattened her palms against the desk to stay their fidgety tapping.

"I thought you'd left." Brilliant conversation. Yet what did it matter? His family owned stock in the center. Could the situation be any more Randall-like? She needed to put Eric firmly in the past and keep him there.

If she remained steadfast, perhaps he'd take a hint and leave her alone.

Which was what he'd eventually do regardless. She was definitely like her mother in that regard. Men never stayed long. She'd thought Randall had been different. Steady, dependable Randall. But she'd been wrong. Horribly wrong and just look what that mistake had cost her in the long run.

Not to mention that she'd gone to Eric's hotel room on the night they'd met. She didn't respect herself, how could she expect him to?

"I did leave," Eric admitted. His gaze roved over her in melted chocolate temptation that made her libido growl in hungry response. "I came back."

"Why?" Why did he have to look so wonderful in his black slacks, blue shirt and tie? Like something on the cover of a men's magazine. He'd taken off his suit jacket at some point since she'd seen him earlier and his tie was loosened around his neck, making her want to walk over to him and straighten it.

Or perhaps she just wanted a reason to touch him?

"You."

"Me?" As much as she thrilled at his answer, he had to stop. She'd made a mistake the night they'd met. One she could forgive due to her mother's death. But she couldn't justify a repeat of their amazing night.

His family held power over the medical center.

They were going to be coworkers.

If she'd learned anything from her experience with Randall, she'd learned not to mix personal stuff with one's job.

The consequences were too dire.

"Seeing you today was an unexpected surprise." He stepped into her office, closed the door behind him, overwhelming the tiny room. Even Bones appeared to tremble in his presence. "I enjoyed our night together."

What rabbit hole had she fallen into? Because he looked as if he wanted to touch her. As if he'd like to push her against her desk, hike up her skirt and run his hands along her thighs, along her— Kasey gulped. "No!"

At his startled look, she took a calming breath.

"That night was…" Amazing, wonderful, just what she'd needed. *Embarrassing*. She didn't behave like her mother. Not usually. She wasn't a woman driven by lust and she had no intention of becoming one. She'd worked too hard to make something of herself, to rise above her past, poverty and genetics. "Nice, but we both know it was a one-night stand kind of thing."

"One-night stand kind of thing?"

He towered over her, not in a menacing way, but she fought the desire to lean as far away as possible...to ease the temptation of moving closer to those broad shoulders and talented hands.

"You're wrong," he continued, looking completely aware of her proximity dilemma and pleased by her reaction to him. "That night wasn't a one-night stand. Far from it."

"What would you call it?" *Besides the most humiliating event of my life?* No, that would have been when Skymont Hospital had let her go over her relationship with Randall. Or perhaps when her mother had shown up drunk at her high school graduation ceremony. Either way, her night with Eric had been a mistake. That's what she repeated in her head, not allowing her hormones a word in edgewise.

"The beginning of something worth pursuing." His eyes bored into her, daring her to deny his claim. Unbidden, her gaze dropped to the strong set of his jaw, to his lips. That mouth had kissed her. All of her.

"Stop." She closed her eyes, fighting memories of the tender kisses he'd placed on her hair, her face, the way he'd kissed away her tears. Memories of tenderness that had given way to passion. To urgent kisses. "Our meeting that night was nothing more than a bad coincidence. We should forget it happened."

"What you call a bad coincidence I call a stroke of good fortune. Just as I consider seeing you today good fortune."

His words were sweet to her ears, but what he was really saying was that he wanted sex again. They'd slept together on the day they'd met. He wasn't interested in a real relationship with her. Just sex. Toe-curling, life-altering sex but, still, just sex.

He moved further into the office, crowding her personal space by coming around to her side of the desk and half sitting, half leaning against the corner. His closeness zapped her ability to breathe.

"Why didn't you wake me before you left, Kasey?"

Oh, God, why had he moved so close?

She shut her eyes, counted to ten, prayed for indifference to him. "That night shouldn't have happened and wouldn't have under different circumstances."

Sad, but true.

"Yes, it would have."

Spicy, sexy musk toyed with her senses. She squeezed her eyes more tightly closed because she worried that if she looked at him, she'd have to touch. Absolutely have to.

"I'm sorry you got dragged into my bad day," she plunged on, needing to talk, needing to do anything that kept her from reaching out to run her finger over the cleft in his chin. "I regret the entire evening."

"You regret meeting me?" He sounded as if he didn't believe her.

Knowing they'd be coworkers, she should regret having met him, but her heart ached at the thought of not having the comfort she'd felt as she'd drifted to sleep in his arms. At not experiencing the mind-shattering passion his kisses had evoked. She'd had a bad day. He'd made her feel better. No matter how much she should, she didn't regret them making love.

She couldn't tell him that.

Doing so would only make what she had to do more difficult.

Indifference. She needed indifference.

"Yes," she choked out. "I regret meeting you."

"Open your eyes."

She forced her eyelids open, looked into his dark eyes and swallowed. Hard. Lord, he looked as if he really had been hurt that she'd left him.

"Now, say you regret meeting me and mean it." He shook his head when her lids automatically lowered. "Don't close your eyes, Kasey. Look at me, and tell me you regret what we shared, because I don't believe you."

She wanted to scoot her chair toward the wall to put more distance between them, but she needed to make a strong stand. Her job, her peace of mind was at stake. She should push him off her desk, but didn't dare touch him. To do so would send her few functioning brain cells into sexual dementia.

Focus on your goals, Kasey. She gave herself a mental pep talk. *Career, helping others, social status, being a valued member of society. A fling with a coworker robbed you of that once. Eric is a coworker with an influential family.*

"Is your ego so big you can't accept that I made a mistake in going to your hotel room?" she accused, going on the attack. She had to destroy the chemistry between them. Because she had to deny it. She couldn't go through what she'd gone through with Randall.

Somehow she suspected recovering from Eric would rob her of a lot more than Randall's decision she was good enough to sleep with but not good enough to give his last name to.

"No, my ego isn't that big." He leaned across her desk, staring straight into her eyes, his breath caressing her lips. "But I was there that night."

"I remember." She hadn't meant to sound nostalgic, but her voice held a touch of longing she couldn't deny. She shook off the erotic memories and put on the flat affect she'd perfected in the days following the fiasco with Randall. In the days before Skymont Hospital had let her go. "I took advantage of you that night."

"What?" His forehead wrinkled in surprise.

She sighed. How much could she tell him without also admitting how much being near him affected her? Was this what her mother had battled every time a sexy man had come near? This overwhelming need to touch? To be touched?

If so, Kasey was grateful the first thirty years of her life had passed without her knowing such carnal craving.

"Like I said," she began, wishing he weren't so close,

that she didn't feel every inch Betsy Carmichael's daughter, right down to the burst of pheromones dictating she forget everything except how this man's lips had felt against hers. "I had a bad day."

"Which doesn't explain how you used me."

She shrugged as nonchalantly as she could pull off when she couldn't breathe. "Don't you get it? I didn't want to be alone. You were convenient. End of story."

A glimmer of anger shone in his eyes. "You're saying any man would have done?"

"If it meant not being alone that night?" She called upon all her strength and lied through her teeth. "Any man would have done."

He smoothly shifted to stand by the black leather chair wedged between her desk and the corner of the office. Genuine shock shone on his face. Would he realize she was oversimplifying the night's events? She couldn't give him that opportunity.

"When I saw you with Dr. Douglas this morning…" Sitting forward, she continued her assault before he regrouped his thoughts, an assault directed as much at her libido as at Eric. "I just wished you'd go away. I don't do one-night stands. At least, I never had until that night. If I'd known I'd see you again, I never would have shared a drink with you, much less gone to your hotel room."

How horrible did that admission make her sound?

How much did it brand her Betsy Carmichael's daughter?

Was it even true? No. Eric had made her feel better, made her feel whole. She would have gone anywhere he'd led.

What scared her was that even now, when she was thinking more logically about her mother's death, when she knew she'd slept with a man similar to Randall, Eric still made her feel dazed, made her want to go where he led.

"Then I'm glad you didn't know we'd see each other again." He crossed his arms, his fingers coming so close to touching her she imagined she could feel his body heat sear through her clothes. "I enjoyed making love to you, Kasey."

"I imagine so." She couldn't keep the snideness out of her voice. After all, she'd just compared him to Randall and he was playboy Dr. Douglas's friend. "You should be grateful I left before you woke."

He leaned back, eyed her, his lips twisted with displeasure. "Grateful that you used me for sex and left while I was asleep?"

Was her face as red as it felt?

"Most guys would be grateful to avoid an awkward morning after."

His gaze unwavering, he shrugged. "I'm not most guys."

Yes, she'd noticed that about him.

"The day we met wasn't a good day," she said for lack of knowing what else to say.

"So you've said. Yet you haven't said what was so

bad." His voice held a gentle, concerned quality that made her want to squirm.

She didn't want him to be nice. She didn't want to like him, didn't want to believe in the light shining in his eyes that said she could trust him.

Whatever his game was, she wouldn't, *couldn't*, play along. Neither would she.

"What happened to send you into that bar?" Eric asked. "Into my arms?"

Her gaze dropped to the strong arms that had held her so securely. He sounded sincere. It would be so easy to give in, to lean on those broad shoulders.

She knew better, though. Randall had sounded sincere, had let her lean on his shoulders. Then he'd jerked the carpet out from under her feet and trampled on her while she was down.

"My life is none of your business."

Unfazed by her snappish comeback, Eric stared into her eyes. "What if I want to make your life my business? What if I want to see you again because I wasn't grateful you left without waking me?"

Was it even possible? She hadn't thought so, but what if?

Each and every time she'd leaned on another person, she'd fallen. Even if Eric hadn't been grateful she'd left, eventually the attraction would fizzle and then where would she be? Stuck working with an ex. The good-ole-boy system had already driven home how they dealt with sticky situations.

She would not be forced to start over again.

Not even for a man as appealing as Eric.

"I'd say you were out of luck, because the night we met was a fluke and is never going to happen again." She liked her life in Rivendell too much to risk it.

"Kasey," he began, pinning her beneath dark fire.

"Stop right there, Dr. Matthews." She jumped from her seat, refusing to be trapped by his nearness. She held up her hand to ward him off. "What happened between us was a mistake. I don't appreciate you coming to my office, pressuring me this way. I'm not interested. End of story."

He paused, confusion flashing in his eyes. Not backing away, he stayed within inches of her face. "You're serious?"

"Absolutely." Much better to deny the sexual chemistry between her and the fascinating man tempting her to throw caution to the wind. As much as she'd once cared for Randall, he'd never lifted her to the heights this man had in a single night. She might not recover a second time. Not professionally. Not emotionally.

Although Eric looked like he wanted to say more, he clamped his mouth closed and conveyed his displeasure via his tight facial expression.

Resuming his perch on her desk, he watched her for so long she fought to keep standing. His eyes gleamed a deep brown, threatening to burn her with their intensity if she showed the slightest sign of weakness.

His gaze scorched into her soul.

Finally, he gave a curt nod and left.

Kasey's forehead crashed to her desk and she rolled her head back and forth against the hard, cold surface.

Eric was gone.

But he'd be back.

Every workday, he'd be back.

Just how was she going to stay steadfast when confronted with Eric day in and day out?

CHAPTER THREE

A WEEK later, Eric winced at his twenty-year-old patient's bright red skin. "How long were you out in the sun?"

"My boyfriend works on a horse farm and we were out riding. I ended up sticking around and helping him most of the day. Last night I was miserable. I thought I was going to have to go to the emergency room," the young woman admitted, holding her body stiffly.

"I'll be as easy as I can." He gently lifted her loose clothing away from her skin to peer at the burn. "Did you have on sunscreen?"

As impossible as it seemed, her face grew redder. "No. I was working on my tan."

"I'd suggest you work on protecting your skin from permanent damage. A good SPF 30 sunscreen would have saved you a lot of trouble." He motioned toward her burn.

"Oh, you don't have to worry. I've learned my lesson. I plan to go buy the highest SPF in the store."

Eric shook his head. "No need. SPF 30 provides all the protection you need. Once the sun is blocked, it's blocked. Anything beyond just puts extra chemicals on your skin without any real extra protection."

He slipped on his stethoscope and listened to her heart sounds. Normal S1S2 with a regular rate and rhythm. No murmur. Lung sounds clear to auscultation.

"You're losing a lot of moisture through your burn. Make sure you drink a lot of water over the next few days. You want to stay hydrated."

He tapped the RX emblem on the computer screen and entered a prescription for burn cream. He sent the prescription to the pharmacy and printed out a patient education handout on skin care and sunburn.

His next patient was a thin older gentleman with soulful eyes and slumped shoulders. After less than thirty seconds, Eric realized Shane Bresdan needed more than a prescription refill.

The man took a deep breath, stared at his hands. "My wife left."

"Left?"

"Kapooie. She's gone." Shane's tone was flat, as if he talked about the weather. But his eyes held a world of pain and his hands were clenched tightly in his lap.

"Where did she go?"

Sagging shoulders lifted then fell. "Don't know. She just picked up and left while I was at work one day. Came home to a note saying she was gone and wouldn't be back."

And Eric thought he had female problems.

"Were you having marital issues?"

"No more than normal. She's never left before. Never even threatened to."

Poor man. After waking up in his hotel room alone two months ago, Eric wholeheartedly commiserated. He'd never had a woman walk out on him. He hadn't cared for the experience.

He'd thought he and Kasey had hit it off that night. They had. But whereas he'd gone into the hotel room thinking they were starting something special, she'd gone in thinking of the ending to her bad day.

Eric sighed. Thinking about Kasey was futile when she refused to acknowledge they'd shared anything more than a one-nighter. Was he really such a bad judge of women? Hadn't he learned to read who was sincere and who wasn't? He'd thought so, but perhaps not.

He turned back to his patient. "How are you dealing with her leaving?"

Unpacking his few personal belongings, going along with his mother's constant social demands because it made her happy, and making her happy made him happy, hanging out with Jonathan.

Which had worked until he'd been confronted with the living breathing reminder of the woman who'd bailed out on him.

Now he was discontented as hell.

Eric talked to Shane several more minutes, recommended counseling and an antidepressant. Shane denied suicidal ideas and agreed to return to the clinic for reevaluation. He scheduled a follow-up appointment for a week's time.

Eric shook the man's hand and walked into the hallway with him.

His Kasey radar bleeped. Why was he so aware of a woman who wanted nothing to do with him? He should be grateful. He hadn't come home to start a relationship. He'd come home for his mother, because he'd heard the need in her voice.

Unable to keep from looking at Kasey, he resigned himself to her reaction. Had four years out of the States really made such a difference in his social skills that he'd gone from fighting off women to chasing after one who denied wanting anything more to do with him? Why didn't he believe her?

She wouldn't have taken off from his hotel room bed if she'd wanted a relationship. Or would she? If she'd known who he was, known they'd be colleagues when he eventually took his place at the clinic, would she have left to throw him off kilter? To leave him wanting more?

He caught her looking at him. Her big green eyes were soulful behind her glasses. Her lower lip was sucked in between her teeth. Her fingers tightly clutched her stethoscope.

Why was she pretending their chemistry didn't exist when it so obviously did?

His gaze roved over the woman standing a few feet away, staring at him with a deer-in-the-headlights expression.

Gold digger or not, he wanted Dr. Kasey Carmichael. More than he remembered ever wanting a woman. She wanted him, too.

With time, she'd admit she wanted him.

"How long has your back been hurting, Mr. Oliver?" Kasey asked, making a notation on the sixty-year-old's electronic chart. Mr. Oliver came in every few months with a variety of complaints. Over the time she'd been taking care of him, Kasey had grown fond of the older gentleman, who qualified to come to the ambulatory clinic through a special charity fund sponsored by the Rivendell Ladies Society.

Shoulders covered in dirty coveralls, he shrugged. "On and off for years. Just something I live with, you know. With no insurance, I ain't had much choice."

Pushing her professional, no-nonsense, black-rimmed glasses up the bridge of her nose, she nodded. Mr. Oliver worked two jobs, trying to support his family. Although his children were all grown, one of his daughters and her three children lived with them. They struggled to make ends meet on the best of days. "When did your back get worse?"

"A couple of weeks ago. I was at work and lifted a car battery. Heard my back pop and then had to have Joe help me straighten." His weary eyes met hers. "You know Joe. He and his wife come to see you. He drove me here today."

"Joe's a nice man." Kasey typed his response into

the patient database. "Have you ever had an X-ray of your spine?"

His forehead wrinkled with thought. "Nope. Had one on my shoulder once when I was younger, but that's it."

Kasey examined his back, running her fingers along his spine, noting the abnormal curvature and areas of spasm. "I'd like to order an X-ray of your lumbar and thoracic spine. That's your low and middle back. You've got some scoliosis that's probably congenital, meaning you were born with it, but I'm concerned you've lost some vertebral height as well."

"Whatever you say, Doc." He shifted uncomfortably on the exam table. "I'm not sure I can afford X-rays, though."

"They're included in your visit today," she reminded him, glad that cost wouldn't keep Mr. Oliver from getting the care he needed. Yet another reason she volunteered with the Rivendell Ladies Society, a group of Kentucky women who gave back to their community. RLS was the social club, just what she'd dreamed of belonging to while growing up. Kasey's reality had been more along the lines of Public Housing is Us.

Mr. Oliver's brows lifted. "The X-rays are included? I didn't realize."

She nodded, doing her best not to make the proud man feel uncomfortable. She understood he didn't like accepting charity. All too well she understood. Hadn't she once survived on others' charity? Between her booze and her men, Betsy had had little time for her daughter.

No, Kasey wouldn't think of her mother.

To do that would lead to thinking of her death which led to thoughts of meeting Eric. She was having a difficult enough time not thinking of him.

What had his look in the hallway been about? She'd swear when he looked at her he saw right through to her soul. The sensation made her very uncomfortable.

"Have you noticed any burning or tingling in your legs or feet?" she asked her patient, refocusing on the issue at hand.

"No burning, but my feet stay cold. Particularly on the left side." Mr. Oliver lifted the offending foot from the floor, rotating his ankle. She had him flex his foot toward his knee. No pain. Negative Homan's sign.

She indicated for him to take off his shoes. He did so. She took out a sensory tine often used to measure diabetic neuropathy and asked him to tell her when she touched his foot with the bristlelike instrument.

Mr. Oliver had decreased sensation in three of his toes.

She pressed against each toe, closely watching how quickly the nail bed and flesh returned to pink. His capillary refill was within normal limits. Unfortunately, his great toenails bilaterally were yellow, thick and malshaped from a fungal infection. She'd check on pharmaceutical samples. If his liver enzymes came back okay, she'd treat the fungus with an oral medication that would slowly clear the infection. With the decreased sensation, she'd do all she could to protect his feet.

"We may need to do an MRI scan, but I'll wait and see what the X-ray shows." She straightened, filled out an order slip and handed the paper to him. "Take this to the radiology department. It's just beyond the elevators on the right. I've also ordered a urinalysis and a few blood tests that you can stop back by the laboratory in the morning and have done. You need to fast, for at least eight hours before you have the blood drawn so I can check your cholesterol, too."

"Okay." The man stared at the paper in his callused hands. Grease permanently blackened his nails, etched out each and every wrinkle, outlining the story of his life. Years of hard labor as a mechanic couldn't be washed away with soap and water. "Thanks."

Kasey respected Mr. Oliver. Circumstances may have prevented him from having a better life, but he didn't expect handouts, didn't want a free ride.

Unlike her mother.

Despite their monumental differences, Kasey had mourned her mother's death, wished she could have felt more loss over the woman than over what might have been. She couldn't change the past. Her mother was gone and there was no longer hope that someday her mother might get her act together where they could have a real relationship. The relationship they'd had, however lacking, was all they'd ever have.

Kasey bit the inside of her lip to stop the new line of maternal thoughts heading her way. She forced her mother to the recesses of her mind and smiled at her patient.

"When you're done getting the X-rays, stop by the pharmacy, which is one door down from the radiology department. You'll have two prescriptions waiting. One for an anti-inflammatory and one for a muscle relaxant." She told him what the generic prescriptions would cost. "Don't forget to come back as soon as you can for the blood tests, preferably tomorrow. If your labs show anything requiring further treatment, I'll call you."

Gripping his front sheet, he left the exam room. Kasey headed to her office.

Sitting at her desk, she riffled through a stack of papers on her desk, ignoring an announcement of the addition of Dr. Eric Matthews to the ambulatory clinic of Rivendell Medical Center. Instead, she reviewed a cardiology consult letter on Bill Ridner. The words blurred before her eyes. Her mind was filled with the man who haunted her every thought.

The announcement had been sitting on her desk for a couple of days. Not that she'd let herself read the postcard-sized message. She hadn't. Wouldn't. The less she exposed herself to Eric, the better. The less she knew about the man behind the gorgeous body and quick smile, the better.

An image of that gorgeous body, his passionate kisses while he'd made love to her—had sex with her—caused her to inhale sharply. He'd started at the clinic the day after his surprise arrival a week ago and was working directly with her. How was she supposed to ignore that? Ignore him?

Perhaps she should read the announcement just to learn about her enemy better.

Technically, as head of the ambulatory clinic, she was Eric's superior, but time and again Clive Evans sought out Eric, as did several longtime board members. Had the clinic ever put so much effort into schmoozing a new physician?

The more attention Eric got, the more nervous Kasey became about who would take Herbert's board position.

She rubbed her temple, massaging the dull throb that erupted any time she thought of Eric.

She had a permanent headache these days.

"Okay, so I like him," she admitted to Bones, grimacing at the skeleton on her bookshelf. "A lot."

Way more than she should since a relationship between them was impossible. Could she have picked a worse person to be attracted to? A man who not only was someone she worked with but a doctor who was likely vying for the same promotion she was and had strong family ties to the medical center. Why else would he keep having so many private conversations with the administrator and board members?

He was just like Randall. Rich, spoiled, used to getting what he wanted. When push came to shove, he'd rise to the top, even if he had to step on her to do so. She'd do well to remember that.

Kasey massaged her temple with more vigor, wondering if she'd worn the flesh away from her skull yet. She'd always massaged her temples when she got agitated. At the rate she was going, she was going to look like Bones.

"Kasey?"

She glanced up, barely suppressed a wince at seeing Eric in all his glorious manliness standing in her doorway. As usual, he was dressed impeccably in dark tailored slacks and a crisp button-down shirt.

He stood in her doorway, staring at her. His deep brown eyes told her what his mouth didn't. He wanted her. Probably a case of wanting what he couldn't have, but, regardless, his lingering look sent tingles over her body, flushed her skin, and made her squirm. Hopefully, he hadn't noticed.

Yeah, right. Because he'd gone blind and stupid and hadn't noticed she couldn't keep her eyes off him any time he was near.

"Kasey?" Eric repeated, eyeing her with concern.

"Yes?" She dropped her hand from her temple and inflected as much annoyance into the word as she could. Which was quite a lot since her previous thoughts did annoy her. She didn't want to notice Eric. The only way she'd survive working with him was for her to ignore he existed and for him to ignore her.

Which meant she should probably pray to go blind, deaf and lose all sense of smell.

Because he looked like he'd stepped straight off a Hollywood television set showcasing drop-dead gorgeous doctors, sounded like a Pied Piper's tune that played directly to her dancing libido, smelled so heavenly she wanted to grow wings, wear a halo and learn to play the harp.

So heavenly she was instantly taken back to being wrapped in his arms, their bodies tangled, and breathing in his musk.

Did he possibly have a disorder where he oversecreted pheromones meant to drive women into a heated frenzy?

She'd believe it.

"What do you want?" she bit out tersely, hoping to still her hyperresponsive libido. She didn't need to remember what they'd done, how he'd smiled at her, laced their fingers and— There she went again, remembering what she didn't need to remember.

At her curt question, disappointment flashed across his face, but he didn't comment, just seemed to expect her surliness.

Guilt hit her.

He didn't deserve the way she was treating him.

He'd been nothing but kind to her, and she liked him. So how could she explain that she had to force as much distance between them as possible? That she couldn't afford another blow to her career, but mostly she couldn't deal with how he made her feel weak, like her mother?

To give an inch with Eric would be risking everything she'd worked to achieve. Her pride in herself. Her career.

"I've been with Colin Taylor." His eyes searched hers, piercing her sanity with their intensity. "He usually sees you, but you were booked up this morning, so he scheduled with the new guy instead." His lips lifted in a smile, then paused midway. "Do you have a minute to answer a few questions?"

"In regard to one of my patients? Always."

Even if she did suspect her advice on a patient was the last thing Eric needed. She'd already seen and heard enough to know all accolades regarding his skills were well deserved.

It seemed everyone in the building had something to say about him. She'd very quickly begun blocking out any mention of Eric.

Particularly the rumors that the board planned to ask him, a newcomer, to join their ranks.

"What's going on with Mr. Taylor?" She didn't meet Eric's eyes and, thus, managed to keep her voice level.

"You've scheduled fasting labs for him on three separate occasions, but he never shows. Why is that?"

"Shouldn't you ask Mr. Taylor, rather than me?"

Eric's expression tightened and she rushed on.

"Part of it may be that he doesn't believe the tests are important, despite me telling him otherwise. But it's more likely because he doesn't have a ride to the clinic."

"He doesn't drive?"

"He doesn't own a car. His son usually brings him in for his appointments, but he isn't able to in the mornings."

Eric considered her answer. "How does he get to his job?"

"He walks. About two miles each way."

"Oh." Looking thoughtful, Eric tapped his long fingers against her desk. The methodical rhythm mimicking a subtle attack along the lines of Chinese water torture. Each tap wore on Kasey's sanity.

Instead of caving in, she glared pointedly at the expensive gold watch circling his wrist. "You may have noticed the coding on his billing sheet. Mr. Taylor comes to the clinic through a charity fund provided by the Rivendell Ladies Society." Whom she was to meet with the following evening to discuss their upcoming fundraiser—a masquerade ball. "Not all our clients have padded PPOs. Those who see us through the charity are the working poor and don't have the luxury of dropping everything to follow recommended medical guidelines."

His lips twitched with the hint of a grin reminiscent of the ones he'd flashed at Calista Blue's. Her breath caught.

"Feel that strongly about it, do you?"

Her and her big mouth. She'd gotten up on her soapbox and said too much. Had she expected him to become defensive? To argue with her? Had she hoped he was an elitist snob so she could hold it against him? No one knew she'd grown up in the poorest area of Lexington, that if not for government assistance programs and charity, she'd have been homeless, starved.

"I suppose." She didn't elaborate, just went back to studying Bill Ridner's cardiology report. "It's my job to care about my patients."

He crossed his arms and regarded her. "Why is it that no matter what I say, it's the wrong thing? What's changed from the night we met? I'd have sworn you liked me that night, that we had a connection."

"You know what changed," she answered honestly. "We were never meant to see each other after that night. The fact we now work together makes the situation awkward."

"You're right about the situation being awkward, but it doesn't have to be." His eyes sparkled like dark amber. "I'm interested in you. You aren't interested in me. Fine." He shrugged. "Forget that I want to make love to you until you can't see straight. Let's be friends."

Friends? They couldn't be friends. A friend didn't battle urges to run her fingers over broad shoulders. A friend wouldn't be so acutely aware of how his pulse beat at the base of his throat, of how when he smiled a dimple dug into his right cheek. A friend's body didn't explode with pleasure when he— *Friends?* Was he insane? They couldn't be friends.

She wouldn't even touch his "Forget that I want to make love to you until you can't see straight." Like a woman could forget when a sexy man told her that and she knew he had the skills to back up his claim.

"Why would you want us to be friends?" Had her voice squeaked?

His gaze didn't waver, just continued to probe further and further inside her. "I like you."

"You like me?" Why did she hold her breath while waiting for his answer? Lord, she was losing it.

All because of the man standing before her and his irresistible appeal. He wanted to make love to her again. Because he couldn't have her. Everything about Eric said he wasn't used to being told no.

He smiled self-derisively, as if he couldn't help himself for being sexy, as if he couldn't help that he made her want to run straight into the blade of a broken heart.

He probably couldn't.

"I made my feelings apparent on the night we met," he clarified. "Nothing's changed on my part."

Heat crept into Kasey's cheeks. Out of habit she pushed against her glasses, sliding them up as far as they'd go on the bridge of her nose. "You were drunk the night we met."

"You think so?" His dark brow arched, his expression somber. "There wasn't any alcohol in my soda, Kasey."

There hadn't been? "It doesn't matter. We can't be friends."

His forehead wrinkled. "Why not?"

Because he made her want to forgo a lifetime of promises that she wouldn't be like her mother. With Randall, she'd been naïve, believed they'd end up married with a house in an upscale neighborhood, send their kids to the right schools, and grow old together. In the end, she hadn't been good enough for anything beyond sex. He'd married the blue-blooded daughter of one of Skymont's trustees.

She suspected Eric's background made Randall look like a poor ole boy. In the long run, Eric would want someone like him, someone who came from wealth and prestige and good stock. No matter how far Kasey had come, how proud she was of her success and the woman she'd become, she was still poor little Kasey Carmichael from the wrong side of town. She was still the daughter of Betsy Carmichael who'd had a revolving door to her bedroom and a predilection for alcohol.

Kasey bit the inside of her lip and wondered how they'd gone from discussing Mr. Taylor to a conversation about the night they'd met. Discussing work was much safer.

"You were asking about Mr. Taylor?" she reminded him, hoping her voice conveyed that she was no longer willing to discuss anything personal. "Was there something specific you needed to know regarding his care?"

Eric sighed, but let her change the subject back to their patient. "I'm concerned we're missing something. His MRI showed degenerative disc disease. He certainly has symptoms from his back issues, but I'm worried more is going on."

She tried not to let his "we're missing something" comment irk. Since this was his first time seeing Mr. Taylor, what he really meant was that she was missing something. "More?"

"His prostate is enlarged."

Around fifty percent of men over the age of fifty had an enlarged prostate. Kasey stared, waiting for him to say something more enlightening.

"Did he tell you that his father and grandfather both had prostate cancer in their early sixties?"

Mr. Taylor hadn't told her and she'd taken a detailed family history from him on several occasions. Had repeatedly examined him without him mentioning urinary symptoms, erectile dysfunction or symptoms that had made her suspect prostate issues. He'd had a digital rectal exam not long after she'd first seen him at the clinic, but she couldn't recall just how long ago that had been. Eric had apparently done another today since he'd said Mr. Taylor's prostate was enlarged. Had she missed something important on one of her patients?

"I want to get a prostate specific antigen on him as soon as possible. I tried to get him to go to the lab today, but he thought he should wait and do the labs you'd ordered."

"In addition to the comprehensive metabolic profile, complete blood count and cholesterol panel, I ordered a PSA, too. If you read my notes, you saw that I've encouraged him to have the labs drawn while here, even though it meant forgoing the lipid check. He's repeatedly refused." Was he criticizing her skills? Would he twist the care she'd provided to Mr. Taylor in an attempt to make her look incompetent to the board? "Why are you telling me this?"

Eric eyed her, clearly not understanding her hostile tone. "He's your patient."

"He saw you today," she spat out. Did she sound petty? She hadn't meant to, but Eric made her antsy. Among other things.

"Yes, but you know him better than I do. He mentions you with every other breath," Eric pointed out. "He knows you're an excellent doctor, and he trusts your opinion. I thought you could talk to him, convince him to have the PSA drawn even if he isn't prepared to have the other tests."

He was legitimately concerned for their patient.

Eric didn't deserve how she was treating him. Not personally, not professionally. She had to find a balance between keeping him at a distance and being so prickly.

For that matter, she'd felt prickly and emotionally wrought from the moment Eric had arrived on the scene. She blamed her mother's death, but also her unexpected reaction to Eric and the fact she couldn't get him out of her head no matter how much she tried.

Looking into Eric's concerned brown eyes, she couldn't recall why she even wanted to get him out of her head.

What she wanted was to tell him she was sorry, to tell him that he made her want things she was afraid of wanting because the last time she'd let herself have those dreams she'd gotten badly burned.

That she'd been embarrassed she'd slept with him on the night they'd met.

That looking at him, wanting him, made her feel like the little girl she'd once been with her nose smashed against a store window, eyeing the goodies inside.

"If he schedules with me," she started over, making sure to keep her voice polite, professional, not prickly, "I'll talk with him. But if it's regarding his prostate, he's just as likely to schedule with you or Dr. Douglas."

Several of her regular male patients saw Dr. Douglas when the time came to have certain male body parts checked. Vice versa, too. She and Grace, the clinic's nurse practitioner, saw some of Dr. Douglas's patients for their female problems, but at no other time.

"Okay." Eric lingered for several more minutes without speaking, as if he was waiting for her to say something.

What? she wanted to scream.

Instead, she went back to doing what she'd been attempting to do for weeks. She ignored him. Or pretended to. Which was the crux of what she'd been doing.

"Kasey?"

Heart pounding, she looked up, fought gulping back the ball of emotions clogging her throat. "Is there something else?"

"Yes."

Her pulse leaped, her breath caught, her hands clasped together to keep them from nervously fluttering around while she waited for him to make his move.

And waited.

Because he just sat across from her, watching her with an intensity that made her think he was committing every feature to memory. That he wanted her to act on the strong impulse within her to go to him, bury her fingers into his dark hair and pull him to her lips.

What was it Eric wanted of her? Just sex?

Because she was smart enough to recognize that all he had to do was touch her and she'd go up in flames, would likely beg him to make love to her again. He recognized that truth, too. But he didn't press his advantage, which totally confused her.

And frustrated her.

Dear heavens, did she want him to press?

He let out an exasperated sigh. "I'm not going anywhere, Kasey. Which means that eventually you're going to have to deal with what happened between us. What's going to happen between us." He leaned forward, hovering inches from her face.

Her gaze dropped from his expressive eyes to his mouth. Kasey gulped.

"For the record—" his pupils darkened to almost black "—I'm not talking about wanting to be your friend."

CHAPTER FOUR

"DO YOU want to talk about it?" Jonathan asked later that night at the Calista Blue bar where Eric had met him for dinner and to catch a televised baseball game.

The bar where Eric had met Kasey.

He and Jonathan had gotten drinks and ordered their food. Flashing a flirty smile, their waitress placed their order on the table.

"Nope." Eric took a drink of his soda. He rarely drank alcohol these days and never when he was upset.

Kasey upset him. In a big way.

Why did he get the feeling that every time she pushed him away, she was really running from herself?

"There are a million girls in this town who would love to take your mind off Kasey Carmichael." Jonathan took a swig from his longneck. "Like those two hottie blondes over there."

Not acknowledging his friend's mention of Kasey, Eric followed his gaze. Sure enough, two women were giving them come-hither looks. Once upon a time, he might have been interested, but he hadn't had a fling in over four years.

During his mission work, he'd had two committed relationships, one with an Australian doctor who'd volunteered with the group for a year and the other with the daughter of a British diplomat who'd funded the vaccination program Eric had helped implement. Later, he'd learned both had known who he was, his family connections. Just as well that he hadn't been under any illusions that either relationship would lead to marriage.

In his heart, he'd always known he'd go back to Kentucky and find a balance between the life his heritage demanded of him and the life he wanted for himself.

Eric motioned toward the smiling women. "Go ahead. I'm not interested."

Jonathan's jaw dropped. "You can't be serious?"

"I don't need you to start matchmaking, too," Eric snapped.

Jonathan shook his head. "Ouch. Somebody sure is testy."

Knowing his friend was right, Eric grimaced. "Sorry."

"It's your mother doing the matchmaking?" Jonathan took a drink. "Or do I want to ask?"

"Probably not." Eric inhaled a deep breath. "And, yes, it's my mother. Despite my insistence that I'm not interested, she's setting me up with one of her cronies' daughters. Not that she calls them dates. They're 'social functions'."

Jonathan laughed. "And you aren't interested in these social functions."

"No."

"Because you're interested in a particular coworker of ours."

Eric didn't answer.

Jonathan eyed him a minute before saying, "You should go to Aruba with me tomorrow. The sun and babes will take your mind off the Ice Queen."

Glaring at Jonathan's use of the nickname, Eric shook his head. "I've only been on the job a week. I can't take off for Aruba." Once he would have taken up the offer without a thought to his responsibilities, without a care in the world. That had been a long time ago. "If you'd wanted to do Aruba together, we should have gone before I started at the clinic."

Eric stared at his friend's amused expression. "Besides, I didn't say I was thinking about Kasey."

"You didn't have to," Jonathan snorted. "The entire office knows you have the hots for her. Probably the entire building. Why haven't you asked her out on a date?"

"Good question and one I wished I knew the answer to." He needed time with her, time to explore the uncharted emotional waters he was currently drowning in. "She won't have me."

Taking a sip of his beer, Jonathan grunted. "She had you on the night you met."

"I never said that," Eric replied. He'd been very closemouthed about the night he and Kasey had met. A few times he'd wondered if Jonathan could shed some light on where he'd gone wrong with Kasey. But as good a person as Jonathan was, he'd have agreed with Kasey about being grateful she'd left without waking him. To Jonathan, that would have been the perfect night. Phenomenal sex with no strings attached.

"You didn't have to." His friend stuck a fried pickle in his mouth. "The Ice Queen gave you brain freeze and now you're warped."

"Apparently, and I told you not to call her that."

Not looking in the slightest reprimanded, Jonathan grinned. "No worries, pal. I've seen how she looks at you. She's got the same warped brain disease you do." Jonathan lifted his beer in salute. "Go get healed together or something."

Right. All he had to do was convince Kasey. Piece of cake.

"It's not that simple."

"Of course it is. You want her. She wants you." Jonathan shrugged. "Just make your sleek Eric Matthews move and reel her in."

His sleek Eric Matthews move? Had he ever had such a move? He'd never had to work for a woman. He wasn't even sure he knew how. Maybe that's what he was doing wrong.

"You weren't paying attention," he admonished. "I've already made my move. She turned me down flat."

Jonathan almost choked on his appetizer. "You're kidding?"

"I wish."

Jonathan threw his head back in laughter. "I never thought I'd see the day when a chick shot you down."

"Yeah, well, you have now."

Jonathan took a swig of his beer, then shrugged. "Maybe you should count yourself lucky. Kasey's all about her career. It's no secret her sights are set on the board."

"How do you know that?"

"Advancement is a big deal to her. Honestly, it's surprised me that she's stayed in the ambulatory clinic as that isn't the most politically advantageous spot to work within the facility." Jonathan shot him a look. "At least, it wasn't until Lena Matthews's son took an interest in the clinic."

"So, why is Kasey still in the ambulatory clinic if she's all about her career?"

"The only thing I can figure is that she honestly believes in the charity fund's work."

After her heartfelt defense of the fund, Eric could believe that.

"I know you've not made a big deal of who you are, but does she know?"

Eric shrugged. "I'm not sure. I didn't think so, but sometimes I wonder."

"You think that's why she hooked up with you that night?"

"I didn't say we hooked up. But I will admit that if it had been Kasey who'd invited me to Aruba, I'd be packing my bags."

Grinning, Jonathan held his hand over his heart. "I'm crushed."

Eric laughed. "Yeah, I can tell."

The waitress put their food in front of them just as a cheer went up around the bar. Someone had just knocked a home run.

Eyeing the television monitor closest to them, they dug into their food and for a few hours Eric forgot about Kasey Carmichael.

The following Monday, Kasey handed Lora a lab request for a patient she'd spoken with on the phone. "Thanks."

"You're welcome." A pretty pink blossomed in the blonde's cheeks. "We got a postcard from Dr. Douglas today."

Kasey blinked in surprise. *Dr. Douglas had sent a postcard?*

"That's nice," she said for lack of knowing what to say. Dr. Douglas didn't seem like the postcard-sending type. Had he ever sent a note before during one of his frequent vacations?

Perhaps the card was in Eric's honor.

"He says Aruba is awesome, and he wishes we were there." Lora sounded wistful, as if she wished she was there. For the view or for Dr. Douglas, Kasey wasn't sure. Lora had been one of the many women to go through the revolving door of Dr. Douglas's life. Kasey hadn't ever been convinced the nurse had gotten over him.

"Aruba sounds fairly tempting after the last two

patients we've seen this morning." A bipolar patient who'd gone off her medications and another in for the removal of an ingrown toenail. The removal of toenails was one of Kasey's pet peeves. She'd yet to do one where her own toenails didn't curl tightly into her shoes.

"Tell me about it. Give me the sun, a beach and a good book and I'm so there," Lora mused, turning when an exam-room door opened behind her.

Eric stepped into the hallway, a serious look on his face. Usually his eyes twinkled, but no merriment danced in his deep brown gaze now. Not that Kasey was looking *that* closely.

"Just who I was needing." He was looking at her, too. That closely. "Can we talk a minute?" At her obvious hesitation, he gave an exasperated sigh and added, "Regarding the patient I'm currently seeing."

A room that had been used for storage on the opposite side of Dr. Douglas's office was being renovated for Eric. Currently, the two men were sharing Dr. Douglas's office. Whereas Kasey's office was tidy and trendy, Dr. Douglas's was crammed full of books, medical magazines, sports memorabilia and various educational wall posters sponsored by pharmaceutical companies.

Kasey followed Eric, turning suspicious when he closed the door. However, his expression remained somber, piquing her curiosity.

"I'm with Maggie Payne," he began. He stood in front of the overflowing desk, arms crossed, staring expectantly at her. "Do you recall who she is?"

"Yes." A too-thin woman with sad eyes came to mind. "I've seen her a few times over the past couple of months. Isn't she a construction worker?"

"So she says." His tone disbelieving, he blew out a frustrated breath. "You last saw her for injuries resulting from a fall off a ladder. I'm seeing her today for trauma from a roof beam giving way."

Immediately, Kasey knew what he was getting at. One accident could be written off, but two major accidents in such a short time was suspicious for abuse. Heat dampened her body, making her palms clammy. "Perhaps she's just unlucky."

"Perhaps she's being abused and is covering for the bastard." His face red, Eric's hands clenched at his sides.

Kasey's stomach knotted into a tight ball. "Did you ask her?"

"She insists no one hit her, but her bruises indicate otherwise."

Kasey took a few deep breaths, forced her voice to remain steady. "You can report your findings to the police, but if she denies it and won't press charges, there's nothing we can do."

Looking pensive, he nodded. "You should talk to her."

"Me?" she squeaked, feeling light-headed. "Why me?"

Did he somehow sense her past? Somehow see right through her to the life she'd desperately put behind her?

"Because you're a woman."

Her nerve endings sizzled throughout her body. "What does that have to do with anything?"

"I'm a man, and she probably sees me as the enemy. As a woman, she might open up to you."

For many reasons, Kasey hated dealing with abuse cases. She understood her phobias, understood the whys, but understanding didn't make her job any easier. She always made sure her patients were taken good care of, but she referred abuse cases out fast.

The thought of confronting Maggie made her feel squeamish.

"Okay," she agreed hesitantly. "If you think it'll make a difference."

"If I didn't, I wouldn't have asked," he said, staring oddly at her.

Battling personal demons, Kasey followed him into the exam room and tried to keep from wincing at the woman's black eye and swollen upper lip. She was dressed in a hospital gown and through the gaps deep purple bruises marred Maggie's ribs. More could be seen on her upper arms. Like someone had grabbed her, shaken her. Fading yellow-green bruises dotted her thin body.

Eric was right. Maggie hadn't fallen from a roof and although her injuries hadn't been nearly so severe or clear-cut, she likely hadn't fallen from a ladder before her last visit.

"Maggie, you've met Dr. Carmichael," he said in such a gentle voice that Kasey was pulled from her thoughts and looked at him. His face shone with compassion. "I thought, under the circumstances, you might be more comfortable if she examines you."

Tearing her eyes away from Eric, Kasey looked at the woman to see if she, too, had been moved by his sincerity. If the woman found herself wanting to lean on him and pour out her heart.

"Look." Frustration shone in Maggie's eyes. "It really doesn't matter who examines me. I fell from a roof. I just came to the clinic because it hurts to breathe."

Eric met Kasey's gaze. "She'll probably need a chest X-ray."

Unable to stand the intensity in his eyes or the way her heart sped up in response to that intensity, Kasey patted Maggie's hand. "Dr. Matthews is going to leave so I can examine you. We'll talk woman to woman while he's gone."

Eric took the hint and left the room.

Kasey examined the woman, battled tears at the extent of her injuries, battled tears that always threatened when confronted with abuse. Tears from the past.

"Maggie," she began. "I know you told Dr. Matthews that you fell, but that's not what happened. If you don't want to report who did this to you, that's your choice, but my choice is your safety."

"What about my choices?" Maggie shivered, shaking her head back and forth in denial. "If you tell the police, he'll kill me."

"Who?" Kasey asked gently.

"My old man. He only gets mean when he drinks," Maggie said defensively.

"Then he needs to quit drinking."

"Tell me about it." The woman sighed, then whimpered in pain at Kasey's touch. "He busted me up pretty bad this time, didn't he?"

"Yes." She continued her exam, being as gentle as possible. "I can't feel any displaced ribs, but that doesn't mean there aren't fractures. Did he kick you?"

Kasey continued talking with Maggie, examining her, documenting objective findings and asking questions, becoming more and more emotionally involved in the woman's plight.

"I can't leave him. I love him," Maggie sobbed.

"Loving someone doesn't mean you have to stay in an abusive relationship. Taking a stand that this is wrong doesn't lessen your love."

Maggie's head lowered. "Someone like you can't understand."

"I understand better than you think." Kasey took a deep breath. She'd treated abuse cases before, but this was the first time she'd spoken of her shameful past out loud. She ignored the voice asking, *Why now?* "My mother was an alcoholic and a mean drunk, too. I grew up having a lot of *accidents.*"

So many that the state had stepped in several times to remove her from her mother's care. Somehow Betsy had always managed to straighten up long enough to regain custody. Until the next time.

"I was ashamed to admit to anyone that my own mother would do such things to me. I even remember thinking that perhaps I deserved the way she treated me.

As soon as I was old enough to know better, to take care of myself, I left because no one deserves to be treated this way." She gave a pointed look at Maggie's bruises. "Being under the influence doesn't make hitting another person okay."

Maggie stared at her, surprise at Kasey's admission shining in her eyes. "You think I don't know it's not okay? I know that. That doesn't mean I can leave. Where would I go? I can't support myself. I didn't even graduate from high school."

Abusers often convinced their victims of their inability to get by without them, cutting them off from all sources of support. It was all part of the abuse, all part of how they kept the victim under their thumb. As a child, Kasey hadn't had a choice. This woman had choices.

"I can call someone to help you, Maggie. Someone who will give you a place to stay and help keep you safe. What your boyfriend is doing is wrong. He needs help. If you allow this to continue…" she indicated the bruises on the woman's body "…you're not helping him or yourself. I know it isn't easy, but nothing worthwhile is. I made myself a better life. So can you."

Kasey heard a noise behind her, turned and saw Eric standing just inside the door. Her lips parted, but nothing came out.

How long had he been standing there?

How much had he heard?

The soft glow in his sympathetic eyes said he'd heard too much.

Although she'd never revealed the cause of her tears, she'd cried in his arms on the night they'd met, grieving over her mother's death. Now Eric knew her deepest, darkest secret. What next?

She didn't want him to *know* her, to look at her and see beneath the polished surface she'd spent years perfecting.

Most definitely she didn't want his pity.

Sensing Kasey's discomfort, Eric fought his own unease.

She'd been abused as a child.

Fury like none he'd known, not even during the most unjust conditions he'd been exposed to while in Africa, stormed his chest. Fury that Kasey's mother had hurt her, betrayed the trust a child so innocently gave to a parent.

"I, uh…" Kasey looked flummoxed, but as if she was trying to stay calm. Her eyes held the same panicked look as on the day he'd shown up at the office. "I'll order X-rays, Maggie. And a blood count just to be sure your levels don't indicate internal bleeding."

She gave a nervous laugh, totally inappropriate and a sign of how upset she was that he'd overheard her conversation.

Damn it, why wouldn't she let him in? She had on that one night. She'd said she had a bad day. Had something happened with her mother? Was that what had upset her so much she'd come to that bar and found him?

Part of him had wondered about her motives for spending the night with him, for leaving before he'd awakened. But more and more he suspected her reasons had had nothing to do with him, nothing to do with who he was, and everything to do with Kasey and who she was beneath all the layers she'd carefully constructed.

"Think about what I said, Maggie," she said with one last comforting touch to the woman's hand. "You can make a better life for yourself."

With that Kasey pushed past him, obviously expecting him to stay with Maggie. Instead, he excused himself and followed Kasey out of Maggie's room and into an empty exam room. Her head was in her hands.

Was she crying?

"Kasey?"

She turned, eyes flashing with tears. "You had no right to eavesdrop."

"I wasn't eavesdropping." But he had been. "At least, not intentionally," he corrected. "I did knock before opening the door."

He stepped toward her, his spirits lifting when she didn't back away. "I'm sorry about your mother, Kasey."

Her eyes narrowed into tiny slits. "Don't tell me you're sorry when you know nothing."

"I'd like to know," he admitted, closing the distance between them. "Let me know you, Kasey."

"No." She bit into her lip. "No." A tear slid down her cheek. "No. No. No."

Not letting her push him away, he wrapped his arms around her and pulled her close. Feeling inadequate, he held her, planning to let her cry. "Shh, it's okay."

It would be okay, because he'd protect her from the world. Always. Even as he thought it, he recognized that he should be afraid, more afraid than he'd ever been, but he wasn't.

He'd come home for a reason. He'd thought it was his mother. To honor the family legacy he'd once scorned.

Now he wondered if he'd come home for a woman he'd never met.

A woman who reached places he hadn't known existed inside him.

The next day, Kasey saw an upper respiratory infection patient and refilled another patient's hypertension medications. Another three patients and she'd caught up for the morning, but the receptionist registered two more drop-ins.

"Sorry, Kasey," Lora said, "but Agnes couldn't bear to turn them away."

"No problem. She's good at screening who can wait and who can't. I'll see them."

She didn't want a single moment's downtime. Not when she'd made such a fool of herself following her consult with Maggie yesterday. Thoughts of how she'd once again cried in Eric's arms receded to the back of her mind when she was with patients.

Thank God she'd managed to avoid him the rest of the day.

"Do you want me to have them come back after lunch?" Lora asked.

Kasey shook her head. "There's no reason for them to wait that long. I'd rather go ahead and see them now."

She needed all the distractions she could get, because her brain seemed to be on a single track these days.

As if her thoughts had conjured him up, Eric stepped out of an exam room. "I'll take one of the patients so Kasey will have time for lunch."

She started to deny him, say that she'd see both, but when their eyes met, she just nodded.

There was an odd light in his eyes. A light she'd seen in his eyes yesterday when he'd held her after her encounter with Maggie. A light that warned change was in the air. Hah, change had been in the air since the night she'd met him.

When Kasey had finished examining her late arrival, she saw the gentleman, almost crippled with rheumatoid arthritis, to the front of the clinic. She turned to go to her office to grab her purse. Eric stood directly in her path.

Had he been waiting on her to finish?

"I think I got the easy patient. She only needed a medication refill." He grinned, but his eyes searched her face. As if he was worried about her, as if he, too, kept thinking of yesterday. "Are you headed to lunch?"

Wanting to get away from his penetrating gaze, she absently nodded.

"Great. Me, too." Smiling, he took a step toward her. "We'll go together."

No way did she want to go to lunch with him.

"You go ahead." Had her voice gone up an octave? "I'm not going to the clinic's restaurant."

The bottom floor of the clinic boasted a small in-house cafeteria that served a variety of menu options. Most of their coworkers and a few of their patients would be dining there. Unfortunately, they didn't serve organic, but a small privately owned café a couple of blocks away did.

"Even better." A self-satisfied smile curved his lips and his eyes sparkled so intently she took a step back. "Let's go. On the way there I can tell you about what Colin Taylor's tests showed."

She couldn't think of a single reason why she could say no without looking petty in front of Lora, who'd stepped into the hallway. Or perhaps she couldn't think period.

Not with Eric looking at her that way.

A way that had Lora glancing back and forth between them. Oh, yeah, her nurse was curious.

No wonder. All the staff adored him, especially the women. They went out of their way to chat with him, to fetch this or that for him, to bat their eyelashes at him. Not Kasey. She'd intentionally have walked on nails to keep from bumping into him.

However, minutes later she was nestled into the front seat of Eric's expensive sedan and soaked in the mixture of fine leather and even finer man.

God, was it so wrong that she wanted to be with him?

Even if she could only do so in a professional capacity?

"Nice car."

He glanced around as if noticing his vehicle for the first time. "It's a ride."

The car looked brand-new. Not a spec of dust anywhere and no way could you fake that new-car smell. "Oh?"

"It was a coming-home gift from my mother, but not what I usually drive," he admitted, giving her a sideways glance. "My truck is in the shop, getting a tune-up."

A gift from his mother. What kind of mother gave a luxury car for a "coming home" gift?

"You drive a truck?" She shouldn't ask, shouldn't care, but he'd piqued her curiosity.

"An SUV, actually." Eric glanced at her and shrugged, oblivious to her inner turmoil. "It's what I drove before I left the States. I like it. Lots of room to haul stuff—or unsuspecting women." He waggled his brows at the last, then put his attention back on the road. "Something I can get muddy, pull a horse trailer with or take a date to a nice restaurant."

Muddy. She had a difficult time picturing Eric muddy, but no doubt he'd look great coated in mud.

She swallowed the lump that formed in her throat.

He parked his car outside the restaurant. She glanced at him in surprise. He'd driven straight to Barnaby's.

"Eat here often?" She headed here most days that she could get away from the clinic, but rarely did she see any of her colleagues. Never had she seen Eric. She definitely would have noticed if he'd been anywhere in the vicinity.

"No," he continued, oblivious to her thoughts, "but I've been meaning to try it. Jonathan mentioned you ate organic so I figured this was where you were headed. I hear the food's good."

Kasey's insides tingled. "You and Dr. Douglas talk about my eating preferences?"

Not seeming in the slightest ashamed at his admission, Eric pocketed his keys.

"I asked about you. He told me what little he knows." He ran his palm over the buttery leather of the steering wheel, then turned toward her, his face sincere. "I'll say this again in case you've somehow misunderstood. I can't stop thinking about you and want to know everything about you."

He looked at her as if she were flawless, an enthralled look that made her feel…priceless.

Which was utterly ridiculous.

She rolled her eyes and got out of the car before she said something she shouldn't. Like that she couldn't stop thinking about him, too, and what were they going to do about it?

The restaurant was crowded. Kasey thought she'd glimpsed a member of the Rivendell Ladies Society leaving when they'd first arrived, but otherwise she didn't see anyone she knew.

Which was probably good since she was dining with Eric.

By the end of the meal, she felt equally flustered and flushed with excitement.

Life was lonely when you'd become afraid to let anyone close to you for fear of disappointment and pain. Yet she'd never been close to anyone who didn't eventually disappoint and hurt her.

For one night, she had let Eric close.

She'd felt alive. When she looked at him, she felt electrified. Aware of every breath she took. Aware of every cell in her body.

He did that to her.

She met his intent gaze.

Deep in her heart she wanted to give him a chance to prove he wasn't like Randall, wasn't like the men who'd come and gone from her mother's life.

But if she gave him that chance, would he only end up breaking her heart and quite possibly destroying her career?

A scenario that was all too likely to happen.

Yet could she live with the knowledge that she'd let the fear of failure trap her inside a glass box of her own making?

Eric leaned back in his chair, watching emotion after emotion flash across Kasey's beautiful face. Each day he found something to ask her, some way of spending a few moments with her, knowing that eventually he'd wear down the wall she'd erected.

Yesterday, as he'd held her, a few chunks had fallen away from that protective wall.

What would she do if he leaned across the table and

kissed her? Probably slap him. The chunks hadn't been that big.

Still, she needed a little shaking up.

Or was that what had happened that night?

"You never told me what upset you the day we met."

"Didn't I?" she answered vaguely, taking another sip of her water, not glancing his way. Her cheeks held a high glow, as if she was overly warm.

"What happened to cause you to come to that bar and order a beer when you obviously don't drink?" he pushed, giving her that shake. Did her reasons have to do with what she'd told Maggie yesterday?

Kasey stared at her fork as if the tines held the formula to cure all man's afflictions. "Why?"

Because that night she'd liked him, wanted him, clung to him. "I want to understand you."

"Why would you want to do that?"

Because he wanted her to like him again, to want him again, to cling to him again. "Why wouldn't I? We're friends."

"No," she denied, with a low laugh. "We're not. Otherwise you wouldn't have said you want to be friends. That implies we aren't friends."

"Fine." He exhaled a deep sigh. "We're not friends, but we are coworkers. Coworkers are allowed to be concerned about one another."

"Rivendell employs hundreds of people. I don't share my personal information with them."

"Okay." Tiring of whatever game she played, he went

for broke. "We're more than coworkers, more than friends, and whether you admit it or not, you know we would be lots more if you weren't so stubborn."

Her eyes flashed green sparks. "What would we be if I weren't so stubborn?"

"Lovers."

She swallowed. "We can't be lovers. We work together."

He arched a brow. An interesting denial. "Technically, we already are."

Her cheeks glowed a bright shade of pink. "One night doesn't make us lovers."

"Perhaps not," he admitted, staring directly into her eyes. "But I've dreamed of making love to you every night since we met. That should count for something."

"Face it." She swallowed again, her voice low, steady. Surprisingly, she didn't look away, didn't try to hide the swirling desire in her eyes. "You only want me because I've not fallen at your feet."

"I'm willing to test that theory, Kasey." Placing his palms flat against the table, he leaned forward. "Fall at my feet."

She hesitated for the briefest moment. "I can't fall at your feet. It would hurt my career."

Eric frowned. Dating him would hurt her career? Surely she didn't believe that. He was striking out with Kasey for the very reason people usually wanted to be with him. Her comment struck him as ironic. Did she think if things didn't work he'd hurt her professionally? That stung.

"You won't date me because we work together?" He pinned her with his gaze, refused her the right to look away. "That's the reason you keep saying no?"

Pensive, she nodded. "It's a reason."

Finally they were getting somewhere. "Let's say we didn't work together, then what? Would getting rid of working together be enough for you to go out with me?"

She hesitated, then inhaled sharply. "Yes."

Eric mentally high-fived himself. "Fine. I'll give my notice when we get back to the office. How does dinner at six-thirty sound?"

Kasey's eyes widened, her jaw dropped, and she stared at him as if he'd lost his mind. Then a wide smile spread across her face and she burst out laughing. "You're crazy."

"So it would seem." He smiled back, lifted his glass and saluted her. "About you."

Her full lips stilled, curved. She shook her head. "What am I going to do about you?"

"Let me show you why you should have said yes all along," he suggested, knowing from the glow in her eyes that he had her. Whatever had been holding her back had shifted. She'd quit fighting the chemistry sparking between them.

She pursed her lips. "Lunch isn't enough?"

"Not by far." He swept his gave over her face, settling on her mouth. "Just so you're prewarned, dinner won't be enough either. I've missed you."

"Dinner will have to be enough," she informed him,

her eyes shining with a glow he hadn't seen before. "I'm not going to sleep with you, Eric."

"I've heard that before," he teased. "A few hours later, I'm trying to play the role of the gentleman and you beg me to—"

She wadded up her napkin and tossed the paper at him. "You'd have to play the role. You're no gentleman."

No, much to his mother's disappointment, he never had been. "You can't blame a guy for trying."

"Oh, I blame you all right. I blame you for all of this." Although she smiled and the twinkle still glowed in her eyes, there was a heavy dose of reality in her words.

"What do you blame on me, Kasey?"

"I wasn't looking to meet anyone on the night we met," she admitted, her gaze downcast at her water glass. "I was in that bar to keep from being alone, but I wasn't looking for what happened or for a relationship."

"But we did meet." He reached across the table, laid his hand over hers. "I'm glad we met, that we happened. We were good together."

"You've complicated my life in ways you don't even begin to understand," she said, seeming to carefully measure each word.

"You think I like being caught up in a woman who doesn't want anything to do with me?" He stared straight into her eyes and refused to let her look away, refused to let her wiggle her hand out from under his.

"I am caught up, Kasey. Crazy caught up. What happened the day we met?"

"My mother's funeral."

CHAPTER FIVE

"YOUR mother died?" Eric's heart lurched in his chest, pounding against his rib cage.

"Well, I didn't bury her alive, if that's what you're thinking." Face pale, she squeezed her eyes shut, regret at her admission evident.

She hadn't meant to tell him, hadn't meant to share her grief.

Her mother's funeral. That explained the tears on the night they'd met.

"Why didn't you tell me? Why would you keep that to yourself?" Damn it, why had she pushed him away when he could have been there? She shouldn't have had to grieve alone. "Why didn't Jonathan tell me about your mother when I asked him about you?"

"When I took off work to go to Lexington, I didn't tell anyone I was going to my mother's funeral. Just that something unexpected had come up and I needed time off work a few days." Her gaze dropped to where he held her hand, his fingers clutching her trembling ones.

Eric let her softly spoken admission register. She'd admitted to Maggie that she'd left home as a teenager. Had she seen her abusive mother since?

"She'd had liver disease for a long time," she continued. "The medical examiner's report said she died from liver failure."

Clearly, the news had left her devastated.

So devastated she'd spent the night with him.

"We weren't close, but her death shocked me. I guess death shocks everyone." She closed her eyes and took a deep breath. When her eyes opened, raw pain shone in the green depths. "I never wanted her dead, Eric."

Not caring who in the restaurant saw, Eric lifted her hand and kissed her fingertips. "Sometimes things happen and we don't understand the reasons."

No wonder she'd looked distraught when she'd sat down next to him. No wonder she'd cried while he'd held her. As interfering as his mother was, he loved her dearly and couldn't imagine not having her meddling in his life. Even while he'd been in Africa, she'd always let him know he was loved, missed.

"I hadn't seen her for almost two years," Kasey admitted, swiping at her eyes with an embarrassed glance around the restaurant. She needn't have bothered. No one paid them any attention.

He stroked his thumb across her hand, marveling at how soft she felt when he knew what strength lay in her capable touch.

"When I left the funeral home, I felt so alone. She

was the only family I had and she was gone. With her death went all my dreams that someday she'd sober up and we could be a real family. As I drove home from Lexington, all I could think was that I didn't want to be alone." Sadness filled her eyes. "Still, I shouldn't have picked up a stranger in a bar."

"You didn't pick up a stranger." He laced their fingers and gave a squeeze. "You picked me."

Her eyes glimmering with tears, she shook her head. "Same difference."

"Big difference."

Her gaze dropped to their hands. He did the same. Her hand looked so delicate entwined with his larger, darker one.

"If you say so." Glancing up, she laughed nervously and pulled her hand from his. She lifted her water glass to her lips and took an unsteady sip.

"We were never strangers, Kasey. That's why that night happened. Say what you will, but if we hadn't connected, had the attraction not been there, you wouldn't have gone with me. I'm sorry about your mother." Desperately he wished he could take away the pain she'd felt, still felt. "But I'm glad you came into Calista Blue and sat down beside me."

Biting her lower lip, she nodded, although he wasn't sure which part of his comments she was agreeing with.

"Let me be a part of your life."

"A relationship between us would make things messy." The green shade of her eyes grew darker.

"Eventually, we'd part ways and then what? We'll have to work together every day and that could be disastrous."

There was more than what she was saying. She clearly spoke with the voice of experience. What else had happened to make her so skittish?

"I'm not going to promise you things I'm not sure I can keep. Neither am I sure what will happen between us in the future," he admitted, "but I care about you."

Her eyes softened at his admission. "You have no idea how much I want to say yes."

Not nearly as much as he wanted her to say yes.

"How about we take things one day at a time and see where that leads us?" He stared deep into her eyes, not hiding how much he wanted her to say yes. "If you want to keep things low-key because of work, fine, I'm game. Just give us a chance."

The afternoon flew by, which was a good thing because Kasey had a difficult time concentrating on her patients. She couldn't recall ever being distracted from her work before Eric. Not even Randall had interfered with her job. Not until after all hell had broken loose at Skymont, at any rate.

Pushing her glasses up the bridge of her nose, Kasey glanced up from the junk mail she flipped through to clear off her desk.

"Busy?" Eric leaned against her doorjamb, looking sexier than any man had a right to.

Seeing him in her doorway was getting to be a habit. One she'd be lying if she didn't admit to liking.

Her heart kicked up a beat. No wonder she'd been distracted all afternoon. Eric wanted her. What woman wouldn't be distracted?

"Just finishing for the day." She waved the conference flyer.

They'd gone back to the office after he'd suggested a low-key relationship. He'd promised to stop by her office before leaving for the day. Which explained why she'd lingered.

Trying to keep her eyes locked with his and not roaming over his broad shoulders, flat abs and narrow hips encased in his slacks, she waited for him to say more.

Unfortunately, her gaze wandered when he stepped into the office and closed the door.

So did her mind.

She'd kissed those lips. Clung to those shoulders as she'd cried.

He'd held her. Tight. For real. As if he cared.

All she had to do was say *yes* and he would be holding her again.

She wanted him to hold her.

She pushed against her glasses, swallowed the lump in her throat.

"Why do you wear those?"

Her clothes? Certainly they'd grown too tight, as if she should rip them off. Just as they'd ripped off each other's clothes on the night they'd made love.

"My glasses?"

He nodded.

The better to see you with.

What was wrong with her? Why couldn't she look at him without remembering how he'd felt deep inside her body, how his strong heartbeat had mesmerized her.

"Why do people usually wear glasses?" she asked, knocking back the desire swamping her. He moved closer, and she got a whiff of pure testosterone-laden Eric. The man should bottle that and make his fortune.

"They're prescription?" he asked.

"Yes." There, she'd said yes. Yes. Yes. *Yes.* Now, would he please hurry up and kiss her?

Instead, he studied her face. "You didn't have them on the night we met."

She'd accidentally left them in her car seat when they'd fogged over from tears. She'd taken them off to clean her runny mascara. As steamed up as her insides had felt, she was surprised her glasses weren't fogged over right this minute.

"I wear them for reading and at work. I'm legal to drive, but definitely things are clearer when I have them on." Wow, she sounded normal, not like every nerve ending strained toward him, wanting an individual stroke. *Yes.*

He continued his slow perusal. "You had your hair down that night, too."

She touched her tightly pulled-back hair. "Loose hair gets in the way during work. My stethoscope gets tangled."

Too much information. Flustered, she shuffled through the stack of mail, gave Bones a don't-look-at-me-that-way look, anything to give her a moment to pull herself together.

Eric reached across her desk and did the unthinkable. First, he pulled the pins out of her hair and then her clip. Her dark hair fell to her shoulders. She wanted to run her fingers through the tangled mess in hope of restoring some kind of order. But she didn't move, she was so mesmerized by the look in Eric's eyes.

Hot liquid desire burned in his gaze.

Hot liquid desire burned inside her, paralyzing her. She waited to see what he'd do next.

Not one to disappoint, he retrieved the glasses from her face. With great care, he folded and placed them on her desk. "Better."

Better? What was with the critique? And why wasn't he kissing her? She'd said yes. "If you don't like how I look, don't look."

"I do."

"You do what?" She moistened her dry lips.

"Like how you look." Eric pulled her to her feet. With exaggerated slowness he grazed his fingertips over the smoothness of her cheek, along her jaw, then brushed over her slightly parted mouth.

"You are beautiful, but you try to disguise that beauty with those." He gestured to the glasses on her desk. "And those." He nodded at the hair clips. "It doesn't work, Kasey. Your beauty shines through."

She snorted. "That's why men are beating down my door."

"Well," he agreed with a crooked smile, "I didn't exactly beat down your door, but I do show up here quite often."

His fingers slipped into her hair, cupped the base of her head, massaged her scalp.

Heat blazed in her cheeks, in her chest, lower.

He bent his head, pausing within centimeters of her lips. Staring into her eyes, he waited, his hot breath moist and tempting.

She knew what he wanted, what he waited for.

She closed the distance between them, pressing her lips to his, taking what she'd wanted for what seemed like forever.

Tension she hadn't been aware he'd been giving off eased. Tension she hadn't noticed because her own had been so overpowering.

He might have let her take the initiative, might have given her the opportunity to stop him had his kiss not been what she wanted. But he took her kiss as the key to open the floodgates of chemistry between them.

With every brush of his lips over hers, every thrust of his tongue into her mouth, Eric stole bits of her soul.

"Kasey," he breathed into her mouth, his hands roving over her neck, her shoulders, her back. "I've wanted to kiss you like this for so long."

Weren't they her thoughts exactly?

His mouth covered hers again.

Kasey forgot where she was, why she was, who she was. All she knew was Eric. Eric's mouth, his lips, his tongue, his minty taste. Had he brushed his teeth or eaten a mint? Had he known he would kiss her? Had they really come that far with just one lunch date where he'd asked her to give him a chance?

If they hadn't come that far, why wasn't she lambasting him instead of kissing him back?

Because this was what she wanted. To touch him, kiss him, feel his long, hard body pressed to hers.

Dear sweet heaven above, he was hard.

With another lingering kiss he pulled back. "I have to stop before I forget where we are and we do something we shouldn't. Before I take you right here, right now, because I'm damned tempted."

He glanced meaningfully at her desk and a vivid vision of the two of them, naked, tangled together on her desk, popped into Kasey's mind, blending with the emotional flood she was already drowning in.

She blinked, awed by the magic that he'd wielded with the sweep of his tongue into her mouth. How had he done that?

Sure, she had memories of their previous kisses, but she'd been devastated, drinking that delicious fruity concoction he'd ordered for her. She'd been sure her imagination played tricks on her recall of those kisses.

Her memory hadn't done him justice.

The man could kiss. And how.

* * *

"Kasey?" Eric tilted her head toward him and stared into her glazed eyes. "Say something, sweetheart. Tell me you aren't going cold on me."

"Cold on you?" She pulled free of his embrace and scooted back, almost knocking the framed diploma from her wall. Her movements were jerky, evidence that he wasn't the only one shaken by what they'd shared. "Cold is the last thing a woman could feel after kisses like those."

She covered her mouth with her hand, her wide eyes staring at him in disbelief at what she'd said.

He grinned. Damn, she was cute. And extremely kissable. He'd like to kiss her some more. Lots more.

"Does that mean you're ready to go to dinner? Or that you'd like to forgo food altogether?"

"I…" She paused, inhaled deeply, shook when he took her hands into his. "We agreed to tread lightly until we know this isn't a mistake."

He heard her words, but it was the pain in her eyes that spoke the loudest. "What's his name?"

"Who?" She didn't look away, but her eyes became shielded all the same.

"The man who made you so afraid of relationships."

"What makes you ask that?" She blinked.

"It's obvious some guy did a number on you and now you've closed yourself off from the world." Even as he said the words out loud, he recognized their truth. "That's why you hide behind your glasses. You don't want to be noticed, do you? Not as a desirable woman, at any rate. Being ignored is much safer. Keeping me at arm's length is safer than admitting you enjoyed making love with me."

She jerked her hands free. "You have no right to say those things to me."

"But I'm right, aren't I?" he pushed. "I may have only been here a few weeks, but I suspect I know you better than anyone who works at the clinic."

"You are so arrogant," she accused.

"Tell me I'm wrong."

"You're wrong," she immediately spat at him.

"And you're a liar."

Her mouth fell open, and she gawked at him. "How dare you say that to me?"

"You'll find I dare a lot of things," he promised, tweaking her nose. "It's time someone started making you face the truth, made you start living life again. Part of living is taking chances."

He was probably the last person who should offer advice on living life. Hell, he'd run from his life, spent as much time away from Rivendell as possible. Years. Perhaps it took one to know one, but Kasey had only been scratching the surface of who she was. A simple life helping others, finding the person beneath his heritage had made Eric realize who he was, who he wanted to be. He wasn't so sure Kasey really knew the beautiful woman who stared back at her from the mirror.

If nothing else came from them having met, he hoped he could help her see the wonderful, strong woman he saw.

"I have a good life."

He cupped her face, caressing her cheek with his thumb. "Which is why you came in search of a stranger on the night of your mother's funeral."

Whatever Kasey thought of Eric's comment, she'd only grabbed her purse and asked where they were going to dinner.

Eric opted not to take her to any of the restaurants where they might run into someone who knew them. Instead, he drove into Lexington. They ate at an Italian restaurant he hadn't visited since returning to the States.

"This is really good," Kasey mused, taking a bite of a bread stick not long from the oven.

"It used to be one of my favorites."

"Used to be?"

"I spent four years in Africa."

"I'd heard something along those lines when you first started." She smiled. "The rumor mill is well and alive at the Rivendell Medical Center. What exactly did you do in Africa? I always thought working overseas would be fascinating."

"Working overseas is fascinating." He told her about some of his jobs while there. "Of course, there were a few occasions where it was a little too fascinating."

"Oh?"

"I worked in Darfur for a while."

Kasey's face paled. "But isn't there a war there?"

Eric shrugged. "The poor of war-torn countries tend to be those who need medical care the most."

Dropping the remainder of her bread stick onto her plate, Kasey eyed him suspiciously. "Are you really as great as you seem?"

He grinned. "I'm better, but you already know that."

Smiling, she rolled her eyes. But she didn't deny his claim.

He told her about the months he'd spent working in a Sudanese medical camp, the months he'd spent in a Ethiopian medical convoy, about his favorite memories of the time he'd spent overseas.

"I've never traveled outside the U.S., but hope to some day."

"What's keeping you from doing so now?"

A puzzled look came over her face. "I'm not sure," she admitted. "I tend to work long hours."

"Unless you really mismanaged your practice contract, you should have generous vacation time," he pointed out.

"I do, but somehow I end up at the clinic even when I'm scheduled off."

"That's no fun."

"No." She shook her head, looking surprised at her admission. "It isn't."

Later that night, she gave him her home phone number. He already had her cell-phone number from the clinic.

Standing in the vacant Rivendell Medical Center parking lot where they'd left her car, he kissed her good-night, then watched her drive away.

He hadn't pressed for more. He suspected if he'd pressed she wouldn't have turned him away. He also suspected that if they made love before she trusted him, he'd never have her trust.

He wanted Kasey's trust.

Later that night he lay in his bed, phone pressed to his ear, and swapped medical school stories with a woman who would someday trust him.

A trust he'd work hard to earn and do his best never to lose.

Two weeks later, at the ambulatory clinic, Kasey saw a diabetic who'd stepped on a sharp rock while outside barefoot despite her distinctly recalling discussing that diabetics should never go barefoot, particularly outdoors.

Next, she performed a gynecological exam on a young woman who was having pelvic pain. As the woman's cytology exam hadn't been performed in over a year, she ran the liquid preparation and made three microscope slides to do an in-house vaginal survey.

Kasey applied the appropriate solution to each slide, placed them inside a transport container, then headed to the clinic's small lab to do the gram stain. They could do simple laboratory tests in-house, like a urinalysis, glucose, rapid Strep, pregnancy and a vaginal survey, without having to send to Rivendell's main laboratory.

"Hey, you. I've not seen you today," Eric said, stepping into the lab. "Need any help?"

Kasey's breath caught in her throat. Her heart leaped with joy as it seemed to always do when he was near.

Since the night he'd driven them to the Italian restaurant in Lexington, they'd either dined together or met after she worked on the masquerade ball.

Each night ended the same surprising way. With Eric kissing her goodnight. Admittedly, hot and heavy kissing, but she'd expected him to push for a repeat performance of the night they'd met.

He hadn't.

They spent their time talking, laughing, getting to know each other. Which threw her. If he only wanted a physical relationship with her, why invest the time to get to know her?

"I've still got a few patients to see, if that's what you're asking."

"Me, too."

No matter how much she tried to focus on what she was doing, she couldn't. She glanced up, found her lips lifting into a smile.

"Then perhaps you should finish with yours, instead of watching me," she suggested. She couldn't help but smile. Not when he was looking at her like she was the lollipop that was going to send him into a diabetic coma and he'd die a happy man. She took a step back, knowing that if he kissed her, she'd be a goner. Work was no place for such shenanigans.

Grinning, he stepped closer. "Rough day?"

"I've been swamped." And she had a meeting with

the Rivendell Ladies Society fund-raiser committee tonight. A meeting she wasn't looking forward to since Gladys Anderson had yet to return her calls regarding publicity for the event. "Haven't you?"

"Steady stream of gastrointestinal disturbances," he told her. "Not my favorite thing to treat."

"You have a favorite?"

"Yes, but we'd have to discuss that in private." He waggled his eyebrows.

She rolled her eyes.

"Have dinner plans tonight, Kasey?"

"I do." She'd hoped to have time to go home, shower, look her best before heading to the fancy restaurant where the RLS met. She'd be lucky if she had time to apply a fresh coat of lipstick.

"Lucky bastard." Eric grinned smugly. "Anyone I know?"

"I don't think so."

His grin faltered. "You weren't referring to dinner with me?"

"No. I really do have plans."

His face an unreadable mask, he considered her a moment. "With a man?"

"With a group of ladies I volunteer with. I'm on the fund-raiser committee. We're meeting to discuss progress and to make sure everything is set."

He relaxed a little, toying with a strand of her hair he'd worked loose from her clip. "Sounds exciting."

Did it? Being on a committee, helping plan activities,

that had been her dream for so long. Now she was a fully fledged junior member on her way to becoming a fully fledged member of the RLS. She was rising above her background, becoming somebody. Lord, she was even dating the most gorgeous man in Rivendell.

She lifted her chin with pride. "It's for a good cause."

His eyes glittering with a mischievous gleam, he arched one brow. "Dinner with me isn't?"

"I suspect dinner with you would cause more bad than good."

"Don't you believe it," he warned, taking another step toward her, their bodies almost touching from where he stood beside her. This playfulness reminded her of how they'd talked at the bar. They'd sat in that booth for hours, talking, flirting, enjoying each other's company.

Wanting to put a halt to his advance, she glanced at the slide she'd placed under the microscope clips. Hmm. Had that been a sperm or a parasite she'd seen wiggle its tail? She hadn't gotten a good look, but she suspected a parasite based upon the woman's symptoms.

Kasey used the knobs on the microscope to move the slide so she could get a better view. There. Definitely a parasite. And the patient's other symptoms and her history fit the diagnosis.

"See something interesting?"

"Yes," she answered, glancing up from examining the slide to let her gaze slide over him.

"May I?" He leaned beside her to peer into the microscope eyepiece. "Fascinating little creatures, aren't they?"

Fascinating? She could think of a few other descriptive terms she'd apply.

"Do you see a lot of sexually transmitted diseases at the clinic?" he asked, straightening up but not moving away from how close he stood. His body heat practically enveloped her.

"Most go to the gynecologist, but a fair amount do see us. Particularly if they aren't sure what's going on. Or if they're seen through the charity fund."

"I thought those being seen through the charity could go to the specialists, too."

"They can if we refer them. We're the starting point for all care provided through the charity. Which is why it's important I go to my meeting tonight. Without funds being raised, the charity wouldn't be able to provide care to the working poor of this community."

Disappointment lit his eyes, but he nodded. "Okay."

"I can't have dinner with you, but I would like to see you tonight."

"We could get together after you finish," he suggested, obviously surprised by her admission. "We could meet for coffee."

Kasey smiled. "That sounds perfect. After my meeting I'll likely need someone to vent to."

"Oh?" His brow quirked. "Are you having problems?"

Kasey sighed, wondering if she'd imagined Doreen Von Buren's hostility at the last meeting. "Nothing I can't handle."

* * *

That evening, Kasey sat at the table with half a dozen longtime Rivendell Ladies Society matrons. What was it she'd been thinking earlier about rising above her upbringing?

With a single haughty look from Doreen Von Buren she'd been reduced to feelings of incompetence.

She tapped her pen against her notebook and stared at the list of things she needed to accomplish prior to the charity fund-raiser for the clinic. She was competent, capable, their equal in every way. She'd do such a great job on this fund-raiser that they'd beg her to be a member of their group.

"Have you spoken with the *Rivendell Gazette* yet?" asked the petite platinum blonde, who constantly looked as if she wore a too-tight ponytail, even when she wore her hair loose.

Doreen Von Buren.

If not for the fact the woman had a daughter in her early twenties, Kasey wouldn't begin to be able to guess her age. Her skin was flawless. Doreen dressed immaculately, attended all the right social functions, knew all the right people. Doreen was exactly what Kasey had dreamed of as a child, what she'd aspired to someday become. A wealthy, respected member of society who gave back to the community and made the world a better place by being in it.

Someone who was the opposite of Betsy.

"I bumped into Gladys Anderson of the Lifestyles section," Doreen continued. "She mentioned she hadn't heard from you. We're less than a month out. Don't you think you're cutting the press too close?"

"The initial press release has run." Needlessly, Kasey scribbled down the all-too-familiar name on her list. She'd meticulously kept notes of even the tiniest detail in regard to the masquerade ball. "I've left messages a couple of times about Gladys doing a feature on the event. She hasn't called me back. I faxed another news release to the main editor and plan to do so again this week."

"Oh, dear." Doreen inflected her voice with great concern. "She probably doesn't recognize your name and has just been busy. She did do that wonderful write-up on my daughter last week."

Gladys was an RLS member wannabe, just like Kasey. Until this year Kasey had merely been a lackey, someone to take tickets at the front door, someone to set up the chairs, someone to go door-to-door collecting donations. Not this year. This year she'd been asked to serve as a junior member on the fund-raiser committee. A big step in the right direction and perhaps one that had caused a bit of jealousy.

A commotion at the entrance of the restaurant caused all six women to turn. Ella, Doreen's daughter, who Gladys had apparently gone on and on about in the social section, entered the restaurant. Late as usual, she paused dramatically for everyone to bask in her pale blond glow.

Kasey was struck with a mixture of admiration and jealousy. Admiration of the way Ella accepted the world as her due, how she belonged no matter where she went, at how she oozed class and sophistication. She'd bet her eyeteeth Ella had never gone to bed hungry, that she'd never hidden in a closet to escape one of her mother's drunken rages, that she'd never shopped at garage sales for clothes with money she'd made from doing odd jobs for neighbors, or worn long sleeves in the dead of summer to hide bruises.

Ella lived the life Kasey had grown up dreaming of to escape the reality of her own sad life. Ella looked like High Society Barbie. All she needed to complete the look was a tall, dark and handsome man. Eric popped into Kasey's mind. Eric and Ella would make a beautiful couple. Actually, Ella was exactly the kind of woman Kasey imagined Eric would someday end up married to. Young, beautiful, sophisticated, well bred.

But Ella couldn't have Eric. Kasey reached up to touch her temple, but resisted the urge to massage the pounding there. No, Ella couldn't have Eric because for the moment he belonged to *her*.

For two weeks he'd treated her like the queen of the world. His world, at any rate.

Just as soon as this meeting was finished, she'd meet him for coffee. Right then and there she promised herself that she'd give him a huge hug for the joy he'd added to her life.

Sure, she worried about his meetings with Mr. Evans and some of the older board members, but her life had become Technicolor the moment she'd agreed to let Eric be a part of it.

On Sunday afternoon he'd even convinced her to get on a horse. Her. On a horse. She hadn't even fallen off. Then again, Eric had been on the horse, too. All she'd had to do was keep her arms wrapped around his waist while they'd ridden over the lush Kentucky hills to where he'd arranged a picnic lunch.

The memory put a smile back onto Kasey's face.

Ella air-kissed her mother's cheeks. "Tell me what I've missed."

"Only that Kasey hasn't been able to get in touch with Gladys from the *Gazette*."

Ugh. There went her smile again.

"No problem," Ella assured her before Kasey could speak, sliding into the vacant chair and shaking out a white napkin into her lap. Their waiter miraculously appeared, placed a water glass and a glass of white wine in front of her, earning himself a gracious smile from the platinum blonde. "I'll call Gladys in the morning. What do we need? A feature story on the masquerade ball and a couple of well-placed advertisements?"

"I don't mind calling her again," Kasey said, hating the wave of incompetence washing over her. She'd visit the paper during her lunch break if that's what she had to do to get the issue cleared.

"There's no need," Doreen cut in, her tone brisk, condemning. "My daughter will see that our publicity gets done. Some have a natural talent for these things. Some don't."

Kasey felt the sting of the reprimand.

"Fine." She smiled brightly at Ella. "That'll give me more time to work with the caterer."

"The caterer?" Reva Talley asked from her seat at the table. Again, her age was fairly undeterminable and her plastic surgeon likely a wealthy man. Reva might be forty. She might be sixty.

"I've hired Dellarosa's."

"Didn't we have problems with them?" Doreen's nose curled. "You should have gone with the one we used last year."

"They were already booked," Kasey reminded her, knowing she'd already gone over this with the committee months ago. She'd gone with Dellarosa's at their emphatic recommendation.

"Then perhaps you should act sooner next year instead of waiting until the last minute. If you're even asked to serve."

Kasey blinked at the woman in confusion. Where had that come from?

"Now, Mother." Ella patted her mother's bony arm sympathetically. "You must remember Kasey is new to this. After all, she isn't really an RLS member."

Outwardly, Kasey cast a fake smile of gratitude. Inwardly, she winced.

Just when she was starting to feel like her life was coming together professionally, personally and socially, people like the Von Burens brought her crashing back down to reality.

Not that she didn't sometimes feel like there was a

drastic social chasm between Eric and herself. Not that he ever came across as a snob, he didn't. No, he just did things like calmly announce that the elaborate horse farm they'd visited belonged to his family. No big deal. And because he'd truly acted as if it weren't a big deal, Kasey had eventually relaxed.

Perhaps his years of simple living in Africa had stamped out whatever elitism he might have once had.

That's what she told herself, at any rate.

That a man who would spend four years in third-world countries when he could be sitting at home in the lap of luxury wasn't the kind of man to care if she'd been born with a silver spoon in her mouth or a copy of the *Trailer Park Gazette* in her hands.

Most of the time she convinced herself. Because it was what she desperately wanted to believe.

A week later, Eric smiled at the young woman sitting on the exam table. She couldn't be more than twenty-five. Three small children buzzed around the room with more energy than any one person should have to cope with and a year-old baby squirmed in her lap. Three girls and a boy who looked to be the oldest and was oblivious to all the commotion his sisters were causing. He played with two toy cars in the floor and was lost in his pretend world of play.

"What brings you into the clinic?" he asked, smiling as the toddler dug her fingers into her mother's shirt, clinging tightly to the material while she eyed him suspiciously. Her big, almost black eyes followed his every movement and she didn't return his smile.

"I need a refill on my thyroid medicine." Belinda Peters pried the little fingers loose from her shirt and shifted the wiggling little girl on her lap.

Eric glanced down at the medical record. Sure enough, she was on a thyroid tablet and an antidepressant.

"No problem. I'll write the prescription and a lab slip for you to have your thyroid levels checked." His gaze continued to skim over her record. Her other medication usually needed to be renewed at the same time. "What about your antidepressant? Do you need a refill on that, too?"

"Jackie! Get down from there," she called to the little girl who looked to be about three and was attempting to climb onto the table that housed numerous medical supplies.

Jackie shot her mother an assessing look, decided tempting fate was safe, and kept right on climbing.

With an exasperated sigh, Belinda jumped from the exam table, sat her youngest in the floor and scooped Jackie into her arms. "Sit here, and be good."

The little girl didn't seem happy with her mother's interference. Actually, she seemed downright upset as she twisted and arched in her mother's grasp. "Let go," she howled over and over. The baby on the floor glanced from Eric to her screaming sister to her mother. Her lower lip trembled and big tears welled in her eyes. The third little girl eyed her brother's toy cars, a mischievous gleam in her eyes.

First waylaying the baby's tears with a squeaky toy, Belinda dug in the diaper bag, produced another toy car, which she handed to her other daughter, wrapped her arms protectively around Jackie, then smiled weakly at Eric.

"Sorry. You were saying?"

No wonder the poor woman looked exhausted.

He'd never thought much about kids, although certainly his mother had been hinting enough that it was past time he produced a grandchild for her to spoil. Hinting? More like she'd been parading a constant bevy of possible daughter-in-law candidates. All upper-crust young beauties who were mainly the spoilt daughters of her various well-to-do acquaintances.

Now that he felt comfortable Kasey wasn't using him, he needed to tell his mother about her. Last night, when his mother had questioned him about who was taking up so much of his time, he'd been evasive, not wanting her interference where Kasey was concerned. Not at this stage in their relationship.

His mother could be forceful if you didn't know how to deal with her. Forceful being a bulldozer until she wore you down. She'd learned long ago those tactics didn't work on Eric, but the rest of the world was fair game.

"I was asking about your antidepressant. Do you need a refill of that one, too?"

Squeaking the baby's discarded toy duck and placing it in the baby's hands, Belinda made a quacking noise as she shook her head. "I'm not taking it anymore. Quack. Quack."

"Did Dr. Carmichael discontinue it?" The chart didn't show Kasey having done so, and she documented meticulously. When he saw one of her patients, all the pertinent details were usually right in her notes.

Jackie continued to squirm in her mother's lap, but Belinda kept a firm grip on her daughter while she eyed her two-year-old who, bored with the toy car, contemplated the table her sister had wanted to scale. The baby had stuck the squeaky toy in her mouth and was currently content to gnaw on the head of the rubber duck. "Quack."

"That's right, baby girl. Quack. Quack. I took myself off," the young mother admitted, only half her attention on Eric. "Sara, come over here. Now."

He smiled at the middle child, who apparently wanted to mimic her big sister's every move, and won himself a toothy grin in response. Taking out a couple of tongue depressors, he lifted the child into his lap and handed them to her. Before the little girl got bored with the sticks, Eric turned back to his patient. "Why? Are you feeling better?"

Not wanting to be ignored, Sara wiped a wet stick across his hand. He glanced at the slobber on his fingers, at the little girl in his lap. Unable to resist the mixture of innocence and mischief, Eric smiled. Sara rewarded him with a sloppy kiss on his cheek. "Quack. Quack," she announced merrily.

Eric's heart melted. He'd taken care of kids in the past, thousands while working in Africa. But he didn't recall having one plant a kiss on him. The oddly nice feeling made him wonder if he shouldn't rethink his no-kids thing.

Just like that, an image of him and Kasey making a baby shot into his head, closely followed by the image of a little girl with Kasey's gorgeous green eyes and his dimples popping a kiss on him, melting his heart, wrapping him around her little finger.

Never had he visualized having a child, but the image in his mind was so vivid his heart ached at the knowledge she didn't exist.

Eric reeled, almost to the point he forgot to breathe.

To the point he almost missed what Belinda Peters was saying.

"I didn't like being on another medication, and I didn't like the side effects." Belinda's arms remained securely around her daughter. Jackie twisted and turned in her mother's arms to no avail. "So I quit taking it."

Clearing his head of his unexpected paternal longing, Eric forced himself to focus on his patient. "Can you feel a difference since you've come off the medicine?"

The woman's eyes cut to the two kids on the floor. The squeaky toy held the baby's attention, and the four-year-old little boy pushed the toy car Sara hadn't wanted along the floor, making engine noises and unaware of his mother's watchful eye.

"I cry a lot and don't sleep as well, but I didn't like feeling medicated. It's an okay trade-off. I get by. I saw on the news where this woman was taking the same antidepressant I was on. She lost her mind and hurt her kids." She described the incident in question. "Thoughts like those are the last thing I need at this point in my life."

With Sara content in his lap, Eric spent the next ten minutes discussing the pros and cons of antidepressants. Should he suggest she restart on a different medication that hopefully wouldn't cause side effects? Two minutes more and he knew he should. Still, if he didn't hurry along he'd be behind for the rest of the afternoon and wouldn't be able to see his share of the drop-in patients.

Which meant Kasey would have to pick up the slack. Thinking of Kasey caused his earlier vision to flash through his head again before he could stop the disturbing image.

As unexpected as it had been, the image of him and Kasey having a child together had been…nice.

Which scared the hell out of him.

Maybe he just needed sex. Hell, he did need sex. With Kasey. Badly. But until she said she was ready, he'd restrain himself. On Sunday he'd wanted to push her back onto the blanket they'd picnicked on and make love to her. He hadn't, but he'd wanted to.

After finishing his discussion with the young mother, Eric went to set Sara down. She surprised him by wrapping her arms around his neck, clinging tightly and shaking her head.

"Hey, sweetheart," he said in soft voice. "It's time for you to go home."

"No." The little girl clung tighter and began showering him with more wet kisses.

"Sara, don't do that," her mother ordered, handing her son the diaper bag into which they'd placed the toys. She picked up the baby and grabbed hold of Jackie's hand. Just in the nick of time as Jackie had made a beeline toward the cabinet. "She's getting you all wet. I can take her."

How? he wondered. Her hands were already full. He wasn't sure what type of support Belinda had, but he planned to find out, see if he couldn't get her into a parenting class or support group to make her life easier.

"No problem. I'll help you get this sweetie pie to the car." He stepped into the hallway and immediately bumped into the object of his thoughts. The constant object of his thoughts.

Kasey smiled. Eric's heart sang.

"Hi." He beamed, amazed at how her smile brightened the place like a beam of sunshine.

Her gaze dropped to the toddler in his arms, then back up to stare. Her eyes held an awed wonder. As if the image of him holding the little girl caused baby visions in Kasey's head, too.

Now, that really should scare him.

The last thing he needed was Kasey or any woman getting baby thoughts involving him.

"Can you say hello to Dr. Carmichael?" he said to the toddler, who continued to coat his cheeks with two-year-old high gloss.

"What's your name, sweetheart?" Kasey asked in the softest, kindest voice he'd ever heard.

"This is Sara."

"That's a beautiful name," Kasey said. "Would you like a sticker?"

"Me. Me. I want a sticker," Jackie piped up from where her mother held her hand in a tight grip. Her free hand waved wildly through the air.

"Me, too," the quiet little boy said.

Sara nodded, suddenly acting shy and burying her face into Eric's shirt.

"Here, Dr. Carmichael, I think these are just what the doctor ordered." Lora handed Kasey a handful of stickers to distribute then left to call another patient.

The little boy tugged on his shirt, indicating a spot for Kasey to put a sticker. She applied an airplane one and handed him a few others to attach wherever he saw fit. She stuck a funny-faced bumblebee sticker to Jackie's shirt. The girl clapped in glee and burst into a rendition of "Bringing home a baby bumblebee, won't my momma be so proud of me".

Kasey put a bright red flower sticker on Sara's shirt. "There. You look gorgeous." She bent forward and pretended to smell the blossom. "And don't you just smell sweet as a rose?"

Sara giggled.

Laughing softly, Kasey's gaze met Eric's and a mischievous gleam lit her eyes. "I think Dr. Matthews deserves a sticker, too. What do you think?"

Sara nodded and Jackie clapped again, beginning another round of her song while she danced around in hyper circles.

Kasey flipped through the remaining stickers, smiling when she found the one she wanted. A big, puffy "SUPER." Peeling the protective backing off, she pressed it right above his heart. Her fingers lingered, smoothing the surrounding material. "Perfect."

Did she feel how his heart galloped as if he ran the Kentucky Derby? At the rate he was going he'd win the roses.

Belinda turned to him. "Thank you, Dr. Matthews. I'll take Sara from here."

Eric offered to help them to the car, but Belinda seemed to have everything under control as Jackie led her siblings in another verse about the bumblebee.

When the family had gone, Eric met Kasey's gaze and waggled his brows. "You think I'm super?"

Smile in place, she dramatically rolled her eyes. "It was either that or a fuzzy white bunny who said 'Have a hoppy day'," she fibbed, heading back toward her office.

"Right." Following her, he pointedly looked at the stickers still in her hands. "Hoppy has some company there."

Kasey laughed and stuck them in her lab-coat pocket. "Okay, you got me."

The moment they were inside her office and the door was closed, he leaned toward her, breathing in her sweet scent. "So, answer my question. Do you think I'm super?"

She put her finger to the side of her mouth and pretended to give his question some thought. "Can you leap tall buildings?"

"No." Eric took her into his arms.

"Are you faster than a speeding bullet?"

"No." He pulled her to him.

"Stronger than a locomotive?"

"Depends on what you mean by strong." He shifted his body against hers.

Kasey ignored his blatantly suggestive gesture. "Hmm, you're not doing too well on the superhero quiz."

"Maybe you should ask me better questions," he recommended, nuzzling her neck.

"Do you have a cape and wear your underwear on the outside of a pair of tights?"

Eric laughed. "Not since I was five."

She sighed in exaggerated disappointment, simultaneously arching her neck to give him better access. His tongue traced over the delicate skin, laving her earlobe in a caress.

"There's only one superhero test left," she said a bit breathily. "If you fail, I'm afraid it's hoppy time for you."

"Uh-oh." He sucked her earlobe into his mouth, giving the tender flesh a gentle nip. "This sounds serious."

"Very." Her hands moved to his shoulders. She splayed her fingers, holding tightly to him. "Do you have any fatal weaknesses? You know, like kryptonite?"

"Nope, but I'm hard as a rock," he admitted, shifting his hips against hers to prove his point. "Does that count?"

Pink tinged Kasey's face. "Uh, no, but I'm pretty sure that…" she moved against him "…is automatic qualification for super status."

Eric kissed her mouth, fully and freely, just as he'd kissed her every day for the past three weeks. And as with each of those times, kissing Kasey left him wanting more.

"Maybe I do have a fatal weakness." He paused for effect. "Kaseynite."

Her smile slipped. "I make you feel weak?"

Maybe his attempt to be cute hadn't come out right.

"That's not what I meant," he told her, wrapping his arms around her waist and holding her to him. He stared into her eyes and hoped she saw the truth. "Especially since you make me feel like I could leap those tall buildings and run faster than a speeding bullet."

As he'd hoped, Kasey smiled.

She stretched onto tiptoes and kissed his cheek. "Nice save, my superhero."

CHAPTER SIX

THE clinic was swamped with gastrointestinal disorders. Some real. Some imagined. A bad shipment of tomatoes had hit the supermarkets and the media was having a sensationalist field day with it as nothing else newsworthy was going on.

Over the past few days, the number of cases had slowed, but the clinic remained busy. So did Kasey. With preparations for the fund-raiser and with Eric.

She worried about what she saw as their inevitable breakup, but she wasn't a coward. She'd take each day, enjoy her time with him and deal with whatever the future held.

"Dr. Carmichael?" Lora poked her head into the exam room where Kasey was finishing entering prescriptions for a forty-five-year-old's seizure medications. "Sorry to interrupt, but I just put an acute abdomen in room four."

Another food poisoning?

"I'll be right there." Kasey smiled at the epileptic

patient, handed him his billing sheet and followed Lora. "What's going on?"

"Mr. Oliver is in room four."

"With abdominal pain?" Poor Mr. Oliver. She hoped he hadn't gotten the stomach bug.

Lora nodded. "Dr. Matthews is in with him, but he asked to see you. Dr. Matthews told me to get you."

Dr. Matthews. Eric. Kasey's heart flip-flopped in her chest.

"Thanks," Kasey told Lora.

She knocked on the door, pasted a smile on her face and entered the exam room. Kasey's gaze touched on Eric, her heart beating faster as it always did when she saw him, before turning her full attention to the older gentleman lying on the exam table. "Hi, Mr. Oliver, what's going on?"

"That's what I'm here to find out from you." He winced every time Eric pressed on his abdomen.

"When did your stomach start hurting? You were in the office a few weeks ago about your lower back. Was your stomach hurting then?"

"Not really." He didn't sound convincing.

"Not really? What does that mean?"

"It means it was bothering me, but not bad enough to mention."

"When did it get bad enough to bring you in? This morning?"

"I got to hurting last night. Threw up several times. Nasty bile-looking stuff. Thought I was going to have to go to the emergency room. I took extra of my back medicine. The pain eased up enough to hold off. This morning I tried going to work, but the vomiting started again. Joe drove me here." He placed his hands over his abdomen in response to Eric's palpations. "That hurts."

"Right there?" Eric asked, pressing over the man's upper right quadrant.

Mr. Oliver nodded. "Like a knife is cutting into me straight through to my shoulder blade."

Eric pressed deeper, pushing his fingertips slightly up under the edge of Mr. Oliver's rib cage. The man's breath caught.

"Hard to breathe when you touch me there," he gasped.

Eric and Kasey exchanged looks. A positive Murphy's sign.

"Have you ever had any abdominal surgeries, Mr. Oliver? Specifically, do you have your gallbladder?"

"I have everything God gave me," the man claimed between winces. "Can you fix me, Doc?" His gaze went back and forth between Kasey and Eric. "'Cause I can't work like this and I can't afford not to work. Family has got to eat."

"You need an ultrasound of your gallbladder, Mr. Oliver. While Dr. Matthews continues to examine you, I'm going to call radiology and see if they can squeeze you in this afternoon."

"Is he okay?" Lora asked when Kasey stepped into the hallway. Mr. Oliver was one of those patients the entire clinic adored. Probably because he worked so hard to take care of his family and his love for them always shone through.

"Who?" Jonathan asked, coming out of a patient room. His skin glowed from his vacation. His gaze settled on Lora and lingered.

Interesting.

"An acute abdomen who came in earlier," Lora said, her cheeks glowing but not from the sun.

Not acknowledging Lora's blush or her explanation, Jonathan averted his gaze to Kasey and smiled. "We've had too many abdominal issues lately."

His friendly tone surprised Kasey. He had never paid her much attention. Why would he now?

Unless he and Eric had been talking again. Unless Jonathan knew who Eric had been spending his evenings with, sometimes until near midnight.

"I need to call Radiology," she said, and walked away. When they'd agreed to keep their relationship quiet, had Eric included his best friend in that agreement?

Did it matter if he hadn't?

"Kase?" Jonathan came into her office just as she finished getting the okay for sending Mr. Oliver for the needed test. "Can I talk to you a minute?"

"About?"

"Eric."

"Why would you want to discuss Dr. Matthews with me?"

"Look, I made some comments I shouldn't have on the day I introduced you two." He had the grace to look ashamed. "I owe you an apology."

"Weeks have gone by. Why would you apologize now?"

"You're seeing him, aren't you?"

"I see him every day. At work."

"You know what I'm saying." His gaze narrowed and an apologetic expression morphed into an accusatory one. "The thing is, you've made no secret that you want a spot on the medical board and you belong to that women's club. You can't blame me for wondering if you have ulterior motives where Eric's concerned."

Ulterior motives? What was he talking about? No, she wasn't going to ask. Gut instincts she'd learned to listen to long ago told her not to discuss Eric, that, despite his apology, Eric's friend was who had ulterior motives.

"I'll be honest. I'm still not a hundred percent convinced you're for real. I know about Skymont." He dropped his bombshell. "That you'd do anything to move up the career ladder. Despite the easygoing man you see, Eric has had his share of problems. I don't want to see him get hurt."

Kasey reeled. She hadn't known anyone at Rivendell knew what had happened at Skymont. Hadn't she once worried that becoming involved with Eric would somehow dredge up her past? Had Dr. Douglas become worried about the woman his friend was seeing and hired an investigator to dig up the skeletons in her closet? What else had he found?

"Dr. Douglas." She kept her tone crisp, but polite. "I don't think we should discuss my relationship with Dr. Matthews."

"Perhaps not, but he cares about you. I care about him. He's a good guy. Don't hurt him."

Eric's best friend leaned against the cabinet Bones stood on. Both wore staunch expressions.

"Jonathan?" Eric said, stepping into the room but not making it further than the entrance due to the room's size. Immediately sensing the hostility, he looked back and forth between them. "What's going on?"

Dr. Douglas shook his head. "Just checking on the acute abdomen."

Eric's forehead wrinkled. "You know Mr. Oliver?"

"He's seen members of the Oliver family," Kasey interrupted, watching as Dr. Douglas stepped out of her office.

After one last look at his friend, Eric met her gaze in question.

"Radiology says to send Mr. Oliver now."

Standing in his office, Eric peered over Kasey's shoulder as she read Mr. Oliver's radiology report on the computer screen. The last of the patients had been seen for the day and she'd stopped by his recently finished office to see if he'd heard anything.

"Acute cholethiasis."

He'd just read the report a few minutes prior to her knock.

"It's what we suspected," Eric said, watching Kasey study the monitor. "I've called the surgeon, but apparently the only one working through the charity is on vacation for two weeks. Dr. Willis is covering for him, but isn't willing to rearrange his schedule for a patient he won't make anything on."

"Dr. Willis?" Kasey curled her nose. "He wouldn't be my first choice, anyway, but I suppose we have no choice. So, when is he willing to work in Mr. Oliver?"

"Next Monday."

Kasey grimaced. "A week from now? We can't let Mr. Oliver suffer that long. Even if we heavily medicate him to ease the pain, he'll end up dehydrated or worse. Plus, he'll keep trying to work."

"I agree."

She stood, paced across his office. "I'll call one of the other surgeons. See if I can convince one of them to agree to do the surgery."

"Or I could do the surgery," he suggested, watching her face for her reaction. In a large facility like Rivendell Medical Center where specialists abounded, doctors working in ambulatory care didn't ordinarily perform surgical procedures.

Green eyes widened. "You?"

"Don't look so shocked," he teased. "I'm trained. When I was working overseas, I never knew what was going to walk into my tent. I've done a little of everything. A gallbladder removal in a state-of-the-art surgi-center really isn't that big a deal."

"You'd do his surgery?" She sounded incredulous. "Here, at the surgi-center?"

"If you'll go in with me."

Her brows knitted into a vee. "You might be a trained surgeon, but I'm not. I've never performed anything as extensive as a gallbladder removal."

"I'd like you to be there with me. Will you?"

Her expression became thoughtful, then she nodded. "If it'll get Mr. Oliver taken care of sooner? Absolutely."

He grinned. "Good. I'll call Clive, and let him know what I want to do."

"Clive?" Her brows rose at his easy use of the administrator's first name. "Do you think he'll agree?"

"I don't think he'll say no." Eric grinned, for once extremely grateful his grandfather's name was on the building. "Do you?"

"He might. There will be liability issues to consider."

"He won't say no." Even if *he* had to agree to fund the entire procedure. "It'll be good press for the clinic and for that fund-raiser of yours, too."

She'd told him about the masquerade ball she'd been put in charge of organizing. Not that his mother hadn't already told him a dozen times. Mostly while she simultaneously touted Ella Von Buren's many charms, including her excellent Kentucky blue-blood roots. He'd started to ask Kasey what she thought of his mother— no way could any member of the RLS not know Lena Woolworth. But he still wasn't ready to have his mother interfering in his and Kasey's relationship. Not until he felt more confident his mother wouldn't inadvertently undo the delicate threads of what Eric had worked so hard to achieve the past few weeks. Kasey's faith in him.

Kasey stopped pacing. "Good press?"

"You can use us doing this surgery as a hook to get the press to write a piece highlighting the fund-raiser. They love human-interest stuff. If Mr. Oliver prefers to remain anonymous, no names have to be used." At her open mouth, he winked. "I know a guy over in Editorial and bet we can get a front page write-up if no one gets killed or holds up a bank."

A smile spread across her face, excitement lighting her beautiful eyes. She threw her arms around his neck and kissed his cheek. "Oh, Eric, that's perfect. Thank you."

Caught off guard by her reaction, he took a step back, wrapping his arms around her to steady himself.

His arms around her soft, receptive body knocked him even more off-kilter.

As did her exuberant kiss.

It was the first time since the night they'd made love that she'd touched him of her own accord, touched him without him having first touched her.

It felt damned good. Perfect.

"If this is the thanks I get, book me for anything you like," he teased. "I'm yours to command."

She pulled back, smiling at him like he was brilliant. "Be careful, or I might take you up on that."

As if to clinch the deal, she kissed him again.

CHAPTER SEVEN

"Do you talk about me with Dr. Douglas?" Kasey asked Eric that night after her piano lessons. When they'd first started dating, she'd admitted to taking the lessons for two years, but that she wasn't very good. Still, she smiled when she'd talked about playing and obviously enjoyed the lessons.

Not that the opportunity had presented itself, but she'd yet to offer to play for him. Something he looked forward to as he knew she saw doing so as exposing herself.

While she'd been at her lesson, he'd eaten with his mother. A big mistake. She had invited Ella and the Von Burens. Halfway through the meal, Gladys Anderson arrived to do a piece for her gossip column. His mother had been delighted, as had the Von Burens. Eric had drawn the line at having his photo taken.

The only positive to the entire ordeal was that he and Kasey arrived at the coffee shop where they'd arranged to meet at exactly the same time. That and him confronting Gladys in front of his mother and the Von Burens on not doing her part to help the RLS. After all, she'd yet to get back in touch with Dr. Carmichael. The woman, the Von Burens and his mother had been quite stunned. His mother had also gotten a curious gleam in her eyes that said she'd homed right in on his mention of Kasey. No doubt she'd put two and two together and realized Kasey was the woman he'd been spending his time with.

Eric had left as quickly as he could.

Rather than go inside the coffee shop, Kasey had invited him to her house so they wouldn't have to rush off as the shop closed at ten and it was already almost nine.

Trying not to read anything into the invitation, he'd driven to the trendy neighborhood of mid-sized brick houses, taking in every detail of her home with its small but immaculate yard.

"Jonathan and I talk about you occasionally," he admitted, following her into her living room. Tonight was the first time she'd invited him to her house.

Full-blooded male that he was, he wanted to whisk her off her feet and carry her over the threshold and straight to her bedroom.

She meant more to him than just sex, but every look, every touch left him wanting her more and more. Even though they had made progress, she hadn't let him inside that protective shield many had mistaken as an icy heart.

"What do you tell him?" she asked, placing her purse onto a black marble inlaid table just inside the doorway.

Eric took in the high-end furnishings that screamed success, but not much more. Not a single personal item or photograph in the entire room. He could be in a hotel suite for all the personalization. "He's curious about my relationship with you."

"And?" She stood in front of the table, looking uncertain.

He walked over to a bookshelf, glanced at the titles. All classics he'd been assigned to read throughout prep school. "Jonathan is more than a coworker. He's my best friend and has been for years. He asked me point-blank if we were involved. I wasn't going to lie to him."

"I suppose I understand that," she conceded.

"He won't say anything, if that's what worries you." He continued to take in her home. "He knows we don't want anyone at the clinic aware we're seeing other."

"Okay." She nodded. "So, Dr. Douglas knows." A nervous smile flittered across her face. "Coffee?"

The fact she didn't argue, didn't seem upset that he'd told Jonathan the truth said they'd made even more progress.

"Actually, water would be great. All this coffee late at night is interfering with my sleep."

"Oh." She bit the inside of her lip, shifted her weight. "Sorry."

She turned to go toward what he assumed was the kitchen.

He grabbed her wrist, turning her toward him. "Kasey?"

She looked at him with her big eyes. Her lips parted and she moistened them.

"I don't really want anything to drink."

She swallowed, her gaze dropping to his mouth. "What do you want?"

He ran his fingers over the bare skin of her arm until he reached the edge of the lacy camisole top she wore. "You."

She shivered, moved closer to him, stared into his eyes.

"I want you, too, Eric." The admission came freely. She wanted him. "I've wanted you from the beginning. So much I've ached."

"Thank God." He pulled her against him, kissed her lips, her throat. Slow, torturous kisses meant to tantalize, to torment, to arouse her as fully as he was, but which only succeeded in driving himself into further need.

Kasey kissed him back, matched him touch for touch, dug her fingers into his hair, his nape, his back. She slid her hands inside his shirt, up his back, pushed the tailored material off his shoulders.

"I want to touch you, Eric. All of you." Her breathy plea ripped into Eric and tore his resolve to go slow all to hell.

Dropping his shirt to the gleaming hardwood floor, he scooped her off her feet. "Where's your room?"

"That way." Burying her face into the crook of his neck, she pointed toward the hallway leading off the living room.

Tiny kisses rained over his throat. Her hot, moist tongue dipped into the groove at the base, causing him to misstep.

"Which room, Kasey?" he growled, wanting to lay

her on her bed and strip her naked, feast on the way she looked waiting for him to make love to her.

She pressed another kiss to his collarbone, then lifted her head. "There."

Without setting her down, Eric fumbled in the dark until he found the light switch. Soft light flooded the peach room.

With a gentleness that almost brought tears to Kasey's eyes, he laid her on the bed, cupped her face and kissed her. With each touch, he worshipped her body, her soul.

When she lay naked before him, his eyes met hers, darkened. He dipped his head and ran his tongue over her belly in slow, sensual strokes, over and over until her entire body pulsed. Her fingers dug into the patterned quilt on her bed, bunching the material around her. He laved her navel as if branding the area as his own mark upon her body.

He moved on, loving other parts of her body, letting her finish undressing him, letting her love him in sweet exploration of their reactions to each other.

He paused to put on a condom.

Staring into her eyes, he thrust into her body, melding them into one, and all rational thought disappeared.

She sensed the longing to go faster trembling inside him like a caged beast roaring to be let loose. Yet every time she tried to increase their pace, to give him release, he reined her in with a whispered, "Not yet."

Sweat beaded on his forehead.

Lying on her with his weight partially supported on his elbows, he clasped her hands, thrust deep. Looking into his eyes, seeing the passion, seeing more, something she'd never seen in any man's eyes, Kasey had the biggest revelation of her life.

She trusted Eric.

With all her heart and all her soul. With everything she was.

Because she loved him.

And, maybe, just maybe, what she saw reflected in his eyes was love, too.

Still spiraling down from heights she'd never known, Kasey lay in Eric's arms, her ear pressed to his chest as she listened to his pounding heartbeat.

When he'd quit saying not yet, she was sure they'd left her bedroom, had floated off into Neverland or some other magic, mystical place.

Just as they had the first few times in his hotel room, they'd left the light on during their lovemaking. Part of her had felt self-conscious about doing so now that they weren't strangers, but another part had reveled in being able to see Eric, to look into his eyes and watch his reaction to her touch, his reaction to touching her.

He kissed the top or her head. "I think it's time we come out of the closet."

She lifted her head off his shoulder to look at him. "But—"

"I want to date you, Kasey. I have from the beginning. I acknowledge your fears about our working together, but I want the world to know you're mine."

Elation lifted her spirits. She rolled on top of him and smiled, her hair cascading around her head to shade their faces. "Does that mean the world will know you're mine?"

"I've been yours from the night you sat down beside me at Calista Blue's."

"You have?"

"From the moment I looked into your sad, green eyes."

Not daring to believe what she was hearing, she laughed lightly. "What man could resist?"

Which brought to mind one who had been able to resist. One Jonathan had mentioned in her office. Just how much did Eric's friend know? How much had he shared with Eric?

She rolled off him and stared up at her textured ceiling. "I was in love once."

She waited to see how he'd take her admission. Was it poor bed etiquette to reveal your past while still recovering from phenomenal sex? Probably, but it seemed imperative that she come clean about her past.

He rolled onto his side, took her hand in his and brought it to his lips. "He was a lucky man."

"He didn't think so. He dumped me for another woman." Just saying the words out loud made tears sting her eyes. "A woman with a background similar to his."

"What kind of background would that be?" Eric caressed her fingers.

"Wealthy. Old money. The kind that speaks without

a nickel being spent." Kasey took a deep breath. "He came from a wealthy family just outside Nashville, where I was working at the time. So did she. Her father was on the board of trustees at the hospital where I worked in a fast-track career advancement program. After Randall and she became engaged, I was called to task for inappropriate behavior within the workplace."

Bile soured her mouth at the memories of how she'd been terminated at Skymont.

Eric remained silent, his finger tracing over hers.

"Inappropriate being that I slept with another doctor in the privacy of my home, a doctor I dated for almost a year." A wasted year of her life in so many ways. "I was given the choice of voluntarily leaving with a full recommendation or being dismissed without severance pay."

Eric sat up in the bed. "There are laws against that. You could have taken them to the cleaners."

"Sure there are laws, but who would have hired me if I'd sued, Eric?" She'd given great thought to the decisions she'd made during that time. Her natural instinct had been like Eric's: to fight. But when she'd approached the situation with logic rather than anger, she'd kept coming to the same conclusion. "Even if I'd won a lawsuit, what employer would take a risk with me? My reputation would have been ruined."

"Their reputation would have been ruined."

"Possibly, but I had more to lose than they did."

"You could have gone into practice for yourself."

"True, I could have," she admitted, had even briefly

considered doing just that. Going into solo practice wouldn't have salvaged her wrecked reputation. "But my goal has always been higher than owning a private practice."

He sat in silence for a moment, before asking, "You want to replace Herbert on the medical board, don't you?"

"Yes," she admitted, relieved that he understood how important her career was to her. "I know I'm young, but my résumé is impeccable and so are my qualifications."

She glanced at Eric, unable to read his thoughtful expression. She went on. "Anyway, I wanted you to know about Randall."

"Why, Kasey? Why tell me this now? Tonight?" His terse questions surprised her.

Did he think she was trying to pressure him emotionally?

"Because I want you to understand what a risk it is for me to be here with you, for you to understand that I didn't lightly make the decision to invite you into my bed." She tasted blood and forced her teeth to let go of her lower lip. "Because if we're going to do this, we need to be honest with each other, not have so many secrets between us."

Eric scooted up in the bed, propping pillows behind him. He studied Kasey's face, looking for any sign that she knew his secret.

The one culminating this afternoon when he'd talked to Clive about scheduling Mr. Oliver's surgery for the following morning.

Herbert had officially retired. The spot on the board was Eric's. His mother had been ecstatic.

Had Kasey somehow learned of his discussion with Clive? Was that why he was here in her bed? Why she'd told him of Randall? Of how she'd been betrayed by love?

Love.

The word brought his thoughts to a halt.

Did he love Kasey?

Certainly, he felt things for her he'd never felt before. Crazy, irrational things that made him pull strings to arrange to perform a gallbladder surgery. Things that had him thinking about the future, about the things his mother said to him about his family responsibilities.

Things like how betrayed Kasey was going to feel when she learned he'd been given the board position.

How betrayed his mother would be if he turned down the position she considered his legacy.

"I should tell you something," he began, searching for the right place to begin and not coming up with a good start.

"You don't have to tell me," Kasey surprised him by saying. "I already know."

"You do?"

"You're from old money, too, and I know you've got inside connections with the board." She gave a breathy sigh. "Just like Randall. That's why I was scared of history repeating itself, but you're not like him."

Aw, hell. They were talking about two different things. He was talking career and she was talking heart.

Which told him quite a lot about where Kasey's feelings lay.

Unless she was manipulating him. Giving him what he wanted so he'd give her what she wanted.

Sex for the board position.

He weighed the thought in his mind, recalling how many times in the past he'd been wrong about women, about how many times he'd been used by those close to him.

Kasey was different. What they shared was different. Was something special and fragile and worth believing in, worth protecting.

"I care about you, Kasey. A lot." Telling her about the board position when they'd just made love was wrong. He couldn't let her throw her icy shield between them again. He'd find a way to tell her about Herbert, to tell her the dilemma he was in regarding the position. She'd be upset, but would understand once he explained.

Fear entered her eyes, as if she sensed a "but" coming. He didn't say it. Couldn't say it.

"I don't want to hurt you, ever."

She closed her eyes. "Then don't."

She was right. There were too many secrets between them.

"You should know it's the one thing I do well in life, hurting those I care about."

Her eyes opened, looking at him in confusion.

"When I was younger, I rebelled against my parents, did everything I could to embarrass them."

"Sounds like you were a typical teenager."

"Drugs, sex, partying, even some petty theft." At her shocked expression, he grimaced. "Not things I'm proud of, but I was still doing those things in my early twenties. I was so high at my father's funeral that I don't even recall having been there. I was a wreck."

"I'm sorry you were in such a bad place." She touched his shoulder. "You couldn't have been that bad, though, otherwise, you'd never have gotten into medical school."

"My mother bought my way into medical school."

"Bought your…?" She stopped, the enormity of what he was saying apparently sinking in. "Just how does one buy a child's way into medical school? Is that even possible? How much money would that take?"

"Apparently at that time it took enough to build a new dormitory and nursing school."

"An entire dorm and nursing school?"

Eric nodded. "It wasn't like the school was going to not let me in, was it? Much less kick me out no matter what I did when my mother funded whatever pet project they came up with."

Kasey's gasp stung.

"I didn't realize," she admitted. The shock on her face said there were a lot of things she hadn't realized. Like just how wealthy his family really was.

"Jonathan saved me."

"Dr. Douglas?" Her shock continued. "That seems…unlikely."

"He likes to have a good time, but he's never done

the hard-core things I did. It wasn't until he sat me down after my father's funeral and told me to either get my act together or find a new best friend that I admitted I was on a path to self-destruction."

"Dr. Douglas did that?" Disbelief rang in her voice.

"Lots of people did, including a judge, but Jonathan was the one who got through."

"How?"

"He moved all my stuff out of our apartment and hung a wanted ad for a new best friend and roommate on the door."

"I'm…blown away."

"He's a good friend."

"Apparently." She stared at him in awe. "How did you become the wonderful doctor you are today?"

"After I went into rehab—"

"You went to rehab?" she interrupted, pulling the bedspread higher over her chest.

"I'd been doing hard drugs for months. I went to rehab." He swallowed his pride, swallowed the pain caused by the disillusionment in her eyes. "Other than the occasional alcoholic drink, I've been drug-free for seven years."

"I'm glad."

"Me, too." Eric finished telling her about how he'd turned his grades around, impressed even the most un-impressionable of his professors, known he had to do more with his life than immediately step into his father's empty shoes or the ones his mother had so nicely laid out for him to wear.

When he'd finished medical school, he'd signed up with a medical mission group and gone overseas. He'd learned to live without all the things he'd taken for granted, learned about who he was beneath the Woolworth fortune. Who he really was beneath all the spoilt layers the world saw.

It was that man who'd come home to Rivendell.

That man Eric liked looking into the mirror and seeing each day.

CHAPTER EIGHT

KASEY semi-floated the next day. Eric had stayed until just before dawn. She'd slept spooned against his hard frame only to be awakened by morning kisses.

They'd shared so much of themselves last night, revealed painful truths, clung to each other throughout the night. When she'd awakened this morning, she'd felt closer to Eric than she'd ever felt to anyone.

Because she loved him.

"You sure are perky this morning," Lora observed, grinning at Kasey. "You must be looking forward to going into surgery with Dr. Matthews."

"Must be." Kasey didn't reveal more, but the smile Lora gave her said she didn't have to. Lora recognized the glow of a woman in love.

Just as well that she and Eric had decided going public was okay. Not that they'd make an announcement or anything. She wasn't exactly sure how going public worked. She and Randall had openly dated from the beginning.

Randall. How could she have thought she wanted to marry him? What she'd felt for him was so much less than what she felt for Eric.

Making love with Eric, knowing they'd both overcome demons, all of it was so much…more.

"There you go again," Lora teased, looking happy for Kasey. "He's a great guy."

"Yes, he is," Kasey agreed with a bright smile. "I should get to work. Who's next?"

"A new patient in room three. She wouldn't say why she's here, but she hasn't had health care in years."

"She's here through the charity fund?"

"Yes. Nice enough lady, but she gave vague answers to some of her health history questions. You may have to clarify a few items."

"Okay, guess I should get in to see her."

"Hey, Kasey?" Lora stopped her. "If you're ever free for lunch, maybe we could go to that café you like. I ate there last week and, boy, have I been missing out. Great food."

Surprised by the offer, Kasey smiled. She and Lora had grown closer over the past few weeks. She liked the nurse she suspected had feelings for Dr. Douglas. "I'd like that."

Due to the reshuffling of their schedules to clear the afternoon for Mr. Oliver's procedure, Kasey didn't see Eric until right before they headed to the surgical center.

When he met her in her office, he wore scrubs and looked dreamy. Eyes twinkling, he grinned. "Miss me?"

"Just a little," she teased, moving toward him.

He pulled her to him, holding her close. His arms felt so good. She rested her head against his strong chest. The embrace lasted only a few seconds, but it was enough to reassure Kasey that what they'd shared during the night had been real.

He waggled his brows, checking her out. "I like your scrubs."

"I was thinking the same thing when you came in here."

"That you liked your scrubs?"

"Something like that." She laughed, wondering how in just the span of a few months she could have gone from not knowing this wonderful man to him being the center of her world.

They left her office to head toward the surgi-center.

"I spoke with Mrs. Oliver earlier," Eric told her as they stepped into the hallway. "She and her daughter are both in the waiting area. I told her we'd stop by after the surgery to let her know how everything went."

Kasey smiled. "That was thoughtful of you."

He shrugged. "They were worried about him. I wanted to reassure them."

"You know the gossip mill is buzzing about you doing this surgery, right?"

"Is it?"

She nodded. "I was too busy this morning to catch

much of what was being said, but I overheard a couple of nurses talking."

He grinned. "Did they like my scrubs, too?"

"Probably." Laughing, Kasey rolled her eyes. "Is it true that you asked to work in the ambulatory clinic, but were originally supposed to have worked in a different department?"

He stopped walking, regarded her. "Does it matter?"

"Not really," she admitted. "I was just curious as to why you would do that. Was it to work with Jonathan?"

"He is my best friend," Eric agreed, opening the stair-well door so they could go down to the surgi-center level. When the door closed behind them, they stood on the landing. "But I'd be lying if I didn't admit that I wasn't thinking of Jonathan when I made the request to work in the ambulatory clinic."

"You weren't thinking of him?"

He shook his head.

Warmth spread through Kasey's chest. "You wanted to work with me?"

"Under the circumstances, working together seemed like the best way to get to know you better."

Because she'd been so adamant about not wanting anything to do with him.

"I'm sorry I pushed you away when you arrived at the clinic, Eric. I was so sure that you would think poorly of me for sleeping with you that I never gave you a chance."

"Did you think poorly of me because I'd slept with you?"

"Sleeping with you made me think of you, but not poorly. More like with longing for a repeat."

"Were you disappointed?"

"With the repeat? Are you kidding? Last night was amazing." She hugged him. "You are amazing."

"You were pretty amazing yourself." Eric held her to him for several heartbeats. "Come on. It isn't a good idea for us to hang around in this stairwell. Alone. Being amazed by each other. No telling what that might lead to and Mr. Oliver is waiting on us."

Together, they took the stairs, then headed toward the back of the building so they could go to the surgical center to get scrubbed.

In the sterile surgery suite, Eric maneuvered the staple gun to the correct position and clipped Mr. Oliver's gallbladder stem. Moving slightly lower, he placed another clip. When he'd secured the area, he used the laser to cut between the clips, bagging the gallbladder then pulling the stone-filled pouch free via a trochanter.

The nurse did an instrument count, a gauze count. Kasey stood on the other side of the surgery table, watching in fascination. Clear goggles shielded her eyes, a surgical mask covered her lovely face. But when her gaze met his, he knew she was smiling.

His breath caught with a blast of emotion that tightened his rib cage almost painfully.

He needed to tell her the rest of the story. About his mother. About the clinic. About how he felt about her. Tonight.

He also needed to talk to his mother, to tell her that he wouldn't risk losing Kasey over Herbert's vacant spot.

Woolworth, Inc. owned controlling stock in the clinic. If Eric wanted a position on the board, the board would create a new position. Kasey desperately wanted Herbert's spot, had set that as her marking point for success. He wouldn't deny her that success.

Turning down the position was the right thing to do.

"Would you like to do the honors?" he asked, indicating the removal of the trochanters.

Her eyes lit with excitement. "Can I?"

"Sure. You know the motto."

"The motto?"

"See one, do one, teach one," they and several of the operating room nursing staff finished in unison.

Eric demonstrated proper removal with the first trochanter and allowed Kasey to do the remaining two.

Together they secured the punctured flesh. Moments after they were finished, the nurse released where Mr. Oliver had been secured to the table to keep him from moving during surgery, and anesthesia was being reversed.

"We're finished with our part," Eric informed their groggy patient. "Now you just have to wake up well enough in Recovery that you can be put into a room so your family can visit."

Looking dazed, the man nodded, then grabbed Kasey's hand. "Thank you."

She bent down, kissed his cheek. "You're welcome,

but Dr. Matthews is who really deserves your thanks. Without him, this wouldn't have happened."

They left the operating room to find Mr. Oliver's family to tell them his surgery had been a success.

"That was amazing," Kasey enthused once away from the others. Her eyes sparkled with excitement. "Enough so I think I could go back to school and do a surgical fellowship."

Eric laughed, loving the look of pure happiness on her face. Oh, yeah, he'd turn down a hundred board positions before he'd be the one to wipe the smile off her face.

The only position that really mattered was the one of being an integral part of her life.

"Let's pick up takeout and eat at your place tonight," he suggested as they walked toward the waiting room. "We can discuss your plans to make me date a college co-ed then."

She grinned, smacking his arm playfully. "Okay, so surgery might get boring if it was all I did, but being in the operating room with you was brilliant."

"Because I'm brilliant?"

"Absolutely," she agreed. "And a gifted surgeon whose talents aren't being put to full use in the ambulatory clinic."

"I like the ambulatory clinic," he reminded her.

"And I like you being in the ambulatory clinic." She shot him a look that said she liked a lot of things about him. "But perhaps the clinic isn't the best use of your many talents."

"I like the ambulatory clinic," he repeated.

"Good," she acquiesced. "We can't do takeout tonight, though. It's only two weeks until the RLS masquerade ball. I'm meeting with the ladies tonight for one last committee check-in. I mentioned it to you yesterday."

With everything that had happened over the past twenty-four hours, he'd forgotten.

Which meant she'd be dining with his mother rather than him.

Why did that put a nervous feeling in his gut?

"We need to talk before you go to your meeting, Kasey." He purposely kept his tone light, not wanting to rob her of the joy on her face. "In private."

A mischievous look came over her face. As if she thought he wanted to do something besides talk in private. Hell, he did want to. Particularly since her look wasn't one of aversion to the idea. He'd been having fantasies about that desk of hers since the first time he'd stepped into her office. Of course he'd have to turn that skeleton around. He'd swear at times the thing was watching him.

"Are we going to discuss private matters, Eric?" she teased, shooting him a flirty look.

"If you don't quit looking at me like that we're going to do more than talk." He waggled his brows.

Kasey giggled. Looking at her, Eric wondered how anyone could have ever called her an ice queen. Her smile warmed him all the way to his center.

"Tell you what," she said in a sultry tone. "Since we

both have an office full of patients to see, you can reveal all your private matters tonight after I finish my meeting with the masquerade ball committee."

He didn't like waiting. Particularly not as his mother had called him this morning to check on him since he'd not come home last night. The perils of having agreed to live with her rather than in a place of his own. At the time it had seemed like a good idea since living under the same roof meant he was able to see her more. Now he knew the reasons for not living with your mother at the age of thirty-two.

"Call me after you're finished," he said, resigned that their conversation would have to wait. "I'll come over and I'm bringing clean clothes this time so I don't have to rush off in the morning."

Her eyes darkened to a deep green. Her gaze dropping to his mouth, she nodded. "I'll call the moment we're through."

Despite her happiness, Kasey fought to keep her smile that night. Doreen Von Buren once again laid into her. The woman had never been overly friendly. Overly friendly wasn't the RLS style, but never had Kasey felt so blatantly attacked. From a woman she'd long admired from afar.

"You haven't talked to the florist?" Doreen snapped. "What are you thinking? The ball is in less than a fortnight. We'll end up with weeds on the tables if you don't get with the program."

"I'm not handling the floral arrangements. Daphne Moore is," Kasey said through a clenched teeth smile.

"Daphne?" Doreen glanced around the table, but Daphne hadn't shown that evening. "Well, then, I'm sure it's been taken care of."

"I'm sure." Kasey mentally added calling the florist to her list of things to do. Just in case.

Doreen made a snide remark about incompetent hired help beneath her breath.

Hired help? Kasey opened her mouth to confront the woman. She'd had enough. But before a sound came out of her mouth, someone else spoke up.

"Kasey has been volunteering with our group for several years and has recently been given status as a junior member." The classically beautiful woman sitting at the head of the table commented with her usual elegance and grace. She'd been sitting quietly, as had the other five women, watching the exchange. "On whatever level she's served, Kasey has always gone above and beyond to make sure our events are successful. I'm sure the masquerade ball will be no exception."

She hadn't realized the RLS matron had noticed all the hard work she'd done for the group since she'd moved to Rivendell.

With those simple words from Lena Woolworth the room suddenly found everything Kasey had done or suggested to be utterly brilliant.

Well, Doreen didn't find her utterly brilliant. Doreen

glowered, but she didn't speak another unsavory word. Not even a veiled one.

The committee adjourned. Kasey gathered her purse from where she'd tucked it beside her chair. When she rose, Lena said, "Kasey, be a dear and walk with me to wait on my car. I'd like to discuss something in private."

"Yes, ma'am." A bevy of nerves rushed through Kasey. Was Lena going to invite her to become a fully fledged RLS member? Surely not this soon? There were other volunteers who'd been junior members far longer than Kasey had been living in Rivendell.

When they stepped outside the restaurant, Lena handed the valet her ticket stub and turned to Kasey. "I have a favor to ask."

A favor? Kasey fought to keep her surprise hidden. "You must know I believe in the work the RLS does and would help in any way that I can."

Lena smiled with her usual regal elegance. "I'm pleased to hear that, but this is personal."

Personal?

Lena watched her closely, expectantly. "It involves my son."

"Your son?" Not long after joining the RLS she'd heard Lena had a son, but that he didn't live in Kentucky. Had he returned home? Did he need medical assistance?

"Yes, I'd like you to convince him to attend the fund-raiser." Lena watched her closely. "Our family is being honored during the ball. He should be there."

Kasey couldn't imagine not wanting to take advantage of an opportunity to be proud of one's family's accomplishments. What was wrong with Lena's son? "Why wouldn't he want to be there when his family is being honored?"

Lena laughed, her lovely eyes still fixated on Kasey. "It's a long story, but suffice it to say that my son marches to the beat of his own drum."

Probably a spoilt kid who had no clue how good he had it.

"I'll do what I can and attempt to convince him." How, she had no clue, but this was a personal favor for Lena Woolworth. How often did that happen in one's lifetime? No way would she say no. "But wouldn't it be more effective to ask someone who actually knows him?"

Lena laughed again in that sparkly way she had. "But, darling, you do know him. Eric mentioned you while at we were having dinner with Ella and her parents. I did a little checking." The woman's eyes twinkled with a light that hinted she'd done more than a little checking. "You work in the same clinic as my Eric."

Eric. As in…

"Dr. Matthews is your son? I thought your son was younger. In his early twenties." That was the impression she'd gotten from the few things she'd heard about Lena's son. Young and irresponsible.

Eric was Lena Woolworth's son.

Eric had had dinner with Ella? The thought almost blindsided Kasey as much as the news that he was Lena's son. She couldn't be more dazed if Lena had struck her head with a baseball bat and stars danced before her eyes.

Eric had never said anything about them being exclusive to each other. She'd just assumed.

He'd had dinner with Ella. And his mother.

Hadn't Kasey once thought he'd eventually want someone like Ella?

Taking measure of Kasey's reaction, Lena smiled. "I know it must be surprising to discover I have a son in his thirties, but time does slip by." She gave another mysterious smile. "I was extremely young when I married Frank."

How had she not put two and two together? Then again, why would she have assumed Eric Matthews was the young and rebellious Woolworth heir she'd occasionally heard tell of?

Why would she assume that the wonderfully, responsible man she'd fallen in love with was the son of the woman who owned controlling stock in the clinic where they worked?

After all, Eric had known for weeks she was a junior member of the RLS.

Hadn't she even mentioned some of the ladies by name? Mentioned his *mother* by name?

He'd never said anything.

Not once had he pointed out that she'd been meeting with his mother.

Because, despite everything he'd said, Kasey Carmichael wasn't good enough to take home and introduce to his mother.

He had Ella for dinners with his mother.

When it came down to it, Eric wanted her for sex. Nothing more.

Just like Randall.

CHAPTER NINE

WHEN Eric arrived at the clinic the next morning, he stopped by Kasey's office first thing. As they'd arranged, she'd called the night before while driving home from her gathering with the RLS. But she'd begged off meeting him, claiming a headache.

She'd denied that anything more was wrong. He'd offered to come over and take care of her, but she'd insisted she just needed to get a good night's rest to get rid of the headache.

A headache? Couldn't she have come up with something more original?

He'd ended up going to Jonathan's and shooting a few games of pool. They'd shot the breeze until the early morning hours.

Despite the fact he'd gotten very little sleep, Eric had arrived at the clinic early.

Kasey's office door stood open, but she wasn't there. Just that damned skeleton that he'd swear guarded the room.

"Looking for Kase?" Jonathan asked from behind him.

Shaking his head, he turned. "You've seen her this morning?"

"Briefly. She went into an exam room a few minutes ago."

He'd hoped to catch her before she got started, but she must have come in early, too.

Jonathan regarded Eric with crossed arms. "Did you talk to her last night?"

He eyed his friend. "It was late when I left your place. Surely you didn't think I'd call her after midnight? If she did have a headache, and I woke her, she'd be upset."

"Rightly so." Jonathan agreed. "But it wouldn't surprise me to hear you had called. Or gone on over to her place. You've got it bad."

Eric didn't deny his friend's claim. He'd admitted as much the night before.

"What did your mother say this morning?" Jonathan asked. "I can't imagine she's thrilled that you're dating someone who grew up in the projects. Or is Lena so happy to have you home she doesn't care who you're involved with?"

Eric had no illusions that his mother cared a great deal. As her only child and sole heir, she'd always felt she had more say in his life than he did. Despite his mother's philanthropic work to better the plight of the poor, she was an elitist in many ways.

"She wasn't out of bed when I left this morning. Like I said last night, I have mentioned Kasey to my mother. I didn't tell her we were involved, though. Just that one of her junior RLS members worked at the clinic with me."

"You've been walking around whistling Dixie, you think Lena hasn't noticed?" Jonathan snorted. "You took a woman to the Wild W for a private picnic. You failed to come home the other night. You think Lena didn't immediately jump to all the right conclusions when you mentioned Kasey?"

Eric grinned self-derisively. "Since she backed off throwing Ella Von Buren in my face after I mentioned Kasey, I'm sure she did."

"Ella? Wasn't she on the cover of that women's magazine a few months ago?" Jonathan whistled with appreciation. "Tell you what, your mother can throw Ella my way. I should be so lucky."

Eric shrugged. "Deal, but I'll warn you, she's more looks than brain."

"Just how I like them," Jonathan bragged, earning a laugh from Eric.

Kasey stepped out of the exam room, spotted the two of them talking, and smiled. A polite smile that didn't reach her tired-appearing eyes.

Eric's stomach knotted. Something was wrong. What had happened from the time he'd kissed her goodbye yesterday evening to when she'd called him to cancel?

His mother.

"Good morning, Eric. Dr. Douglas." She didn't meet Eric's eyes; instead she smiled at Jonathan.

"Jonathan," his friend insisted. "Call me Jon-a-than."

Kasey nodded and stepped past them into her office.

With a go-get-'em-tiger grin, Jonathan slugged him on the shoulder, then disappeared into a patient room. Eric followed Kasey into her office and closed the door behind him.

He avoided looking at Bones. "Feel better this morning?"

The blank look that briefly passed over her face said more than her words, confirming his suspicions.

"Yes, much," she recovered. "Thanks for asking."

She'd lied to him about her headache. To get out of seeing him last night.

Eric didn't like games. Never had. "What's going on? I thought we'd moved past this."

Kasey backed up against her desk, but didn't sit. "This?"

"You think I can't look at you and see that something's wrong? Yesterday you lit up when you saw me," he pointed out. "Today you practically cringed."

"I just have a lot on my plate right now." She didn't deny the cringe, which slam-dunked his stomach with doubts of where they stood with each other.

"With this masquerade ball," she continued, not looking at him. "Please understand."

Could her distance really be that simple?

He'd never organized a masquerade, but his mother had many times over the years. He'd never seen her stress one. Of course, Lena never stressed such things. She had plenty of minions to take care of the details and the stress.

But Kasey did look stressed. Then again, Kasey was one of his mother's minions.

Hell, he'd tell his mother to lay off Kasey, to get some of her minions to lighten Kasey's load. Whatever it took to ease the tension from her face.

But the real question was what had his mother told Kasey?

"What did she say to you?"

Kasey's face paled. "Who?"

He sank back against the cabinet, bumped into the creepy skeleton, then straightened. "My mother."

"Why would you ask me about your mother, Eric?" Kasey's eyes narrowed. "You've never even introduced me to your mother."

"Is that why you're upset? That I never introduced you to Lena?" He'd been protecting her, but it struck him that Kasey might see him not introducing her in a bad light.

"I couldn't care less that you didn't introduce me." She straightened the skeleton he'd bumped, her voice so flat it conveyed more emotion than if she'd screamed at him.

"I can see that."

What he saw was the anger sparking in Kasey's green eyes. And the hurt. And the sheer determination.

She pinned him beneath her intent gaze. "Were you serious about us going public that we're a couple?" she surprised him by asking. "If so, you'll go with me to the masquerade ball."

His mother had been trying to get him to commit for

weeks, but he'd held off. He wasn't overly fond of such occasions, this one more than most. But if Kasey wanted him to escort her to the ball, he'd be honored.

What did Kasey want? Him? His name? His money? Did the social ladder matter to her as much as she sometimes let on?

"Fine, I'll go to the ball with you."

The challenge in her eyes momentarily shifted. "You'll come to the masquerade ball as my date?"

At her surprise, he asked, "Did you think I wouldn't?"

"Actually…" She let the word draw out. "I thought you might already have a date for the evening."

Why would she think that?

"The only plans I have with any woman are with you, Kasey."

She placed her finger against her chin and pretended thoughtfulness. "Gee, and I thought you'd had dinner with another woman."

Oh, yeah. His mother had been talking. "My mother?"

Kasey's eyes narrowed. "Ella Von Buren."

"She was my mother's guest. Not mine."

"Right."

Why did he feel as if he was on trial?

"I'm telling you the truth," he said simply. He was not going to argue with her about Ella. He'd done nothing wrong and wouldn't defend himself as if he had.

"Fine." Kasey shrugged as if it were no big deal. "You're telling the truth."

She stood a few feet away looking at him with impassive eyes. Impassive eyes that hid whatever was really going on inside her head.

"And?" he prompted when she didn't say more.

"You know the old saying."

Eric had no idea what she was talking about. "What saying would that be?"

"The truth shall set you free."

What she was saying, implying, sank in. Stunned him.

"You don't want to see me anymore?" Two nights ago she'd made love with him and now she was dumping him? "Didn't you just invite me to go to the fundraiser with you?"

"I wasn't expecting you to agree to go," she said in a rushed tone, her chest rising and falling in a deep breath. "I'm sorry, Eric. But more and more this is feeling like the past come back to haunt me."

"I'm not like Randall."

"So you keep saying." Kasey turned, the light illuminating the smudges beneath her eyes that said she hadn't slept well the night before. "But let's look at the facts." She paced three steps to the wall and turned back toward him. "You are from old money, work at the same place I do, and failed to acknowledge our relationship to your family." She ticked the items off on her fingers. "Sounds similar to me."

"We agreed to keep our relationship private," he reminded her, moving closer to her, but she backed away, her back pressing against the wall. "I was honoring that agreement."

"Nice," she said with a sarcastic twist to her voice. "It must be great to be able to ease your conscience by saying you were doing me a favor by not acknowledging my existence in your life."

"I told Jonathan," he said.

Kasey snorted. "Bragging about your latest conquest to your best friend doesn't count."

Kasey wasn't just venting anger. She was serious. Eric sighed, wishing he knew the right words to say to make her understand how he felt. "You weren't my latest conquest, Kasey."

"Oh?" A dark brow rose. "You've already moved on to someone else? Perhaps Ella is your latest conquest?" she bit out, a toothpaste-ad smile on her face. "And good news, she comes from good breeding stock and apparently already has your mother's blessing."

Eric crossed his arms, refusing to take her bait. "I haven't done anything wrong."

"Do you really believe that?" She laughed, raking her gaze over him. "Perhaps you do. A rich, spoiled man as yourself has no clue what honor and loyalty mean."

"Do you really believe that?" He tossed her accusation back at her, but her expression remained stoic. "You're being unreasonable, Kasey."

"Do you want to know what's unreasonable, Eric?" She took a step toward him, pointed her finger at his chest, emphasizing her words. "What's unreasonable is that I thought you were different." She poked her finger into his sternum. "What's unreasonable is that you knew

I was meeting with your mother once a week and you failed to say anything."

She was right. He should have told her about his mother, introduced them. How could he explain about Lena's personality?

She jabbed her finger hard against his chest. "What's unreasonable is that I thought we were involved in a monogamous relationship and all the while you were wooing Ella on the side."

He opened his mouth to correct her, but she rushed on.

"What's unreasonable is that until you showed up I thought I was a shoo-in for the medical board position, but the truth is I never had a shot because it's always been yours."

Now still wasn't a good time to tell her about Clive offering him the position.

Because she was right about that, too.

With him out of the picture, she was a shoo-in for the promotion.

"If the position hadn't already been yours, Mommy dearest could always buy you a spot on the board." Kasey hit below the belt, but she didn't look remorseful. She looked like she'd like to physically hit him to go along with her emotional punch. "The board should play their cards right. The clinic could end up with a new wing."

"Don't say things you're going to regret," he warned, knowing she was speaking from anger and hurt. But her words cut deep. Cut to the part of him that had sent him over the edge so many years ago. The part of him that he'd shed while in Africa.

"Stop and think about what you're doing."

"I am thinking about what I'm doing," she insisted. "We come from different worlds. And I'm not just talking about financially. What you did was wrong."

What he'd done? What had he done? Save her from his mother's bulldozing? Cared about her? "You really are being unreasonable."

"What's unreasonable," she continued, picking back up with her earlier train of thought, stabbing at his chest, "is that I believed in you, trusted you with my heart and invited you into my bedroom. Good thing I've seen reason." She stood a few inches taller, her chin thrust forward and her eyes sparkling. "Because what is reasonable is that we are through."

"No." He wasn't going to let her relegate him to being pushed aside at the first sign of trouble. "You're not leaving." He stood firmly in front of her, blocking her exit from the office. "You're going to talk to me. Right now."

"You want to talk?" Acid dripped from her tongue. "Fine, let's talk about how nice it must be to have everything in life handed to you on a silver platter."

"Kasey—"

"But guess what?" she interrupted, pushing against his chest. "You can't have everything, Eric. Because you can't have me. Not anymore. Not ever again."

A cold sweat popped onto his skin. Spears of emotion twisted into his gut. She was seriously calling them quits.

"I've already lost one job due to inappropriate be-havior with a man." She glared at him, daggers of her hatred lancing his heart. "You might have your family name to insure your job, but I don't. Goodbye, Eric."

Dazed, Eric stood in Kasey's office, wondering what the hell had just happened and how things had gotten so out of control.

She'd dumped him.

Because he hadn't introduced her to his mother?

Because he'd had dinner with Ella?

No, their problems went deeper than that.

Much deeper.

The real problem lay with the fact that she didn't trust him, that she lumped him into the same category as her ex.

As if he hadn't done everything possible to earn her trust.

Had he been so wrong about her? He'd thought she saw the real him. The him he'd found in Africa. The him he was proud of. Instead, she saw the old him, the him who might have deserved being rejected.

A knock sounded on Kasey's office door, then, without waiting for a response, Jonathan entered the room.

"I'd ask how your talk with Kasey went, but I heard. For that matter, the entire office heard when she slammed the door in your face. I've never seen her so upset," Jonathan pointed out with a low whistle. "Ac-tually, I've never seen her upset, period. What did you say to her to set her off like that?"

Eric picked up the skeleton's hand and let it drop back to its side. The bony fingers rattled against the skeleton's hip.

What had he said?

He'd gone into her office intent on clearing the air between them. Was that what he'd done? Cleared the air? Because there was a horrible stench floating about. One that reeked of being given the heave-ho.

The stench of him being hurt by Kasey not trusting him. After all this time, she didn't trust him.

He took a deep breath.

"I have to admit I'm surprised at you," Jonathan mused in Eric's continued silence.

Eric glanced at his friend. "Why?"

"Because you never set Kasey straight."

"I told her she was being unreasonable."

"Telling an upset woman she's being unreasonable— isn't that the same as waving a red cape in front of a bull?"

"Says the man who's never had a serious relationship with a woman." Was he being defensive? Most likely, but obviously Jonathan had no clue what he was talking about. Not when it came to Kasey. After all, once upon a time his friend had called her the Ice Queen. That alone proved how little he knew about Kasey.

"Hey, that isn't so," Jonathan denied. "Every woman I've been involved with has been a serious relationship. I've loved 'em, every one." He leaned back against Kasey's desk, his legs crossed at his ankles. "Why didn't you tell her about Lena? Why didn't you make her see 'reason'?"

"She stormed out of here before I could." Literally, she'd stormed out of her office on a cloud of righteous indignation.

"Really?" Jonathan played devil's advocate. "If Kasey was important to you, really important to you, you'd have made her listen, made her see reason. You'd have made her hear what you were saying."

"Just like you're hearing what I'm saying."

"Look." Jonathan uncrossed his legs, stood. "All I'm saying is that Kasey has a point. You've been sneaking around with her for weeks, never mentioning that she was serving on a committee with your mother. That doesn't bode well with any woman. Much less one as highly strung as Kasey Carmichael."

Jonathan had never steered him wrong. Had always laid it out straight. Even when it wasn't what Eric wanted to hear.

"Fine." Eric straightened, shoving his hands into his pants pockets. "I'll go make her listen."

Jonathan shook his head. "Not during office hours. Wait until the patients are seen, then make her listen if that's what you want. Kasey isn't the kind of woman to appreciate the drama of having her private affairs aired in her workplace."

Damn it, Jonathan was right.

"I've never seen you this torn up over a woman. If she's what you want, if you trust her motives, you better figure it out before you have that discussion."

Eric raked his fingers through his hair, eyeing his

friend as if he had no clue who he was. "When the hell did you get so smart?"

Jonathan grinned, socked his arm. "I've always been this smart. You just now figuring that out?"

Kasey finished her day without additional run-ins with Eric. Not that she'd been able to avoid seeing him, but she had managed to avoid being cornered.

Which was a huge relief.

When she'd slammed out of her office, her gaze had immediately landed on Lora and Jonathan standing in the hallway.

She'd gone red-faced in shame.

The guilty look on Lora's face had said they'd heard it all. Everything she and Eric had said to one another.

Mortification hit Kasey.

Mortification like she hadn't felt since her mother had shown up drunk at her graduation ceremony and left in the backseat of a police car.

But Kasey kept her head high and went into the room where her next patient waited.

All day, she kept her head high, her smile in place, and she successfully avoided Eric.

Mostly because she got the impression he was avoiding her, too.

Which hurt.

She'd been right about him all along.

He'd gotten what he wanted a couple of nights ago, and now they were through.

She may have beaten him to the punch, called an end before he did, but Eric hadn't put up a fight.

No, he may have looked stunned, but he hadn't stopped her, hadn't given her explanations of why he'd made the choices he had regarding their relationship.

Because he'd never considered her worth the effort.

Which didn't quite ring true, but her heart ached too much to give full credence to her niggles of doubt.

When she said goodbye to her last patient for the day, Kasey bumped into Clive Evans. The administrator had been lingering outside her office.

Had he been waiting for her?

Why would the administrator be waiting on her?

Had word gotten out about her argument with Eric?

Panic seized her, cut off her air supply. The room spun, causing her to reach out to touch the wall to regain her balance.

Their disagreement had only been that morning. Had Eric already put pressure on the administrator to let her go?

Just as Skymont had?

Kasey lifted her chin.

She wasn't leaving her job at Rivendell. Not without a fight.

A fight the likes of which Rivendell had never seen.

The likes of which Dr. Eric Matthews had never seen.

Determined to be strong, she opened her office door and waited for Mr. Evans to be seated. "What can I do for you, Mr. Evans?"

Her brain raced ahead. She'd hire a lawyer. The best lawyer in Rivendell. In Kentucky.

She'd take the case all the way. To the Supreme Court if she had to.

If Eric thought he could get away with this, he was wrong.

She would fight him.

Mr. Evans looked smug with the news he'd come to deliver. Probably enjoying being one of Eric's gofers. "I came to talk to you regarding the board position being vacated by Dr. Herbert retiring."

Kasey inhaled sharply. The board position? Had Eric sent the administrator to break the news to her?

"What about the board position?" she asked cautiously, wondering why Eric hadn't told her himself. It wasn't as if she didn't already know.

"We'd like to unofficially extend the position to you."

Sure she'd heard wrong, Kasey stared at the lanky man. "Me? You're sure?"

He laughed. "I'm sure, but I have to admit that's not how I expected you to respond."

"I'm a bit stunned, sir." Stunned didn't begin to cover it. She was floored. Blown away. She'd been expecting a battle to keep her job. Not a promotion.

"In a good way, I presume?" her boss asked.

"Of course." She pulled her racing thoughts together. "As I'd mentioned when I interviewed with Rivendell, a seat on the medical board has always been my goal."

"Yes, your high aspirations helped make you stand out from a few of the other qualified physicians we spoke with before hiring you."

Kasey really couldn't believe her ears. She was being offered the board position. Not Eric. How had that happened?

Had someone on the board slipped?

Would Lena be so upset she'd stop funding the charity providing care through the clinic? That would break Kasey's heart as the ramifications would affect so many. Actually, if she knew that's what would happen, that people like Mr. Oliver would be denied health care, she'd let Eric have the position.

"Sir, I'm pleased, but I must admit I'm surprised Dr. Matthews isn't being offered the position."

Mr. Evans's eyes flashed with surprise at her gutsy comment. They also flashed with something more. Something Kasey couldn't label, yet instinctively knew what it was.

"He was offered the position, wasn't he?" she guessed, her heartbeat increasing in tempo.

Mr. Evans met her gaze. "The clinic is fortunate to have a doctor like Dr. Matthews. But the clinic is also fortunate to have a doctor like you. You're being offered the board position, Dr. Carmichael."

An evasive answer any politician would be proud of. If not for her strong suspicions her puffed-up ego would be lifting her body off the ground. She was suspicious, though.

"Was Dr. Matthews offered the board position?" she demanded, her voice no-nonsense.

The administrator's face contorted into a tight mask.

"You are not privy to certain items of business related to the running of this facility."

Another evasive answer.

"You offered him the position and he turned it down." It wasn't a question, but an answer to the question she'd asked. "Why?"

"Dr. Carmichael, I find your reaction to a tremendous opportunity for advancement within this clinic entirely inappropriate."

Inappropriate.

How she hated that word.

How it grated with the past.

"I would advise you to quit looking a gift horse in the mouth and appreciate the opportunity you've been handed," he continued. "Anything else is entirely inappropriate."

Could he have made a more appropriate word choice?

Inappropriate.

The only inappropriateness was that she'd opened her heart to Eric, allowed him into her life. She'd trusted him.

How inappropriate.

CHAPTER TEN

WITHOUT preamble, Kasey barged into Eric's office. "How dare you try to manipulate me this way?"

Looking way too professional and calm, he looked up from what he'd been working on. "Manipulate you?"

"Don't play dumb with me," she warned, crossing over to stand in front of his desk. "You know exactly what I mean."

"This isn't about my mother?"

She paused a moment, giving thought to his question. "No, this has nothing to do with your mother. At least, I don't think so."

"Then what?"

She wanted to strangle him for playing innocent. Of all things, Eric wasn't innocent. He'd used her, manipulated her, was still manipulating her, although she hadn't worked out his reasons. "I know what you did, Eric."

He set his pen down on his desk, leaned back in his leather chair and regarded her. "I've done lots of things during my lifetime. You'll have to be more specific."

She heaved a frustrated sigh. "I know you turned down the board position."

He considered her a few moments, not answering her one way or the other. "Why would you think that?"

"Why?" she scoffed. "Because I was offered the position a few minutes ago."

"Congratulations."

"Congratulations?" she stormed, wanting to slam her fist down on his desk. "You think I took the position? When I knew the only reason it was offered to me was because you'd turned it down? That I was second best?"

"You aren't second best, Kasey."

"Darn straight I'm not," she agreed, losing some of the wind of her anger. Why was he being so nice? She didn't want nice, she realized. She wanted emotion from him. Passion. She wanted evidence that he cared. "Why would you turn down the board position?"

"Because the position meant more to you than it did to me."

His gaze met hers and she got a glimmer of something. Not passion, but something.

"I'm not taking your leftovers."

Leftovers? Not how most people would consider a lucrative spot on the Rivendell Medical Center's medical board.

"Don't cut off your nose to spite your face, Kasey."

"Don't spout clichés at me."

"You wanted the spot on the board, it's yours."

An invisible hand reached up from her belly, locked on to her throat and gave a powerful yank downward.

"I turned the position down."

"Easily remedied. Tell Clive you've changed your mind."

"I won't be changing my mind." She wouldn't. She'd been wrong about Eric. But obviously he was wrong about her, too. "I didn't sleep with you to advance my career."

"I never said you did."

"But that's what's happening, isn't it?"

"No."

"You turned down the position because of what I told you the other night. Because of what happened with Randall."

"Yes." He smiled, apparently pleased she was starting to understand where he was coming from.

"Would you have turned down the position if we weren't involved?"

"That's a silly question. We are involved."

"Answer me. Would you have sent Mr. Evans to me if we weren't lovers?"

"Technically, we aren't lovers. You dumped me this morning."

"Did you turn down the position hoping we'd get back together?"

"I enjoy our time together, Kasey. I wasn't happy when you refused to meet me last night."

"Because you wanted to have sex with me again?"

"I've been waiting to have sex with you again from the moment we met."

She wouldn't be manipulated this way. She'd thought the manipulation was going to be directed at pushing her out of the clinic. Instead it was the opposite. Eric was trying to manipulate her into a sexual relationship with him.

Neither was going to work.

"Nothing's changed. I meant what I said this morning. We're through, Eric." They'd tried, but it was obvious that they couldn't overcome their differences. She wouldn't have to go through life condemning herself for not attempting to make things work with Eric. She had, but he'd already had future plans.

"You're upset I turned down the position?" He gawked at her, disbelief on his face. "I did it for you, Kasey. Because you wanted the position."

"Not like this, I don't."

"Whoever said a man couldn't please a woman was damned right." He stood up, walking across the room in agitation. "I never know where I stand with you. You say you want the position, I give it to you and you hold that against me."

"Gave it to me? You didn't think I'd have a problem with that? Unlike some, I want to earn my way."

"It really burns you up that I didn't live in poverty as a child, doesn't it? That's the real issue here. That you want to punish me for having wealth, a family, for having what you didn't. Sorry, Kasey, but I'm not going to take that punishment."

"You have no idea what you're talking about."

"Sure, I don't." His brown eyes darkened and his lips pursed. "I planned to talk to you tonight, planned to explain about my mother, but there's really not any point, is there, Kasey? You've condemned me without a trial. No matter what I say or do, you're never going to trust me with your heart."

A week and a half later on the evening of the masquerade ball, Kasey buzzed around the banquet hall making last-minute checks. The caterers had arrived on time and set up a delicious spread. The florists had done gorgeous arrangements for each of the tables scattered around the room. The beautiful bouquets of fresh flowers that graced the tables right inside the hotel ballroom smelled so heavenly they'd almost taken her breath away when she'd passed by. The sound system had been checked and double-checked. The emcee, a local television news personality, had arrived moments ago for any last-minute updates on his duties.

All in all, she'd done everything she could to ensure the evening's success. For the RLS and personally.

She'd scheduled an appointment with Lora's sister who worked as a hairstylist in a nearby salon. Lora had insisted that she let Tracy do her makeup, too. Kasey had. Although heavier than normal, Kasey liked how the smoky colors made her eyes appear huge.

Eyes that were no longer hidden behind glasses thanks to the contact lenses she'd purchased earlier in the week. She hadn't quite adjusted to the feel of them yet, but no longer felt as if she had an eyelash in her eye.

Careful not to disturb her fancy hairdo or makeup, Kasey had donned her rented princess gown from a costume shop. She'd reserved the gown several weeks ago before Eric had started at the clinic. She'd even found "glass" slippers to wear with the gown. A dainty white silk purse and a dab of perfume completed her look for the evening.

With her gown, makeup, hair and contact lenses, she felt so much like Cinderella she wished she could orchestrate a magic pumpkin carriage to whisk her off to the ball. But that would have meant she thought her Prince Charming was waiting for her to arrive.

Perhaps he was.

God, she hoped he was.

Guests began arriving and the room quickly filled to near capacity. The noise level from numerous conversations drowned out the soft music playing in the background.

Kasey bumped into a couple of her coworkers, who praised her outfit and hair. When she walked away she could still hear them commenting on her costume.

"Kasey?" Lora came up beside her. "Wow. You look fabulous! I hope you don't mind if I tell everyone Tracy did your hair and makeup. She could use the business.

When folks get a load of you, they're going to be beating her door down."

"If you think it'll help her, go ahead. She did a wonderful job." Kasey touched one of the upswept curls on top of her head. Rather than the tightly pulled-back look she usually wore, Tracy had created a loose mass of curls that framed Kasey's face. A few stray tendrils tickled the nape of her neck and a sparkly tiara framed the front.

"You and the RLS ladies really outdid yourself on this." Lora spread her arm out, indicating the packed ballroom.

Kasey's gaze lit on where Eric, dressed as Prince Charming, stood talking to the administrator and a couple of members from the clinic's board. Kasey had met them. But she'd never relaxed around them. They'd reminded her too closely of the jerks she'd had to deal with at Skymont.

Eric glanced up, caught sight of her. Pausing in midsentence, he lifted his hand to his heart, causing several of his companions to turn to see what had caught his attention. Letting his gaze caress over every feature, he ate her up with his eyes. He didn't hide the possessiveness in his expression, didn't hide the pure desire on his face.

But he made no move toward her.

He wouldn't.

He'd made his stance clear.

He'd laid his cards on the table. She didn't trust him. He found that unacceptable. The next move would have to be hers.

Their eyes clashed.

Kasey's feet stuck to the floor, and she couldn't move. In that moment, with her eyes locked with Eric's, everyone else in the room faded.

She loved him. Why else would her heart have shattered? The question came down to whether she trusted him. Did she trust him not to hurt her?

She'd thought so on the night they'd made love in her bed. She still thought so. So why had she been so quick to end their relationship?

One truth stood out. Not telling Eric how she felt was selfish, would truly put her in the same league as her mother as no other act could.

Eric turned back to the men he was talking to, resuming his conversation without another glance her way.

"You're wasting your time," Doreen Von Buren said, sliding up next to Kasey and following her gaze. "Men like Eric Matthews want their cake and to eat it, too. You're just this month's flavor."

"Pardon?" Not that Kasey was sure she wanted to know what Doreen meant. She suspected she didn't.

"Don't play coy. I saw you at Barnaby's with him about a month ago and decided to do a background check."

Had anyone not done a background check on her?

"A good thing I did, too. You're nothing more than a gold-digging tramp."

Kasey's mouth dropped. "Excuse me?"

"You heard me." Doreen took a long drink from her wineglass. "You've always had your sights set on marrying well."

"You know this how?"

"Randall Covington III," Doreen bit out with a snide smile. "He was more than willing to tell me anything I wanted to know. I passed on his words of advice to Eric."

"What words of advice?"

"That he should be careful or you'd be knocked up before he could say hefty child support." Doreen smiled with snobby finesse.

Drawing upon years of experience at hiding her emotions, Kasey gave a tight smile. "I hope you had a pleasant visit with Randall. Now, if you'll excuse me."

She didn't want to make a scene at the fund-raiser she'd spent so much time organizing. More and more she was thinking she didn't like the women she'd long admired. That perhaps those women weren't so different from the ones her mother had hung out with, only they had more money to mask their flaws.

She did believe in the work the RLS did, though, particularly in the funding of health care for the uninsured. For that reason alone, she'd remain pleasant.

Doreen grabbed Kasey's arm. "Don't walk away from me, you little tramp."

Kasey's gaze dropped to where Doreen grasped her arm.

"That's twice tonight you've called me a name." Smiling brightly in case anyone was looking their way, Kasey tipped Doreen's wineglass over. The liquid poured down the front of Doreen's flapper dress. "You really should be more careful. I bite back."

Okay, so maybe dumping your drink down someone's dress wasn't being pleasant, but Kasey felt quite pleased.

She turned and walked away, her head held high. She'd not gone ten feet when she bumped into Lena.

"Your cheeks are red, dear. Are you feeling under the weather?" Eric's mother asked in such a tone that her accent sounded more British than Southern. To go with the modified accent, Lena was dressed as the Queen of England.

"I'm fine." Other than she'd just poured wine down Doreen Von Buren's dress. No big deal. But, oh, had standing up to the woman felt good. "Just a tad nervous about how everything is going."

"Based on every seat being sold and the donation boxes at the front of the room being stuffed, I'd say everything is going splendidly," Lena praised. "That is a lovely gown, dear. You're Cinderella?"

Kasey nodded, watching from the corner of her eye as Doreen stomped out of the ballroom, the long scarlet feather in her headband flapping with each flounce.

"Perhaps before the stroke of midnight you'll dance with Prince Charming."

Kasey's gaze returned to Eric's mother, trying to read her expression. "Perhaps."

"I'm not sure how much my son has told you, but I almost lost him about eight years ago."

Under the circumstances, talking about Eric with his mother didn't feel right, but Kasey didn't step away. She couldn't. "Lost him?"

"To drugs and a reckless lifestyle. My husband loved the power of the corporate world and from the time Eric was born he pushed Eric. They clashed terribly. I often wonder if Eric didn't initially get involved with the wrong crowd just to strike out at his father."

"Why would he do that?"

"Because he forced a lifestyle on Eric that he didn't want."

"Pardon me for saying it, but the lifestyle you lead isn't a burden by any stretch."

"Don't you believe it," Lena contradicted, her sharp gaze cutting into Kasey. "Eric's father worked from dawn till the midnight hours. By choice, but that didn't make any difference to a son who wanted his father's attention."

"Eric rebelled to get his father's attention?"

"You didn't think he did it because he wasn't intelligent enough to know better?"

"No," Kasey admitted cautiously, wondering where their conversation was headed. Wondering why they were even having this conversation.

"Eric didn't choose his father's world, but mine didn't fit either. Wealth carries great responsibility to society. It also carries the constant gaze of the public eye. Not everyone is equipped to deal with those stressors."

"You think Eric isn't?"

"Eric is equipped to deal with anything he chooses. When Frank died, Eric plunged so low that nothing I did could lift him. But he got past that, left Kentucky and grew into a man any mother could be proud of." Lena's gaze held Kasey mesmerized. "As much as a mother is grateful for parental pride, what she wants more than anything is for her child to be happy."

What did Lena expect her to say? Kasey wanted Eric to be happy, too. He deserved happiness.

"I love my son. Very much. There's little I wouldn't do to make him happy. Little I wouldn't destroy that threatened his happiness."

Was that encouragement or a warning?

"He's very lucky to have you." How had she gotten into a conversation about Eric with his mother? "If you'll excuse me…" she smiled at Lena "…I need to check on the emcee."

Before Lena could stop her, Kasey headed to the opposite side of the room and came face-to-face with Eric and Ella Von Buren. Great. The night just kept getting better and better.

Looking remarkably like Marilyn Monroe, Ella flirted outrageously with Eric, right down to running her finger along the front of his ruffled shirt and leaning in to tell him something close to his ear.

They made a striking couple. Ella gorgeously blond and svelte. Eric the proverbial tall, dark and handsome. Not only did they look good together, but they were from the same world.

But they didn't belong together and Eric didn't look at Ella the way he looked at her.

Because he didn't love Ella.

He loved her, Kasey Carmichael.

The thought broke through Kasey's fears. Eric hadn't told her he loved her. Not with words. But he'd shown her. From the night they'd met he'd been showing her how he felt her. Only she hadn't been paying close enough attention.

Still, she hesitated. What had he thought of Doreen's revelation? Had he given the woman's words any credence?

He loved her. In her heart, she knew he did. Love meant believing in the other person, placing your heart in their hands.

She loved him.

Would trust him with her heart. Even at the risk of having her heart broken.

The music struck up and before she could second-guess herself, Kasey went up to him. "Will you dance with me?"

Ella guffawed.

Eric didn't comment, but he stepped away from Ella and toward the dance floor.

Following him, Kasey bit the inside of her lip. She wasn't going to run from the way she felt about Eric. Or from her job at Rivendell regardless of what happened.

She wouldn't run. Not ever again.

She'd fight for what she wanted.

What she wanted more than anything was Eric.

That dream was worth fighting for.

Near the middle of the dance floor, he turned to her

and Kasey moved into his arms. As always he smelled amazing, felt amazing, was amazing. She wrapped her arms around his neck, toyed with the dark hair brushing his nape and sought the right words.

Thinking wasn't so easy when his powerful body was so close to hers. They moved around the dance floor in perfect accord.

"I'm sorry," she whispered, knowing that was the place to start.

"For?"

"Pushing you away."

"And?"

"I'm going to fight for you, Eric. To my dying breath."

He pulled back to where he could look into her eyes, his gaze narrowed. No light shone in his eyes, no warmth. Had she waited too long? Had he already decided she wasn't worth the effort? Had he believed Doreen Von Buren?

But she owed it to him, and to herself, to lay her heart on the line. "I've kept my heart sheltered because I believed you'd eventually walk away from me and leave me brokenhearted."

"I wasn't the one to walk away," he said, his arms stiff.

"I thought I was beating you to the punch. Up to this point I haven't trusted you with my heart." She stretched and kissed his cheek. "That's why I'm sorry."

Kasey bit the inside of her lip, watching his face.

The emcee called out Eric's name. Kasey glanced around. The music had stopped, apparently some time ago. Lena, the emcee, Clive Evans and several other suits stood on the stage at the front of the room.

They'd completely missed the song ending, the emcee encouraging people to make donations, and that the emcee had turned the mike over to the clinic's administrator and Clive waited for Eric to join him on the stage.

What had Lena said about their family being honored at the ball?

Eric hesitated, searching her face.

A bit misty-eyed, Kasey pushed against his arm. "Go. I'll tell you everything when you've finished."

Clive read off a list of Eric's accomplishments, both academically and during his work in Africa. Considering what she knew about him, that he'd so completely turned his life around, made her appreciate all the more everything the administrator said.

"It's with great pleasure that I officially welcome Eric to the Rivendell Medical Clinic."

Applause filled the room. Pride filled Kasey. Pride in a man who'd taken control of his life and gave back. To the world. To his community.

To her.

If only she had let him. Please don't let it be too late, she prayed. Please don't let her have pushed Eric away one time too many.

Eric's mother kissed his cheek, said how proud she was of him, and he was immediately swamped by well-wishers.

What he really wanted was to find Kasey and finish the conversation they'd started. Despite scanning the ballroom, he couldn't spot her anywhere. Had she left? Why was it that each time he got his hopes up that she really cared, that she'd let him behind her shields, she pushed him away?

She'd left her own ball without a lost glass slipper in sight.

"She went out the side door, into the conservatory," his mother whispered into his ear.

"Who?"

She tsked at him. "Don't give me that."

Eric nodded, then paused. He'd promised himself he wasn't going to chase Kasey, that she had to show effort in their relationship, too. Was going into the conservatory after her chasing?

"Go. You know you want to," his mother ordered, pretending to lean in for another kiss to his cheek. "I'll handle this."

She would. There wasn't much his mother couldn't handle.

Eric excused himself and worked his way across the room, eventually sneaking out the conservatory door. It took him a few minutes to find Kasey.

She sat on a bench with a gazebo directly in front of her. Flowers and vines wrapped decoratively around the intricate wrought-iron design. With her gown and tiara, she was straight out of a fairy tale.

She was straight out of his fantasies.

She glanced up, surprise on her lovely face. "Eric. I was expecting you to be tied up for a while. I stepped out to get fresh air."

Eric sat down on the bench next to her. "We weren't finished with our conversation."

"No, we weren't." She hesitated, then looked up with eyes so big, so green he felt he could fall into them and never escape. "Doreen Von Buren told me she'd talked to you about visiting Randall."

"She did."

"And?"

"And nothing. Doreen is a busybody who stuck her nose where it doesn't belong."

Kasey nodded, glanced down at her hands, then back up at him. "Did you believe her?"

"No. Should I have?"

She slipped the glittery mask from her face. Her eyes sparkled as brightly as the costume accessory she'd removed. "This probably isn't the best time or place, but it's weighing so heavily on my heart, I have to tell you."

Had he read her wrong inside? Had he yet again thought Kasey was going to let him in only to discover that she'd changed her mind? "What now?"

"I love you."

"You love me?"

Kasey stroked her fingers over his jaw, cupped his chin. "More than I ever thought possible. I'm not sure when it happened exactly, maybe I loved you from that very first night, but just refused to see the truth."

Eric's pulse sped up, slamming through his body. "I love you, too, Kasey, but I'm not sure it's enough."

Kasey's face paled, her fingers trembled against his cheek. "It's enough for me."

"My love?"

She nodded. "For so long I thought I had to have it all. All the things I didn't have growing up. Money, respect, success. I obsessed about having those things. Then I met you and was terrified to love a man who has the world at his fingertips."

"The things that matter can't be bought. Surely you know that by now."

"It took meeting you to figure that one out, but I do know now." At his confused look, she explained. "I blamed everything that went wrong during my child-hood on being poor, on being at the bottom of the social food chain. My goals all evolved around making some-thing of myself, having money and social status. I've spent my entire life trying to make up to myself for all the things I never had."

"Wanting a better life isn't a bad thing, Kasey."

"No, except I was chasing after all the things I never had except for the one thing that I'd been missing most. Love."

"What about Randall?"

Kasey took a deep breath. "As much as I'd like to deny it, Doreen was partly right. Randall falls into the successful life category rather than the love. I picked him out as the perfect man to share my life with, spent a year with him thinking that's what would happen. I was too blinded by my goals to see him for the person he really was," she admitted on a sad note. "I'm thankful he didn't think I was good enough for him. If he had, I'd be trapped in a miserable marriage to a man I didn't love and who didn't love me. I'd have missed out on the best thing to happen to me. Falling in love with you. I'm so sorry I pushed you away, Eric."

Eric was an emotional mess and all because of the woman sitting next to him with her big green eyes full of love.

Love. Kasey loved him.

"The only other person to ever push me away was my father," he admitted, knowing he had some explaining of his own to do. "When he realized I would never live up to his expectations, he washed his hands of me. You already know what happened after that. When you refused to let me close, part of me worried I'd never live up to your expectations either. So I didn't fight for you as hard as I should have. I want to live up to your expectations, Kasey. I want to be the man you need in your life. The man to make your world a better place, because you make my world better just by being in it."

Tears streamed down Kasey's cheeks.

He brushed a wet drop away with his fingertip. "Tell me again."

She searched his eyes, caressed his face. "I love you, Eric. With all of my heart, all of my being. I want to spend the rest of my life proving to you how much I love you."

He grinned. "The rest of your life?"

She blushed. "I didn't mean… I…"

"I want the rest of your life, Kasey," he assured her. "I want every breath you take to be mine. Marry me."

Happiness shining in her eyes, Kasey nodded. "Yes."

Knowing love would guide them, Eric leaned down and stole Kasey's breath for all time.

EPILOGUE

WITH shaking hands, Kasey clipped the giant red ribbon adorning the front of RLS's newest pet project, the Betsy Carmichael Health Care for All Center. The clinic was a subsidiary of the Rivendell Medical Center whose sole purpose was to provide health care to the uninsured.

The small crowd cheered as the ribbon ends floated to the concrete walkway.

"I'm so proud of you," Eric whispered close to her ear, their daughter held in his arms.

Erica Carmichael Matthews automatically closed her tiny fists around a lock of her mother's loose hair. Kasey almost always wore her hair down these days. She almost always wore a smile, too.

Just as she was smiling at the moment.

"She's got me again."

"I've got her trained to keep a close hold on you." Eric winked, disengaging their nine-month-old daughter's fingers.

"Here, hand her to me before she musses Kasey's

hair," Lena said, reaching for her granddaughter. "There are still press photos to be taken. As the director for this center, Kasey will want to look her best."

"Oh, a little messy hair never hurt anyone," Eric teased, giving Kasey a look that said he'd quite enjoy mussing her hair.

"Of course not." Lena's voice magically transformed as she turned her attention to the apple of her eye, pressing a kiss to the little girl's cherubic cheek. "They think no one noticed Kasey's hair was no longer pinned up after they disappeared from their wedding reception. Photos don't lie."

Kasey and Eric exchanged a look, both smothering laughter. Lena did her best to keep them presentable. Most of the time they complied.

"If you'll all step closer together, we'll get a family shot for the write-up on the clinic's opening."

Eric put his arm around Kasey, pulling her close. Lena stood proudly next to them, holding their precious daughter.

Kasey knew that their road wouldn't always be easy, but when she smiled at the camera with her family around her, her smile was real.

Just as she and Eric's love was real and always would be.

MEDICAL™ 2-in-1

Coming next month

SECRET SHEIKH, SECRET BABY
by Carol Marinelli

One night with surgeon Karim Zaraq leaves pretty midwife
Felicity Anderson pregnant! As prince of a desert kingdom,
Karim must propose marriage… But Felicity won't say
'I do' unless it's for love.

HIS BABY BOMBSHELL
by Jessica Matthews

When Adrian McReynolds becomes nurse and ex-flame
Sabrina Hollister's temporary boss, he discovers he's a father.
Adrian let Sabrina go once already, now this surprise dad is
back for good – and wants Sabrina as his wife.

HIRED: GP AND WIFE
by Judy Campbell

GP Atholl Brodie is determined to ignore his new colleague,
Dr Terry Younger, but not only are they working together –
she'll also be sharing his cosy cottage! And soon her
fragile beauty is melting Atholl's stubborn heart…

THE PLAYBOY DOCTOR'S SURPRISE PROPOSAL
by Anne Fraser

Caitlin knew Dr Andrew Bedi had a reputation, yet couldn't
resist his charm. When Caitlin discovers she's pregnant…
Andrew finds himself wanting to be husband and
daddy sooner than he thought!

On sale 4th September 2009

MEDICAL™

Single titles coming next month

PREGNANT MIDWIFE: FATHER NEEDED
by Fiona McArthur

Pregnant midwife Mia is expecting a new arrival to
Lyrebird Lake Maternity – but not a six-foot Adonis and
his son! Mia tries not to get involved with rescue medic
Angus, but he knows that, with Mia as his wife,
they could be the perfect family.

FOUND: A MOTHER FOR HIS SON
by Dianne Drake

Jenna never expected to work with the love of her
life again. Now, seeing how devoted Dr Dermott Callahan
is to giving his five-year-old son Max all the love and
care he needs, she wonders if she dare reach out
and risk her heart with them – for ever.

On sale 4th September 2009

Available at WHSmith, Tesco, ASDA, Eason and all good bookshops.
For full Mills & Boon range including eBooks visit
www.millsandboon.co.uk

2 FREE BOOKS
AND A SURPRISE GIFT

We would like to take this opportunity to thank you for reading this Mills & Boon® book by offering you the chance to take TWO more specially selected title from the Medical™ series absolutely FREE! We're also making this offer to introduce you to the benefits of the Mills & Boon® Book Club™—

- **FREE home delivery**
- **FREE gifts and competitions**
- **FREE monthly Newsletter**
- **Exclusive Mills & Boon Book Club offers**
- **Books available before they're in the shops**

Accepting these FREE books and gift places you under no obligation to buy, you may cancel at any time, even after receiving your free books. Simply complete your details below and return the entire page to the address below. You don't even need a stamp!

YES Please send me 2 free Medical books and a surprise gift. understand that unless you hear from me, I will receive 5 super new titles every month including two 2-in-1 titles priced at £4.9 each and a single title priced at £3.19, postage and packing free. am under no obligation to purchase any books and may cancel m subscription at any time. The free books and gift will be mine to kee in any case.

Ms/Mrs/Miss/Mr _____ initials _____

Surname _____
address _____

_____ postcode _____

Send this whole page to: Mills & Boon Book Club, Free Book Offe FREEPOST NAT 10298, Richmond, TW9 1BR